George John Whyte-Melville

Songs and Verses

Bones and I or, The Skeleton at Home

George John Whyte-Melville

Songs and Verses
Bones and I or, The Skeleton at Home

ISBN/EAN: 9783744768504

Printed in Europe, USA, Canada, Australia, Japan

Cover: Foto ©Andreas Hilbeck / pixelio.de

More available books at **www.hansebooks.com**

Frontispiece.

SONGS AND VERSES

BONES AND I

OR

THE SKELETON AT HOME

BY

G. J. WHYTE-MELVILLE

WITH ILLUSTRATIONS BY H. M. BROCK

LONDON

W. THACKER & CO., 2 CREED LANE, E.C.

CALCUTTA: THACKER, SPINK & CO.

1899

CONTENTS

SONGS AND VERSES

ix

CONTENTS

CONTENTS

CONTENTS

BONES AND I

LIST OF ILLUSTRATIONS

SONGS AND VERSES

xiii

SONGS AND VERSES

HUNTING SONGS

THE LORD OF THE VALLEY

Hunters are fretting, and hacks in a lather,
  Sportsmen arriving from left and from right;
Bridle-roads bringing them, see how they gather,
  Dotting the meadows in scarlet and white.
Foot-people staring and horsemen preparing,
  Now there's a murmur, a stir, and a shout;
Fresh from his carriage, as bridegroom in marriage,
  The Lord of the Valley leaps gallantly out.

Time, the avenger, neglecting or scorning,
  Gazes about him in beauteous disdain,
Lingers to toy with the whisper of morning,
  Daintily, airily, paces the plain.
Then in a second, his course having reckoned,
  Line that all Leicestershire cannot surpass,
Fleet as the swallow, when summer-winds follow,
  The Lord of the Valley skims over the grass.

Where shall we take him? Ah! now for the tussle;
  These are the beauties, can stoop, and can fly,

SONGS AND VERSES

Down go their noses, together they bustle,
  Dashing and flinging, and scorning to cry.
Never stand dreaming, while yonder they're streaming,
  If ever you meant it, man, mean it to-day!
Bold ones are riding and fast ones are striding;
  The Lord of the Valley is forward, away!

Hard on his track o'er the open, and facing
  The cream of the country, the pick of the chase,
Mute as a dream, his pursuers are racing;
  Silence, you know's the criterion of pace.
Swarming and driving, while man and horse striving,
  By hugging and cramming scarce live with them
      still,
The fastest are failing, the truest are tailing;
  The Lord of the Valley is over the hill!

Yonder a steed is rolled up with his master,
  Here, in a double, another lies cast;
Faster and faster come grief and disaster,
  All but the good ones are weeded at last.
Hunters so limber at water and timber,
  Now on the causeway are fain to be led;
Beat, but still going, a countryman sowing
  Has sighted the Lord of the Valley ahead!

There in the bottom, see, sluggish and idle,
  Steals the dark stream where the willow-tree grows;
Harden your heart and catch hold of your bridle,
  Steady him! rouse him! and over he goes.
Look, in a minute a dozen are in it,
  But forward! hark forward! for draggled and blown,
A check though desiring, with courage untiring,
  The Lord of the Valley is holding his own.

HUNTING SONGS

Onward we struggle in sorrow and labour,
  Lurching and lobbing, and " bellows to mend " ;
Each, while he smiles at the plight of his neighbour,
  Only is anxious to get to the end.
Horses are flagging, hounds drooping and lagging,
  But gathering down yonder, where press as they may,
Mobbed, driven, and haunted, but game and undaunted,
  The Lord of the Valley stands proudly at bay.

Now here's to the Baron, and all his supporters,
  The thrusters, the skirters, the whole of the tale ;
And here's to the fairest of all hunting quarters,
  The widest of pastures, three cheers for the Vale ;
For the fair lady rider, the rogue who beside her
  Finds breath in a gallop his suit to advance,
The hounds for our pleasure, that time us the measure,
  The Lord of the Valley that leads us the dance !

THE GALLOPING SQUIRE

Come, I'll show you a country that none can surpass,
  For a flyer to cross like a bird on the wing.
We have acres of woodland and oceans of grass,
  We have game in the autumn and cubs in the spring,
We have scores of good fellows hang out in the shire,
But the best of them all is the Galloping Squire.

The Galloping Squire to the saddle has got,
  While the dewdrop is melting in gems on the thorn,
From the kennel he's drafted the pick of his lot,
  How they swarm to his cheer! How they fly to his
    horn!
Like harriers turning or chasing like fire,
"I can trust 'em, each hound!" says the Galloping Squire.

One wave of his arm, to the covert they throng ;
  "Yooi! wind him! and rouse him! By Jove he's away!"
Through a gap in the oaks see them speeding along,
  O'er the open like pigeons: " They *mean* it to-day!
You may jump till you're sick—you may spur till you
    tire!
For it's catch 'em who can!" says the Galloping Squire.

Then he takes the old horse by the head, and he sails
  In the wake of his darlings, all ear and all eye,
As they come in his line, o'er banks, fences, and rails,
  The cramped ones to creep, and the fair ones to fly.
It's a *very* queer place that will put in the mire
Such a rare one to ride as the Galloping Squire.

But a fallow has brought to their noses the pack,
  And the pasture beyond is with cattle-stains spread ;
One wave of his arm, and the Squire in a crack
  Has lifted and thrown in the beauties at head.
" On a morning like this, it's small help you require,
But he's forward, I'll swear !" says the Galloping Squire.

"HE'S TOASTED BY ALL."

So forty fair minutes they run and they race,
  'Tis a heaven to some ! 'tis a lifetime to all ;
Though the horses we ride are such gluttons for
     pace,
    There are stout ones that stop, there are safe ones that
     fall.
But the names of the vanquished need never tran-
     spire
For they're all in the rear of the Galloping Squire.

SONGS AND VERSES

Till the gamest old varmint that ever drew breath,
    All stiffened and draggled, held high for a throw
O'er the squire's jolly visage, is grinning in death
    Ere he dashes him down to be eaten below;
While the daws flutter out from a neighbouring spire
At the thrilling who-whoop of the Galloping Squire.

And the labourer at work, and the lord in his hall,
    Have a jest or a smile when they hear of the sport,
In ale or in claret he's toasted by all,
    For they never expect to see more of the sort.
And long may it be ere he's forced to retire,
For we breed very few like the Galloping Squire.

A RUM ONE TO FOLLOW, A BAD ONE TO BEAT

Come, I'll give you the health of a man we all know,
  A man we all swear by, a friend of our own ;
With the hounds running hardest, he's safest to go,
  And he's always in front, and he's often alone.
A rider unequalled—a sportsman complete,
A rum one to follow, a bad one to beat.

As he sits in the saddle, a baby could tell
  He can hustle a sticker, a flyer can spare ;
He has science, and nerve, and decision as well,
  He knows where he's going and means to be there.
The first day I saw him they said at the meet,
" That's a rum one to follow, a bad one to beat."

We threw off at the Castle, we found in the holt,
  Like wildfire the beauties went streaming away ;
From the rest of the field he came out like a bolt,
  And he tackled to work like a schoolboy to play,
As he rammed down his hat, and got home in his seat,
This rum one to follow, this bad one to beat.

'Twas a caution, I vow, but to see the man ride !
  O'er the rough and the smooth he went sailing along ;
And what Providence sent him, he took in his stride,
  Though the ditches were deep, and the fences were strong.
Thinks I, " If he leads me I'm in for a treat,
With this rum one to follow, this bad one to beat ! "

Ere they'd run for a mile, there was room in the front,
    Such a scatter and squander you never did see!
And I honestly own I'd been out of the hunt,
    But the broad of his back was the beacon for me.
So I kept him in sight, and was proud of the feat,
This rum one to follow, this bad one to beat!

Till we came to a rasper as black as your hat,
    You couldn't see over—you couldn't see through;
So he made for the gate, knowing what he was at,
    And the chain being round it, why—over he flew!
While I swore a round oath that I needn't repeat,
At this rum one to follow, this bad one to beat.

For a place I liked better I hastened to seek,
    But the place I liked better I sought for in vain;
And I honestly own, if the truth I must speak,
    That I never caught sight of my leader again.
But I thought, " I'd give something to have his receipt,
This rum one to follow, this bad one to beat."

They told me that night he went best through the run,
    They said that he hung up a dozen to dry,
When a brook in the bottom stopped most of their fun,
    But I know that I never went near it, not I.
For I found it a fruitless attempt to compete
With this rum one to follow, this bad one to beat.

So we'll fill him a bumper as deep as you please,
    And we'll give him a cheer; for, deny it who can,
When the country is roughest he's most at his ease;
    · When the run is severest, he rides like a man.
And the pace cannot stop, nor the fences defeat,
This rum one to follow, this bad one to beat.

A DAY'S RIDE A LIFE'S ROMANCE

WHEN the early dawn is stealing
O'er the moorland edge, revealing
All the tender tints of morning ere she flushes into day,
Then beneath her window, shaking
Bit and bridle, while she's waking,
Stands a bonny steed caparisoned to bear my love
away;
By hill and holt to follow,
Hound and horn, and huntsman's holloa,
Follow! follow! where they lure us; follow, follow
as we may!

When the chase is onward speeding,
With its boldest spirits leading,
When the red is on the rowel, and the foam is on the rein,
Far in front her form is fleeting,
And her gentle heart is beating,
With the rapture of the revel, as it sweeps across the
plain;
Then I press by dint of riding
Where my beacon star is guiding,
And the laggard spurring madly hurries after us in vain.

O'er the open still careering,
Fence and furrow freely clearing,
Like the winds of heaven leaving little trace of where
we pass;
With that merry music ringing,
Father Time is surely flinging

Golden sand about the moments as he shakes, them
       from the glass:
     Horn and hound are chiming gladly,
     Horse and man are vying madly
In the glory of the gallop.   Forty minutes on the grass!

     Till, by yonder group, dismounted,
     Group that's quickly told and counted,
Hark, the pack are baying fiercely round their quarry
       lying dead ;
     But from eyes that shine so brightly
     Such a spectacle unsightly
Must be hidden, as we hide each thing of sorrow and
       of dread ;
     So she gathers up her tresses,
     And with loving hand caresses
Neck and shoulder of the bonny steed, and homeward
       turns his head.

     Every sweet must have its bitter,
     And the time has come to quit her,
Oh! the night is falling darker for the happy day
       that's done ;
     Now I wish I were the bridle,
     In the fingers of mine idol,
Now I wish I were the bonny steed that bore her
       through the run ;
     For I fain would still be nearest
     To my loveliest and dearest,
And I fain would be the truest slave that ever
       worshipped one !

THE CLIPPER

(*Dedicated to the* HONOURABLE CHARLES WHITE,
Scots Fusilier Guards)

Go strip him, lad!   Now, sir, I think you'll declare
  Such a picture you never set eyes on before;
He was bought in at Tatt's for three hundred I swear,
  And he's worth all the money to look at, and more;
For the pick of the basket, the show of the shop,
Is the Clipper that stands in the stall at the top.

In the records of racing I read their career,
  There were none of the sort but could gallop and stay;
At Newmarket his sire was the best of his year,
  And the Yorkshiremen boast of his dam to this day;
But never a likelier foal did she drop
Than this Clipper that stands in the stall at the top.

A head like a snake, and a skin like a mouse,
  An eye like a woman, bright, gentle, and brown,
With loins and a back that would carry a house,
  And quarters to lift him smack over a town!
What's a leap to the rest, is to him but a hop,
This Clipper that stands in the stall at the top.

When the country is deepest, I give you my word
  'Tis a pride and a pleasure to put him along;
O'er fallow and pasture he sweeps like a bird,
  And there's nothing too wide, nor too high, nor too
     strong;

For the ploughs cannot choke, nor the fences can
    crop,
This Clipper that stands in the stall at the top.

Last Monday we ran for an hour in the Vale,
  Not a bullfinch was trimmed, of a gap not a sign!
All the ditches were double, each fence had a rail,
  And the farmers had locked every gate in the line;
So I gave him the office, and over them—Pop!
Went the Clipper that stands in the stall at the top.

"THERE WERE EIGHT OF US HAD IT, AND SEVEN GOT IN!"

I'd a lead of them all when we came to the brook,
  A big one—a bumper—and up to your chin;
As he threw it behind him, I turned for a look,
  There were eight of us had it, and seven got in!
Then he shook his lean head when he heard them go
    plop!
This Clipper that stands in the stall at the top.

HUNTING SONGS

Ere we got to the finish, I counted but few,
   And never a coat without dirt, but my own ;
To the good horse I rode all the credit was due,
   When the others were tiring, he scarcely was blown ;
For the best of the pace is unable to stop
The Clipper that stands in the stall at the top.

You may put on his clothes ; every sportsman, they say,
   In his lifetime has one that outrivals the rest,
So the pearl of *my* casket I've shown you to-day,
   The gentlest, the gamest—the boldest, the best;
And I never will part, by a sale or a swop,
With my Clipper that stands in the stall at the top !

THE WARD

(*Dedicated, by permission, to* MRS. J. L. MORROGH)

THERE are flowers on the earth, there are gems in the sea,
   There's the pearl and the ruby—the lily, the rose—
But the emerald green is the jewel for me,
   And the shamrock's the dearest of posies that grows.
For the flower and the gem are combined in the sward,
That gives pleasure and pace to a run with the Ward.

Oh ! the harrier makes music that's sweet to the ear,
   And the note of the foxhound rings home to the brain,
But the sport we love best is a spin with the deer,
   O'er the pick of the pasture, the pride of the plain ;
Where the men of the hunt, and the men of the sword,
Are at work with their spurs to ride up to the Ward.

Not a moment to lose if you'd share in the fun ;
   Of a gate, or a gap, not a sign to be seen !
Ere the dancers are ready, the music's begun,
   To the tune, if you like it, of " Wearing the Green " ;
For a horse may be grassed, and his rider be floored,
In a couple of shakes, when they start with the Ward.

Now loose him ! now lift him ! Your soul what a place !
   An embankment between, and a yawner each side ;
What delivered us over alone was the pace,
   Never spare when you're " on an engagement " to ride !
For the whip must be drawn, and the flanks must be
     scored,
If you're called on in earnest to live with the Ward.

HUNTING SONGS

Then forward!   The hounds are still fleeting away,
  How they drive for a scent—how they press for a view!
Now they have it! and strain at the flanks of their prey,
  As he scuds by Dun-shaughlin and on to Kilrue;
While the field are beat off, from the lout to the lord,
For the tail of a comet's a joke to the Ward.

The boldest are baffled—the best are out-paced,
  For " wreckers " and ropes, at each fence there's a call;
What with riders dismounted, and horses disgraced,
  You'd think not a leap was left in us at all!
But the humours your bard hasn't breath to record,
For disasters came thick at the pace of the Ward.

Like fairies we whirl by the fairy-house,—see,
  They are down in the gripe, and the mare's on the man!
But a voice cometh up from the deep, and says he,
  " It's pretendin' ye are!   Sure, ye're schamin' it, Fan!"
So we leave them in hopes they may soon be restored;
There's no time to look back in a run with the Ward.

At the finish how few are there left in the game!
  And the few that are left seem well pleased to be there;
But an Irishman rides for the sport, not the fame,
  And it's little he'll trouble, and less that he'll care
For the stakes, when the pieces are swept from the board;
It's " diversion " he loves,—so he hunts with the Ward.

Then success to the master! more power! and long life!
  Success to his horses, his hounds, and his men
And the brightest of days to his fair lady-wife!
  May she lead us, and beat us again and again
Thus from sorrow to borrow all fate can afford;
With Morrogh, to-morrow, we'll hunt with the Ward.

THE GOOD GREY MARE

OH ! once I believed in a woman's kiss,
   I had faith in a flattering tongue ;
For lip to lip was a promise of bliss,
   When lips were smooth and young.
But now the beard is grey on my cheek,
   And the top of my head gets bare ;
So little I speak, like an Arab sheik,
   But put my trust in my mare.

For loving looks grow hard and cold,
   Fair heads are turned away,
When the fruit has been gathered, — the tale
      been told,
   And the dog has had his day ;
But chance and change 'tis folly to rue,
   And say I, the devil may care !
Nor grey nor blue are so bonny and true,
   As the bright brown eye of my mare !

It is good for a heart that is chilled and sad
   With the death of a vain desire,
To borrow a glow that shall make it glad
   From the warmth of a kindred fire.

HUNTING SONGS

And I leap to the saddle, a man indeed ;
  For all I can do and dare,
In the power and speed that are mine at need,
  While I sit on the back of my mare !

With the fair wide heaven above outspread
  The fair wide plain to meet,
With the lark and his carol high over my head,
  And the bustling pack at my feet,—
I feel no fetter, I know no bounds,
  I am free as a bird in the air ;
While the covert resounds, in a chorus of hounds,
  Right under the nose of the mare.

We are in for a gallop,—away ! away !
  I told them my beauty could fly ;
And we'll lead them a dance ere they catch us to-day,
  For we *mean* it, my lass and I !
She skims the fences, she scours the plain,
  Like a creature winged, I swear,
With snort and strain, on the yielding rein ;
  For I'm bound to humour the mare.

They have pleached it strong, they have dug it wide,
  They have turned the baulk with the plough ;
A horse that can cover the whole in its stride
  Is cheap at a thousand, I vow ;
So I draw her together, and over we sail,
  With a yard and a half to spare—
Bank, bullfinch, and rail—'tis the Curse of the vale,
  But I leave it all to the mare !

Away! away! they've been running to kill,
  With never a check from the find;
Away! away! we are close to them still,
  And the field are *furlongs* behind!
They can hardly deny they were out of the game,
  Lost half "the fun of the fair,"
Though the envious blame and the jealous exclaim,
  "How that old fool buckets his mare!"

Who-whoop! they have him,—they're round him; how
  They worry and tear when he's down!
'Twas a stout hill-fox when they found him, now
  'Tis a hundred tatters of brown!
And the riders arriving as best they can,
  In panting plight, declare,
That "First in the van was the old grey man,
  Who stands by his old grey mare."

I have lived my life—I am nearly done,—
  I have played the game all round;
But I freely admit that the best of my fun
  I owe it to horse and hound.
With a hopeful heart and a conscience clear,
  I can laugh in your face, Black Care;
Though you're hovering near, there's no room for you here,
  On the back of my good grey mare.

THE KING OF THE KENNEL

(Dedicated to JOHN ANSTRUTHER THOMSON, ESQ.)

Clara fuga, ante alios, et primus in æquore pulvis.

THE bitch from the Belvoir, the dog from the Quorn—
The pick of their litter our puppy was born ;
And the day he was entered he flew to the horn
But rating and whipcord he treated with scorn.
> *Gently, Bachelor ;*
> *Have a care ! Have a care !*

So eager to find, and so gallant to draw,
Though a wilder in covert a hunstman ne'er saw.
'Twas a year and a half ere he'd listen to law,
And many's the leveret hung out of his maw.
> *Ware hare, Bachelor ;*
> *Ware hare ! Ware hare !*

On the straightest of legs and the roundest of feet,
With ribs like a frigate his timbers to meet,
With a fashion and fling and a form so complete,
That to see him dance over the flags is a treat !
> *Here, here, boy ! Bachelor !*
> *Handsome and good.*

But fashion and form without nose are in vain ;
And in March or mid-winter, storm, sunshine, and rain,
When the line has been foiled, or the sheep leave a stain,
His fox he accounts for again and again.
> *Yooi ! Wind him, Bachelor.*
> *All through the wood !*

SONGS AND VERSES

He guides them in covert, he leads them in chase;
Though the young and the jealous try hard for his place,
'Tis Bachelor always is first in the race;
He beats them for nose, and he beats them for pace.
Hark forward to Bachelor!
From daylight to dark!

Where the fallows are dry, where manure has been thrown,
With a storm in the air, with the ground like a stone—
When we're all in a muddle, beat, baffled, and blown,
See! Bachelor has it!   *Bill, let him alone.*
Speak to it, Bachelor;
Go hark to him! Hark!

That time in December—the best of our fun—
Not a mile from the gorse, ere we'd hardly begun,
Heading straight to the river—I thought we were done;
But 'twas Bachelor's courage that made it a run.
Yooi! over, Bachelor!
Yooi! over, old man!

As fierce as a torrent, as full as a tank,
That a hound ever crossed it, his stars he may thank!
While I watched how poor Benedict struggled and sank!
There was Bachelor shaking his sides on the bank.
Forrard on, Bachelor!
Catch ye who can.

From the find to the finish, the whole blessed day,
How he cut out the work!   How he showed us the way!
When our fox doubled back where the fallow-deer lay,
How he stuck to the line, and turned short with his prey!
Yo-Yooite, Bachelor!
Right, for a crown!

20

HUNTING SONGS

Though so handy to cast, and so patient to stoop,
When his bristles are up you may swear it's who-whoop!
For he'll dash at his fox like a hawk in her swoop,
And he carries the head, marching home to his soup!
Sess! Sess! Bachelor!
Lap and lie down.

TALLY-HO!

THERE are soul-stirring chords in the fiddle and flute
  When dancing begins in the hall,
And a goddess in muslin, that's likely to suit,
  Is the mate of your choice for the ball ;
But the player may strain every finger in vain,
  And the fiddler may rosin his bow,
Nor flourish nor string such a rapture shall bring,
  As the music of sweet Tally-Ho !

There's a melody, too, in the whispering trees
  When day has gone down in the West,
And a lullaby soft in the sigh of the breeze
  That hushes the woods to their rest ;
There are madrigals fair in the voices of air,
  In the stream with its ripple and flow,
But a merrier tune shall delight us at noon,
  In the music of sweet Tally-Ho !

When autumn is flaunting his banner of pride
  For glory that summer has fled,
Arrayed in the robes of his royalty, dyed
  In tawny and orange and red ;
When the oak is yet rife with the vigour of life,
  Though his acorns are dropping below,
Through bramble and brake shall the echoes awake,
  To the ring of a clear Tally-Ho !

" A fox, for a hundred ! " they know it, the pack,
  Old Chorister always speaks true,

HUNTING SONGS

And the Whip from his corner is told to come back,
  And forbid to go on for a view.
Now the varmint is spied, as he crosses the ride,
  A tough old campaigner I trow—
Long, limber, and grey, see him stealing away
  —Half a minute !—and then—Tally-Ho !

Mark Fanciful standing, all eye and all ear,
  One second, ere, wild for the fun,
She is lashing along with the pace of a deer,
  Her comrades to join in the run.
Your saddle you grip, gather bridle and whip,
  Give your hunter the office to go,
In his rush through the air little breath is to spare
  For the cheer of your wild Tally-Ho !

At the end of the wood the old farmer in brown,
  On the back of his good little mare,
Shows a grin of delight and a jolly bald crown,
  As he holds up his hat in the air ;
Though at heart he's as keen as if youth were still green,
  Yet (a secret all sportsmen should know)
Not a word will he say till the fox is away,
  Then he gives you a real Tally-Ho !

There's a scent, you may swear, by the pace that they
      drive,
  You must tackle to work with a will,
For as sure as you stand in your stirrups alive
  It's a case of a run and a kill !
So I wish you good speed, a good line, and a lead,
  With the luck of each fence where it's low,
Not the last of the troop, may you hear the who-whoop,
  Well pleased as you heard Tally-Ho !

"BROW, BAY AND TRAY"

(A SONG OF WEST SOMERSET)

FIRST came the Harbourer,
    The Harbourer, the Harbourer—
First came the Harbourer,
    Before the dawn was clear;
And here he stooped, and there he stood,
And round the coomb he made it good,
And harboured in the Lower Wood,
    A warrantable deer!
Some twenty score, he said, and more
    The noble beast would weigh,
For he'd brow, bay and tray, my lads—
    Brow, bay and tray!
(*Chorus.*) Then here's to him who leads the
            Hunt,
    With "Tally-ho! away!"
    And brow, bay and tray, my lads—
    Brow, bay and tray!

Next came the Tufters,
    The Tufters, the Tufters—
Next came the Tufters,
    Tufting through the brake,
And opened on him, staunch and sure,
And moved him, where he couched secure,
And drove him forward o'er the moor
    His gallant point to make.

While on his track the zealous pack
    We did our best to lay;
For he'd brow, bay and tray, my lads—
    Brow, bay and tray!
(*Chorus.*) Then here's to him, etc.

Next came the Huntsman,
    The Huntsman, the Huntsman—
Next came the Huntsman
    His jolly horn to wind,
With Finisher, and Foreman too,
And Nelson, who had got a view,
And many a comrade, bold and true,
    That bustled round the find.
" Have at him ! see, the slot !" quoth he
    (" Hold up, my gallant grey !").
" He has brow, bay and tray, my lads—
    Brow, bay and tray !"
(*Chorus.*) Then here's to him, etc.

Next came the Master,
    The Master, the Master—
Next came the Master,
    He seemed a merry man;
His spur was in the chestnut's side—
" Hark forward ! hark !" the Master cried;
" My friends, I'll give you leave to ride
    And catch them if you can !
Before the fun is fairly done,
    You'll falter by the way;
For he's brow, bay and tray, my lads—
    Brow, bay and tray !"
(*Chorus.*) Then here's to him, etc.

SONGS AND VERSES

Next came the Parson,
　　The Parson, the Parson—
Next came the Parson,
　　His shortest way to seek,
And like a phantom lost to view,
From point to point the Parson flew—
The parish, at a pinch, could do
　　Without him for a week!
"But see the kill I must, and will,"
　　Said he, "this blessed day.
For he's brow, bay and tray, my lads—
　　Brow, bay and tray!"
(*Chorus.*) Then here's to him, etc.

Next came the Farmers,
　　The Farmers, the Farmers—
Next came the Farmers,
　　The keenest blades I know!
They pierce the copse's leafy gloom,
They climb the hill and thread the coomb,
Or skim the bog for standing-room,
　　But never fail to go.
By hook or crook they'll have a look,
　　I'll undertake to say,
At his brow, bay and tray, my lads—
　　Brow, bay and tray!
(*Chorus.*) Then here's to him, etc.

Next came the Moor-land,
　　The Moor-land, the Moor-land—
Next came the Moor-land,
　　It stretched for many a mile:

HUNTING SONGS

The spurs were plied without avail,
The best of steeds were seen to fail,
The very hounds began to tail,
    And ran in lengthened file—
Yet forward still, he sank the hill,
    To finish out the play,
With his brow, bay and tray, my lads—
    Brow, bay and tray!
(*Chorus.*) Then here's to him, etc.

    Next came the River-side,
        The River-side, the River-side—
    Next came the River-side
        ('Twas brawling to the brim).
Undaunted in the whirling flood,
To face his foes the champion stood,
While, all about him wild for blood,
    They clamoured, sink or swim;
For weary feet at Watersmeet [1]
    Had set him up to bay,
With his brow, bay and tray, my lads—
    Brow, bay and tray!
(*Chorus.*) Then here's to him, etc.

    Next came the Death-stroke,—
        The Death-stroke, the Death-stroke—
    Next came the Death-stroke,
        The huntsman drove it home.
While here and there, from far and near,
With laugh and shout, and thrilling cheer,
We gathered round the dying deer,
    Beside the torrent's foam;

[1] The confluence of Badgeworthy water and the river Lynn.

SONGS AND VERSES

Till stark and dead, with crown on head,
    The fallen monarch lay,
With his brow, bay and tray, my lads—
    Brow, bay and tray!

(*Chorus.*) Then here's to him who led the Hunt—
      Whom death alone could stop,
      With his brow, bay and tray, my lads—
      And four upon the top!
      With nine times nine for every tine
      He flourished in the fray,
      And brow, bay and tray, my lads—
      Brow, bay and tray!

WARE WIRE!

(A PROTEST)

GOOD fellows, and sportsmen of every degree,
Who live by the land, will you listen to me?
To teach you your business I offer no claim,
But the man who looks on sees a deal of the game.
And your thrift while I honour, your acres admire,
I think you're mistaken to fence them with Wire!

Let us argue the point: If the stock get astray,
If the pig in a panic sets off for the day,
If a herd leaves unfolded, lamb, heifer, or steer,
If the colt from his tackle can kick himself clear,
Your truants to capture you'll hardly desire
That their hides should be torn into ribbons with Wire!

For see! The black bullock halts, shivers, and reels,
The handsome prize heifer is fast by his heels,
Entangled the wether, and mangled the ewe,
The pig becomes pork, as he chokes, pushing through,
And the horse at two hundred, to carry the Squire,
Is blemished for life while he hangs on the Wire!

Moreover—and here the shoe pinches, I know!—
You love to ride hunting, and most of you *go*.
When thickest the fences and quickest the burst,
'Tis a thousand to one that a farmer is first.
But I give you my honour, it makes me perspire,
To think of my neighbour turned over by Wire!

You may bore through the blackthorn, and top the oak-
    rail,
Here courage shall serve, and there craft can avail.
The seasoned old horse does his timber with ease ;
The young ones jump water as wide as you please ;
But the wisdom of age, and the four-year-old's fire,
Are helpless alike if you ride them at Wire !

Great Heavens ! rash man, what a crowner you come !
Your collar-bone broken, two ribs, and a thumb ;
While the pride of your stable lies stretched on the
    plain,
And the friend of your heart never rises again ;
Then bitter the curses you launch, in your ire,
At the villain who fenced his enclosure with Wire !

'Tis cruel to see, in the cream of a run,
A dozen fine fellows enjoying the fun,
Struck down at a moment to writhe in the dirt,
Dismounted, disgusted, both frightened *and* hurt !
While behind them a panic breaks out like a fire,
With the ominous caution—" *Ware Wire, sir ! Ware
    Wire !* "

No ! twist us your binders as strong as you will,
We must all take our chances of cropper and spill ;
There are scores of young ashes to stiffen the gaps,
And a blind double ditch is the surest of traps.
But remember, fair sportsmen fair usage require ;
So Up with the timber, and Down with the Wire !

THE KING OF THE WEST

(*Dedicated to* M. F. BISSET, ESQ., *Master of Devon
and Somerset Staghounds*)

CAPTAIN and leader, and lord of the herd,
Bold and alert when his mettle is stirred—
Lithe as a lion, and light as a bird,
    Royal in crest,
Dashing the dew from his frontlet and head,
Pillowed on purple and russet and red,
Rises in state from his heathery bed,
    The King of the West.

Stands for a second erect in his pride,
Listens before and behind and aside
To the tongue of the tufters that gallantly chide,
    Staunch on the quest ;
While louder and deeper the challenge resounds,
Till it rings through the coomb in a chorus of hounds,
And the music of death with its echo surrounds
    The King of the West.

Like a storm-driven cloud, like a hawk on the wing,
Like a shaft from a bow, like a stone from a sling,
How he shoots over bracken and boulder and ling—
    They may gallop their best !
But the horse and his rider shall labour and strain,
The rowel be reddened, and tightened the rein ;
And the staghound shall droop ere a furlong he gain
    On the King of the West !

SONGS AND VERSES

From acre to acre the moorland is spread,
And acre by acre fleets under his tread,
Untiring and swift, as he stretches ahead,
      For life to contest.
By the ridge of the mountain, the copse on its side,
By tors where they glisten, and streams where they glide,
The swamp that can swallow, the wood that can hide
      The King of the West.

For the yell of their war-cry is borne on the wind,
And the ruthless pursuers are raging behind:
He must scour his dominions a refuge to find—
      Nor fail in the test,
Though before him the bounds of his monarchy lie,
Where the blue of the sea meets the blue of the sky,
And above him the raven is hungering on high—
      For the King of the West.

Where a rent in the precipice yawns on the deep,
Unfaltering—undaunted—he makes for the steep;
With antlers flung back gathers breath for the leap,
      To extremity pressed;
And launched from the brink of it, fenceless and bare,
The fate of each element eager to dare,
He cleaves through the wave, as he clove through the air—
      This King of the West.

Low down on the waters the sunset hath spread,
From sky-line to shingle a pathway of red,
Like a curtain of blood, to close over his head,
      Where he sinks to his rest,
Pursuit and pursuers, outpaced and surpassed,
And about him a mantle of royalty cast,
He dies, undefeated, and game to the last—
      The King of the West.

A LAY OF THE RANSTON BLOODHOUNDS

(*Dedicated to* LORD WOLVERTON)

THE leaf is dead, the woods are red,
   Autumn skies are soft and pale,
Winds are through the copses straying,
Ripples on the water playing.
Hark! I hear the bloodhound baying,
   Down by the river in the vale!

Pacing o'er the slopes of Chettel,
   Ere the sun was high,
Many a hunter, full of mettle,
   Trotted gaily by;
Many a rider, free and gallant,
   Chafing to begin,
All the talk and all the talent,
   Met at Cashmoor Inn.
Still and silent, not a holloa
   Telling where 'twas gone;
Faster than the breeze could follow,
   Flew the red-deer on.
Warily, of coming danger
   Noted every sign,
Marking Friendly, Viceroy, Ranger
   Open on the line.
      For leaves are dead, and woods are red,
      Autumn skies, etc.

How the chorus pealed and gathered
   To an organ's tone!
How the horses steamed and lathered
   But to hold their own!
Like a burst of angry weather
   In the tempest's frown,
How the pack, at head together,
   Swept across the down!
Not the lightest fence confined them;
   Racing fair and fast,
Many a mile they left behind them,
   Ere the plain was past.
Then into the vale defiling,
   Drew the lengthened Hunt;
And the good ones, grimly smiling,
   Settled in the front.
      Leaves are dead, and woods are red, etc.

Field by field came grief and trouble,
   Thicker grew the plot;
Stubborn rail and ugly double
   Weeded out the lot.
Here the horse, and there his master!—
   Where they fell they lay—
Faster ran the hounds and faster,
   Farther seemed the prey;
Till at last a check compelled them
   In his face to look.
Forward then his Lordship held them,
   Right across the brook;
Rose again the joyous rally,
   Clamoured louder still,
Woke the hamlet in the valley
   Echoed round the hill!
      Leaves are dead, and woods are red, etc.

HUNTING SONGS

Pleasure that the most enchants us,
  Seems the soonest done ;
What is life with all it grants us,
  But a hunting run !
Necks were stretched, and mouths were deadened,
  Wind began to fail ;
Sobbing sides and rowels reddened,
  Told the usual tale.
Long before the chase was finished—
  Ridden fairly through,
How that gallant field diminished—
  To a chosen few !
Fain would I relate their glory,
  Name each favourite mount :
But your bard who tells the story
  Wasn't there to count !
      Leaves are dead, and woods are red, etc.

Fill your glasses !   All good fellows,
  Lovers of a burst ;
Sportsmen safe or riders jealous,
  Bruising to be first.
Never spare it !   Let the donor
  Drain his cellars' wealth !
Here's the pack ! and here's the owner !
  Here's his Lordship's health !
Surely now with each November,
  In the yearly rounds,
Ranston shall we all remember,
  And the deep-mouthed hounds ;
How they pressed, how none forsook it,
  Through that brilliant hour !
How they ran their deer and took it
  By the flooded Stour !
      For leaves are dead, and woods are red, etc.

"THE PLACE WHERE THE OLD HORSE
DIED"

In the hollow, by the pollard, where the crop is tall and
    rank
  Of the dock-leaf and the nettle growing free,
Where the bramble and the brushwood straggle blindly
    o'er the bank,
  And the pyat jerks and chatters on the tree,
    There's a fence I never pass
    In the sedges and the grass,
But for very shame I turn my head aside,
    While the tears come thick and hot,
    And my curse is on the spot—
'Tis the place where the old horse died.

There's his hoof upon the chimney, there's his hide upon
    the chair,
  A better never bent him to the rein;
Now, for all my love and care, I've an empty stall and
    bare ;
  I shall never ride my gallant horse again !
    How he laid him out at speed,
    How he loved to have a lead,
How he snorted in his mettle and his pride !
    Not a flyer of the Hunt
    Was beside him in the front,
At the place where the old horse died !

Was he blown ? I hardly think it. Did he slip ? I
    cannot tell.
  We had run for forty minutes in the vale,

HUNTING SONGS

He was reaching at his bridle; he was going strong and
      well,
  And he never seemed to falter or to fail;
     Though I sometimes fancy, too, .
     That his daring spirit knew
The task beyond the compass of his stride,
     Yet he faced it true and brave,
     And dropped into his grave
At the place where the old horse died.

"WHEN MOTIONLESS HE LAY
IN HIS CHEERLESS BED OF CLAY."

I was up in half a minute, but he never seemed to stir,
  Though I scored him with my rowels in the fall;
In his life he had not felt before the insult of the spur,
  And I knew that it was over, once for all.

When motionless he lay
In his cheerless bed of clay,
Huddled up without an effort on his side—
'Twas a hard and bitter stroke,
For his honest back was broke,
At the place where the old horse died.

With a neigh so faint and feeble that it touched me like
a groan,
"Farewell," he seemed to murmur, "ere I die";
Then set his teeth and stretched his limbs, and so I stood
alone,
While the merry chase went heedless sweeping by.
Am I womanly and weak
If the tear was on my cheek
For a brotherhood that death could thus divide?
If sickened and amazed
Through a woful mist I gazed
On the place where the old horse died?

There are men both good and wise who hold that in a
future state
Dumb creatures we have cherished here below
Shall give us joyous greeting when we pass the golden
gate;
Is it folly that I hope it may be so?
For never man had friend
More enduring to the end,
Truer mate in every turn of time and tide.
Could I think we'd meet again
It would lighten half my pain
At the place where the old horse died.

SOLDIERS' SONGS

A CAVALIER'S SONG

(FROM "HOLMBY HOUSE")

Ho! fill me a flagon, as deep as you please,
Ho! pledge me the health that we quaff on our knees;
And the knave who refuses to drink till he fall,
Why the hangman shall crop him—ears, love-locks, and all,
   Then a halter we'll string,
   And the rebel shall swing,
For the gallants of England are up for the King!

Ho! saddle my horses as quick as you may,
The sorrel, the black, and the white-footed bay;
The troop shall be mustered, the trumpet shall peal,
And the Roundhead shall taste of a Cavalier's steel.
   For the little birds sing,
   There are hawks on the wing
When the gallants of England are up for the King!

Ho! fling me my beaver, and toss me the glove
That but yesterday clung to the hand of my love;

SONGS AND VERSES

To be bound on my crest—to be borne in the van,
And the rebel that reaps it must fight like a man!
   For the sabre shall swing,
   And the head-pieces ring,
When the gallants of England strike home for the King!

"A HEALTH TO PRINCE RUPERT!"

Ho! crush me a cup to the queen of my heart!
Ho! fill me a brimmer, the last ere we part,
A health to Prince Rupert! Success and renown!
To the dogs with the Commons! and up with the Crown!
   Then the stirrup-cup bring,
   Quaff it round in a ring!
To your horses! and ride to the death for the King!

V. C.

(*From the " London Gazette "*)

VICTORIA CROSS.   7TH HUSSARS.   MAJOR CHARLES CRAUFURD FRASER.

"For conspicuous and cool gallantry on the 31st December, 1858, in having volunteered, at great personal risk, and under a sharp fire of musketry, to swim to the rescue of Captain Stisted and some men of the 7th Hussars, who were in imminent danger of being drowned in the river Raptee, while in pursuit of the rebels.   Major Fraser succeeded in this gallant service, although at the time partially disabled, not having recovered from a severe wound received while leading a squadron in a charge against some Fanatics, in the action of Nawabgunge, on the 13th of June, 1858."

GLEAMING eyes, and dusky faces ;
　　Brazen guns, depressed for slaughter ;
Track of blood in furrowed places,
　　There the jungle, here the water ;
Eager troop and opening section,
　　Crash of grape, and hiss of ball ;
Trumpets, at a chief's direction,
　　Sounding the Recall.

" Turn again, we shall not heed them,
　　Gallant steed, so loyal and true ;
Others in the rear may lead them,
　　We have something yet to do.
Through the wounded, through the dying,
　　Clear the press and stem the rout :
In that stream a comrade's lying,
　　We must have him out ! "

Chargers bold, and riders bolder,
  None dare stem that torrent's force,
Breaking over girth and shoulder,
  Sweeping downward man and horse.
In its bend the stream runs deeper ;
  Foes about him, friends afar,
Sheltering where the bank is steeper,
  Clings the maimed Hussar.

Off with buckle, belt, and sabre !
  Heedless of a crippled limb,
Scorning peril, stripped for labour,
  In he dashes, sink or swim ;
Now he's whirling round the eddy,
  Now he battles in its roar,
Now with lengthened stroke, and steady,
  Nears the other shore.

Dusky faces peering grimmer,
  Fiery flashes from the wood,
Watery flashes round the swimmer
  Where the bullet rips the flood ;
Now to reach him, foothold gaining !
  Now to drag him safely back,
Through an angry volley, raining
  Death along the track !

Dusky faces blankly staring
  On a prey thus lost and won ;
Muttered curses, fiercely swearing,
  " Allah ! Allah ! bravely done ! "
While the hero, like a galley
  Nobly freighted, stems the tide ;
While a score of troopers rally
  On the hither side.

SOLDIERS' SONGS

Tramp of horse and death-shot pealing,
  Wolfish howl, and British cheer,
Cannot drown the whisper, stealing
  Grateful on the rescuer's ear.
" Wounded, helpless, sick, dismounted,
  Charlie Fraser, well I knew,
Come the worst, I might have counted
  Faithfully on you ! "

Thus the double danger spurned he,
  Bold to slay and bold to save ;
Thus the meed of honour earned he,
  Doubled for the doubly brave.
Badge of succour, badge of daring,
  Gold and bronze, by which 'tis dross,
Next the swimmer's medal, wearing
  His Victoria Cross !

"BOOTS AND SADDLES!"

THE ring of a bridle, the stamp of a hoof,
  Stars above, and a wind in the tree; .
A bush for a billet, a rock for a roof,—
  Outpost duty's the duty for me!
Listen! a stir in the valley below,
  The valley below is with riflemen crammed,
Covering the column, and watching the foe;
  Trumpet-major! sound and be d——d!
Stand to your horses! It's time to begin:
Boots and saddles! the pickets are in!

Though our bivouac fire has smouldered away,
  Yet a bit of good baccy can comfort us well;
When you sleep in your cloak there's no lodging to pay,
  And where we shall breakfast the devil can tell.
But the horses were fed ere the daylight had gone;
  There's a slice in the embers, a drop in the can,—
Take a suck at it, comrade, and so pass it on,
  For a ration of brandy puts heart in a man.
Good liquor is scarce, and to waste it a sin:
Boots and saddles! the pickets are in!

Hark! there's a shot from the crest of the hill!
  Look! there's a rocket leaps high in the air!
By the beat of his gallop that's nearing us still,
  That runaway horse has no rider, I'll swear!
There's a jolly Light Infantry post on the right,
  I hear their bugles, they sound the Advance;

SOLDIERS' SONGS

Faith! they'll tip us a tune that shall wake up the night,
  And we're hardly the lads to leave out of the dance.
They're at it already, I hear by the din:
Boots and saddles! the pickets are in!

They don't give us long our divisions to prove;
  Short, sharp, and distinct comes the word of command,
"Have your men in the saddle! be ready to move.
  Keep the squadron together, the horses in hand!"
While a whisper's caught up through the ranks as they
      form,
  A whisper that fain would break out in a cheer,
How the foe is in force, how the work will be warm;
  But steady! the chief gallops up from the rear.
With old "Death or glory" to fight is to win,
And the colonel means mischief, I know by his grin.
Boots and saddles! the pickets are in!
Boots and saddles! the pickets are in!

CATHCART'S HILL

ONCE again we rally, comrades,
  Comrades of the old brigade!
Welcome to the triple badges,
  Star and Thistle and Grenade.
Once again we take our places,
  Once again the healths we fill,
But we miss remembered faces,
  And we think of Cathcart's Hill.

Round the circle jests are passing,
  Stingless gibe and harmless jeer;
Some are laughing, some are quaffing,
  Mirth is half the soldier's cheer;
Loudly ring the glad young voices,
  But a whisper, soft and still,
Bids the heart that most rejoices
  Spare a thought for Cathcart's Hill.

Needs no colour waving o'er us,
  Many a hazard to bring back
Of the bivouac and the leaguer,
  Of the trench and the attack.
Seems again the Advance is sounding,
  And the minié whistling shrill,
Batteries playing, mortars pounding,
  On the slopes by Cathcart's Hill.

SOLDIERS' SONGS

How those colours have been carried
　　Needs no verse of mine to tell ;
How the loyal rallied round them,
　　How the brave beneath them fell.
Laurel wreaths are snatched by glory,
　　Dripping from a crimson rill :
Some are here to tell the story,
　　Some are there on Cathcart's Hill.

Oh ! the merry laughing comrade !
　　Oh ! the true and kindly friend,
Glowing hopes and lofty courage,
　　Love and life, and this the end !
Yet a balm from grief we borrow,
　　Though the eye with tears may fill ;
Half is pride and half is sorrow,
　　While we speak of Cathcart's Hill.

Noble names, devoted nobly,
　　High ancestral deeds to share,
Lowlier valour, waged as freely,
　　All alike are mouldering there.
Homes are lonely yet without them,
　　Women's hearts are aching still,
Though a glory hangs about them,
　　In their graves on Cathcart's Hill.

While a soldier's name is honoured,
　　While a soldier's fame is dear,
Nowhere shall they be forgotten,
　　Least of all, forgotten here.
In the roll of those who perished,
　　England's mission to fulfil,
None more proudly, fondly cherished,
　　Than the dead of Cathcart's Hill.

MISCELLANEOUS SONGS

MARION

THERE'S music in the gallery,
  There's dancing in the hall,
And the girl I love is moving
  Like a goddess through the ball.
Amongst a score of rivals
  You're the fairest in the room,
But I like you better, Marion,
      Marion, Marion,
I like you better, Marion,
      Riding through the broom.

It was but yester morning,
  The vision haunts me still,
That we looked across the valley,
  As our horses rode the hill,
And I bade you read my riddle,
  And I waited for my doom,
While the spell was on us, Marion,
      Marion, Marion,
The spell was on us, Marion,
      Riding through the broom.

MISCELLANEOUS SONGS

The wild bird carolled freely,
   The May was dropping dew,
The day was like a day from heaven,
   From heaven, because of you ;
And on my heart there broke a light,
   Dispelling weeks of gloom,
While I whispered to you, Marion,
     Marion, Marion,
While I whispered to you, Marion,
     Riding through the broom.

"THEN WE LOOKED ACROSS THE VALLEY,
AS OUR HORSES RODE THE HILL."

" What is freer than the wild bird ?
   What is sweeter than the May ?
What is fresher than the morning,
   And brighter than the day ?"

SONGS AND VERSES

In your eye came deeper lustre,
  On your cheek a softer bloom,
And I think you guessed it, Marion,
    Marion, Marion,
I think you guessed it, Marion,
    Riding through the broom.

And now they flutter round you,
  These insects of an hour,
And I must stand aloof and wait,
  And watch my cherished flower ;
I glory in her triumphs,
  And I grudge not her perfume,
But I love you best, my Marion,
    Marion, Marion,
I love you best, my Marion,
    Riding through the broom.

THE WHITE WITCH

HAVE a care! she is fair,
The White Witch there;
   In her crystal cave up a jewelled stair;
She has spells for the living would waken the dead,
And they lurk· in the line of her lip so red,
And they lurk in the turn of her delicate head,
   And the golden gleam on her hair.

Forbear! have a care
Of that beauty so rare;
   Of the pale proud face and the queen-like air,
And the love-lighted glances that deepen and shine,
And the coil of bright tresses that glisten and twine,
And the whispers that madden, like kisses or wine,
   Too late! too late to beware!

Never heed! never spare!
Never fear! never care!
   It is sweeter to love, it is wiser to dare!
Lonely and longing, and looking for you,
She has woven the meshes you cannot break through;
She has taken your heart, you may follow it too,
   Up the jewelled stair, good luck to you there!
   In the crystal cave with the witch so fair,
   The White Witch fond and fair!

I PASS'D without the city gate,
    I linger'd by the way;
The palm was bending to her mate,
    And thus I heard her say,

" The arrow to the quiver,
    And the wild bird to the tree;
The stream to meet the river,
    And the river to the sea.
The waves are wedded on the beach,
    The shadows on the lea;
And like to like, and each to each,
    And I to thee.

" The cedar on the mountain,
    And the bramble in the brake;
The willow by the fountain,
    And the lily on the lake;
The serpent coiling in its lair,
    The eagle soaring free,
Draw kin to kin, and pair to pair,
    And I to thee.

" For everything created
    In the bounds of earth and sky,
Hath such longing to be mated,
    It must couple, or must die.
The wind of heaven beguiles the leaf,
    The rose invites the bee;

The sickle hugs the barley-sheaf,
    And I love thee.
By night and day, in joy and grief,
    Do thou love me?"

The palm was bending to her mate,
    I marked her meaning well;
And pass'd within the city gate,
    The fond old tale to tell.

"IMBUTA"

THE new wine, the new wine,
　It tasteth like the old,
The heart is all athirst again,
　The drops are all of gold ;
We thought the cup was broken,
　And we thought the tale was told,
But the new wine, the new wine,
　It tasteth like the old !

The flower of life had faded,
　The leaf was in its fall,
The winter seemed so early
　To have reached us, once for all ;
But now the buds are breaking,
　There is grass above the mould,
And the new wine, the new wine,
　It tasteth like the old !

The earth had grown so dreary,
　The sky so dull and grey ;
One was weeping in the darkness,
　One was sorrowing through the day ;
But a light from heaven gleams again,
　On water, wood, and wold,
And the new wine, the new wine,
　It tasteth like the old !

For the loving lips are laughing,
   And the loving face is fair,
Though a phantom hand is on the board,
   And phantom eyes are there;
The phantom eyes are soft and sad,
   The phantom hand is cold,
But the new wine, the new wine,
   It tasteth like the old!

We dare not look, we turn away,
   The precious draught to drain,
'Twere worse than madness, surely now,
   To lose it all again;
To quivering lip, with clinging grasp,
   The fatal cup we hold,
For the new wine, the new wine,
   It tasteth like the old!
And life is short, and love is life,
   And so the tale is told,
Though the new wine, the new wine,
   It tasteth like the old!

OVER THE WATER

I STAND on the brink of the river,
  The river that runs to the sea,
The fears of a maid—I forgive her,
  And bid her come over to me;
She knows that her lover is waiting,
  She's longing his darling to be,
And Spring is the season of mating,
  But—she dare not come over to thee!

I have jewels and gold without measure,
  I have mountain and meadow and lea,
I have stores of possessions and treasure,
  All wasting and spoiling for thee.
Her heart is well worthy the winning,
  But love is a gift of the free,
And she vowed, from the very beginning,
  She'd never come over to thee.

Then lonely I'll wed with my sorrow—
  Dead branch on a desolate tree—
My night hath no hope of a morrow
  Unless she come over to me.
Love takes no denial, and pity
  Is love in the second degree,
So long ere I'd ended my ditty,
  The maiden came over to me!

"YES—I LIKE YOU"

WHEN I meet you, can I greet you
  With a haughty little stare?
Scarcely glancing where you're prancing
  By me on the chestnut mare;

"SCARCELY GLANCING WHERE YOU'RE PRANCING
BY ME ON YOUR CHESTNUT MARE."

Still dissembling, though I'm trembling,
  Thus, you know, we're trained and taught.
For I like you—doesn't it strike you?
  Like you more than perhaps I ought.
For I like you, etc.

When I meet you, must I treat you
   As a stranger, calm and cold?
Softer feeling, half revealing—
   Are you *waiting* to be told?
D'you suppose, Sir, that a rose, Sir,
   Picks *itself* to reach your breast?
And I like you—doesn't it strike you?
   Like you more than all the rest.
Yes, I like you, etc.

When I meet you, I could eat you;
   Dining with my Uncle John,
Sitting next you, so perplexed, you
   Ought to know my heart is gone.
While I'm choking, 'tis provoking,
   You can munch and talk and drink.
Though I like you—doesn't it strike you?
   Like you more than you may think.
Yes, I like you, etc.

When I meet you, I could beat you
   For your solemn face and glum;
Don't you see, Sir, *you* are free, Sir,
   I have all the worst to come,—
Mother's warning, sister's scorning,
   Qualms of prudence, pride, and pelf.
Oh! I like you—doesn't it strike you?
   Like you more than life itself.
Yes, I like you, etc.

GIPSY JOHN

(FROM " BLACK BUT COMELY ")

THE gipsy fires are shining,
  The kettle sings a song,
And stomachs want their lining
  That are empty all day long.
Then welcome if you've lost your way,
  For daylight's past and gone,
And strangers might do worse than stay
  To house with Gipsy John!

    So dip your fingers in the stew,
      And drink a cup to me ;
    I'll fill again, and drink to you
      A health in Romany !

I hope you'll like your dinner—
  But it's not polite to brag—
And as I'm a living sinner,
  It has cost me not a mag !
That loaf is off the bailiff's board,
  A rich cur-mud-ge-on ;
The rest comes mostly from my lord,
  Purloined by Gipsy John !

    Then dip your fingers, etc.

There's fowl of many a feather,
  There's a turkey-poult and hen,
A moorcock off the heather,
  A mallard from the fen,

A leash of teal, a thumping goose,
  As heavy as a swan ;
He ought to wear his waistcoat loose
  Who dines with Gipsy John !
      Then dip your fingers, etc.

And when your brains are turning,
  And you're only fit for bed,
Those lamps in heaven are burning
  To light you overhead :
Till waking up, refreshed and bright,
  When stars grow pale and wan,
You'll swear they pass a cosy night
  Who lodge with Gipsy John !
      Then dip your fingers, etc.

The birds in the air shall call you,
  They are stirring with the day,
No mischief shall befall you
  Till we've set you on your way ;
And when you've left the wanderers' camp
  To travel blithely on,
Be kind to some poor tinker-tramp,
  And think of Gipsy John !
      Then dip your fingers, etc.

IF I WERE A QUEEN

IF I were a queen I'd make it the rule
  For women to govern and men obey;
And hobbledehoys to be kept at school,
  And elderly gentlemen hidden away.
But maids should marry at sweet sixteen—
If I were a queen, if I were a queen!

If I were a queen I'd soon arrange
  For a London season the whole year round;
And once a week, if we wanted a change,
  We would dine by the river and sit on the ground,
When lawns are sunny, and leaves are green—
If I were a queen, if I were a queen!

If I were a queen, the lady should choose,
  Taking her pick of them, round and square;
None selected should ever refuse,
  Bound to wed, be she dark or fair,
Stout and stumpy, or lank and lean—
If I were a queen, if I were a queen!

If I were a queen, on Valentine's day
  Every girl should receive by post,
Flaming letters in full array,
  Of darts and hearts burnt up to a toast;
With bows and arrows, and Cupids between—
If I were a queen, if I were a queen!

If I were a queen, I'd never allow
  Tax on unregistered goods like these—
A woman's reason, a lover's vow,
  A stolen kiss, or a silent squeeze ;
A wish unspoken, a blush unseen—
If I were a queen, if I were a queen !

EPHEMERAL

IT came with the merry May, love,
  It bloomed with the summer prime,
In a dying year's decay, love,
  It brightened the fading time ;
I thought it would last for a life, love,
  But it went with the winter snow,
Only a year ago, love,
  Only a year ago !

'Twas a plant with a deeper root, love,
  Than the blighting eastern tree,
For it grew in my heart, and the fruit, love,
  Was a bitter morsel to me ;
The poison is yet in my brain, love,
  The thorn in my breast, for you know
'Twas only a year ago, love,
  Only a year ago !

It never can bloom any more, love,
  For the plough hath passed over the spot,
And the furrow hath left its score, love,
  In the place where the flowers are not.
'Tis gone like a tale that is told, love,
  Like a dream it hath fleeted, although
'Twas only a year ago, love,
  Only a year ago !

FAREWELL

Farewell! farewell!   How soon 'tis said!
    The wind is off the bay,
The sweeps are out, the sail is spread,
    The galley gathers way.

Farewell! farewell!   The words are light!
    Yet how can words say more?
Sad hearts are on the sea to-night,
    And sadder on the shore.

Farewell! farewell!   Perhaps it screens
    Thy triumph to be free;
Farewell! farewell!   Perhaps it means
    An end of all for me.

NUNC EST BIBENDUM

THE times and the seasons have perished,
　　The years have flown over my head ;
The friends that I honoured and cherished,
　　By scores have gone down to the Dead.
With faces now brighter, now dimmer,
　　Like shadows they waver and pass,
While Memory fills them a brimmer,
　　And I see them again in my glass!

But where is the youth I remember,
　　Confiding, untainted, and free?
In a June so unlike my December
　　'Tis strange to accept him for *me!*
A picture Time could not but tarnish,
　　Its colours are faded, alas!
Till Wine, like a coating of varnish,
　　Restores them again in the glass!

And where are the pleasures I followed?
　　The chase in its sylvan abode,
The hounds that I hunted and holloaed,
　　The horses I stabled and rode?
Has he vanished—the favourite that bore me,
　　To sail on an ocean of grass?
No; he's standing there saddled before me.
　　I see him again in my glass!

SONGS AND VERSES

Have I done with the hope and the rapture,
  The whisper that stole to my heart,
The hour of confession and capture,
  The moment to kiss and to part?
Is she gone to the land of To-morrow,
  That loving and true-hearted lass?
Oh! precious indeed, in their sorrow,
  Are the tears that drop into my glass!

Yet how fair was the promise of Morning!
  And noon in its lustre, how bright!
Now darkness is falling, and warning
  My soul of the coming of Night.
There is nothing that Autumn can offer,
  The blossoms of Spring to surpass,
And I challenge the sneer of the scoffer,
  While I dip a dead flower in my glass!

'Tis done; and old Time is the winner,
  I held him a race to the last!
But the sand dribbles thinner and thinner,
  The notches all count for the past.
What matter? Fresh players shall follow,
  Fresh scores in their turn to amass;
And were this my last bumper to swallow,
  I'd drink them " Good Luck " in the glass!

A WORD FOR CHAMPAGNE

I SIGH not for woman, I court not her charms—
　The long-waving tresses, the melting dark eye—
For the sting of the adder still lurks in her arms,
　And falsehood is wafted with each burning sigh.
Such pleasure is poisoned, such ecstasy pain—
Forget her! remembrance shall fade in champagne!

For the bright-headed bumper shall sparkle as well,
　Though Cupid be cruel, and Venus be coy;
And the blood of the grape gushes up with a spell
　That years shall not deaden, nor care shall alloy.
It thrills through the life-blood, it mounts to the brain—
Then crown the tall goblet once more with champagne!

The miser may gloat o'er his coffers of gold;
　The merchant may balance investment and sale;
The land-holder swell with delight to behold
　How his acres are yellowing far o'er the vale:
But mine be the riches that blush on that plain
Where the vintage of Sillery teems with champagne!

Rejoiced is the sage when his labours are crowned,
　And the chaplets of laurel his temples adorn—
When pure gems of science are scattered around
　A name still undying to ages unborn;
But benumbed are his senses, and weary his brain—
Let him quaff at the fountain which foams with cham-
　　pagne!

Ambition is noble, they tell ye—to sway
  The fate of an empire, a nation to rule;
To be flattered and worshipped, the god of a day,
  And then learn to cringe in adversity's school.
But vexed is the spirit, the labour is vain;
And the crestfallen statesman flies back to champagne!

Then give me champagne! and contentment be mine!
  Women, wealth, and ambition—I cast them away.
My garlanded forehead let vine-leaves entwine!
  And life shall to me be one long summer's day,
With the tears of the clustering grape for its rain,
And its sunshine—the bright golden floods of cham-
    pagne!

SO FAR AWAY

FADED flowers fondly cherished,
      Dearer for decay,
Emblems of the hope that perished
      In a summer's day,
All the path behind me strewing
Mark the track of Life's undoing,
Memories of a Past renewing,
      So far away!

Sunset glory sadly hiding
      In a shroud of grey,
Forest whispers sadly chiding
      Forest streams at play;
Airy voices pleading, sighing,
Airy voice to voice replying,
Mourn because our dead are lying
      So far away.

Yet above us, lustre streaming
      From its silver ray,
See the Star of Mercy beaming
      Softly on our way,—
Vain regrets of earth abating,
Holy hope of heaven creating,
Where the loved and lost are waiting,
      So far away.

COMMUNE MALUM

FEW the days so dark and dreary
  But are brightened by a gleam,
Seldom night so long and weary,
  But 'tis lightened with a dream;
So the fruit that never ripens
  Blossomed once for me,
Far away in bonnie Scotland,
  Down by the sea.

Pale and calm the wave was sleeping,
  Pale and soft the skies above,
All was peace, and all in keeping
  With the holy hush of love;
While the pearl of price beside me
  Promised mine to be,
Far away in bonnie Scotland,
  Down by the sea.

Pearl I never thought could fail me,
  Jewel of my darker lot,
How shall faith and truth avail me?
  All dishonoured and forgot.
Would that death had come between us,
  While we yet were free,
Far away in bonnie Scotland,
  Down by the sea.

Better that than shame and sorrow,
  Trust betrayed and spirit strife,
Longing night and lonely morrow,
  Are not these but death in life?
All the heart I had lies buried,
  There let it be!
Far away in bonnie Scotland,
  Down by the sea.

A LULLABY

SLEEP, my love, sleep ; rest, my love, rest ;
  Dieth the moan of the wind in the tree,
Foldeth her pinions the bird in her nest,
  Sinketh the sun to his bed in the sea.
Sleep, sleep—lull'd on my breast,
  Tossing and troubled, and thinking of me.

Hush, my love, hush ; with petals that close,
  Bowing and bending their heads to the lea,
Fainteth the lily, and fadeth the rose,
  Sighing and sad for desire of the bee.
Hush, hush ; drooping like those,
  Weary of waking and watching for me.

Peace, my love, peace ; falleth the night,
  Veiling in shadows her glory for thee ;
Eyes may be darken'd, while visions are bright,
  Senses be fettered, though fancy is free.
Peace, peace ; slumbering light,
  Longing and loving and dreaming of me.

AN INCANTATION

By the power of the Seven
    Great tokens of light;
By the Judges of Heaven,
    The watchers of night;
By the might of those forces
    That govern on high,
The Stars in their courses,
    The hosts of the sky;
By Ashur, grim pagan,
    Our father in mail;
By Nebo and Dagon,
    By Nisroch and Baal:
By pale Ishtar, contrasting
    With red Merodach,
By the wings everlasting,
    I summon thee back!

From the ranks of a legion
    That files through the gloom
Of a shadowy region
    Disclosed by the tomb;
From the gulf of black sorrow,
    Of silence and sleep,
Where a night with no morrow
    Broods over the deep;
By desire unavailing,
    And pleasure that's fled;
By the living bewailing
    Her love for the dead;

SONGS AND VERSES

By the wish that endears thee,
  The kisses that burn,
And the passion that sears thee,
  I bid thee return !

Thou art cold, and thy face is
  So waxen at rest,
In my fiery embraces
  Seek warmth on my breast,
Through the lips that caress thee
  Draw balm in my breath,
And the arms that compress thee
  Shall wrench thee from Death.
Though he boasteth to spare not,
  For ransom or fee,
Yet he shall not, he dare not,
  Take tribute of me.
Then if love can restore thee,
  Though bound on the track,
From the journey before thee,
  Beloved, come back !

THE MONKS THAT LIVE UNDER THE HILL

WOULD it lighten your conscience, sweet Leicestershire
      maid,
   To be shriven, though guiltless of ill?
There's a snug little priory lurks in the glade,
Like a nest in a meadow, and don't be afraid.
For remorseful young ladies are quite in the trade
   Of the Monks that live under the hill.

'Tis a brotherhood zealous and pious, no doubt,
   And their duties they seem to fulfil,
By creating a good deal of racket and rout,
By despising repose and ignoring the gout,
And by keeping the steam up within and without:
   These Monks that live under the hill.

They are seldom in bed before Matins or Prime,
   Though they often rise early for drill;
But at luncheon a " Pick-me-up " brings them to time,
Till their Vespers ring out with the dinner-bell's chime;
And by Complines, the form becomes truly sublime,
   Of these Monks that live under the hill.

They are given to dancing in London, men say,
   And to flirting, I'm told, with a will;
But in Leicestershire trifling like this wouldn't pay,
Where the business of life is to hunt every day,
And the nights must take care of themselves as they
      may,
   With the Monks that live under the hill.

So their riding is reckless, their courage is high,
  And regardless of cropper or spill,
Their "oxers" they rattle,—their "raspers" they fly,
At the widest of water they *will* have a shy ;
And while horses can wag, it is " Never say die ! "
  With these Monks that live under the hill.

Till at even-song homeward like rooks they repair,
  When they've ended the day with a kill,
And they'll chant you some canticles, racy and rare,
And they'll tell you some tales would make many men
      stare,
And they'll bid you to dine on the daintiest fare,
  Will these Monks that live under the hill.

Then the Prior will press you to taste of his best,
  Of the sweet, and the dry, and the still ;
While the jolly Sacristan will pass you his jest,
And the Father Confessor will fill for the guest,
And you'll vow such a life is a life of the blest,
  With these Monks that live under the hill.

Then long may it be so ! and long may they thrive !
  Uncaptured by feminine skill,
For the bachelor-bees have the best of the hive,
And our Priory-priests are too precious to wive ;
And the pick. of the choicest companions alive
  Are the Monks that live under the hill.

"THERE LEAVE THY GIFT UPON THE ALTAR"

ONCE in the promise and lustre of morning,
  Little I dreamt that defeat would be mine,
Panting for trial, regardless of warning,
  Love was like music, and life was like wine.
Now that the doom of the vanquished is spoken,
  Now that the sun hath gone down to the sea,
Now that the heart hath been trampled and broken,
  God of the helpless! I bring it to Thee.

Earth was so fair, and so lavish of treasure,
  Nature emblazoned her pages in gold;
Vain was the glitter, illusive the pleasure,
  A phantom to vanish, a tale to be told.
Here, where the glory of summer was glowing,
  See, the dead leaf quivers bare on the tree,
Blasts of a desolate winter are blowing,
  God of the homeless! I shelter with Thee.

Gone the glad hope in a dawn of to-morrow,
  Faded, forgotten, the noon of to-day,
Night drawing closer in sadness and sorrow,
  Gloom in the valley and ghosts on the way;
All the bright hours of the past I can reckon,
  Memories of anguish bequeathing to me,
Man cannot guide me, nor angel can beckon,
  God of the hopeless! whom have I but Thee?

"GOODBYE!"

FALLING leaf, and fading tree,
Lines of white on a sullen sea,
Shadows rising on you and me;
The swallows are making them ready to fly,
Wheeling out on a windy sky.
Goodbye, Summer!—Goodbye, Goodbye!

Hush! A voice from the far-away!
"Listen and learn," it seems to say;
"All the to-morrows shall be as to-day."
The cord is frayed—the cruse is dry,
The link must break, and the lamp must die.
Goodbye, Hope!—Goodbye, Goodbye!

What are we waiting for? Oh! my heart!
Kiss me straight on the brows! And part!
Again! Again!—my heart! my heart!
What are we waiting for, you and I?
A pleading look—a stifled cry.
Goodbye, for ever!—Goodbye, Goodbye!

MISCELLANEOUS VERSE

HELP AND HOLD

(A LEGEND OF THE HOUSE OF ST. CLAIR)

"Now fie! now fie!" quoth Robert the king—
  And the red blood flew to his brow,
And the weight of his hand bade the beakers ring—
  "I am shamed this day, I trow!

"In stable and hall I have steeds and men,
  I have hounds both staunch and free,
But the white faunch deer of the hawthorn glen
  Makes light of my woodcraft and me!

"And I vow to St. Hubert as I sit here,
  To St. Andrew, St. Rule, and St. Bride,
Till I've sounded the mort o'er the white faunch deer,
  No more in the woodland to ride!"

Then up and spake the bold St. Clair,
  Was drinking the red wine free,
"The lands of thy vassal are scant and bare,
  My liege, as they should not be.

"But had I the space by wood and wold
    To breathe them a summer's day,
I'd ask but my two hounds, Help and Hold,
    While I brought the white deer to bay!"

"Ye are stout," quoth the King—"ye are stout, my lord,
    As behoves a St. Clair to be,
But there's many a brag at the evening board
    Winna stand in the morn on the lea.

"The lands of the Strath, both far and near,
    Shall be yours if her flight ye can turn,
And bring me to grips with the white faunch deer
    Ere she win through the black march burn.

"But a man may not take if he dare not lose,
    And the venture is yet to be said:
Should your good hounds fail, then ye shall not choose,
    My lord, but to forfeit your head!"

"A wager! a wager!" cried bold St. Clair;
    "See, bring me both hound and horn;
Go saddle the bonny black Barbary mare,
    The fleetest that feeds on corn.

"A wager! a wager! on Help and Hold!
    Was never a lord of my line
But would wager his life against lands and gold:
    My liege, the broad Strath shall be mine!"
    .   .   .   .

They saddled their steeds at mirk o' night,
    They mounted when dawn was near,
And they slipped the good hounds with the dim grey
        light,
    On the track of the white faunch deer.

The white faunch deer like an arrow flew,
  The good hounds followed fast ;
I trow they drove her from slot to view,
  Ere noon was fairly past.

Still first in the chase rode bold St. Clair,
  The Bruce spurred hard in his track,
And the foam stood white on the Barbary mare,
  And the King's bonny bay grew slack.

"STILL FIRST IN THE CHASE RODE BOLD ST. CLAIR,
THE BRUCE SPURRED HARD IN HIS TRACK."

" She fails," quoth St. Clair, "and the good hounds gain ;
  St. Katherine speed their flight !
Now cote [1] her ! and turn her across the plain,
  For the black march burn is in sight !

The black march burn falls steep at the bank,
  To the pitch of a horseman's chin,
But Hold's grey muzzle is hot on her flank,
  And the white faunch deer leaps in.

[1] "Cote," a term of chase meaning to be alongside ; from the French *côte—côtoyer.*

SONGS AND VERSES

Light down! light down! thou St. Clair bold!
   Or never go hunting more;
Now have at her, Help! now hang to her, Hold!
   And they turn her back to the shore.

The King's bonny bay a good bow-shot mark
   Stopped short of the Barbary mare,
And the hounds stood grim and the deer lay stark
   At the feet of bold St. Clair.

"My liege! my liege! will ye take the knife?"
   The St. Clair bent his knee;
"By St. Katherine's aid, both lands and life
   Have my good hounds won for me.

"And I vow to St. Katherine I'll build a shrine
   In the Hopes[1] by the western wave,
And I vow to St. Hubert these hounds of mine
   Shall be carven in stone on my grave!"

The bold St. Clair he sleeps in Spain,[2]
   For with good Lord James he had part,
When they hewed a red path through a host of slain,
   To follow the Bruce's heart.

But Help and Hold, as I've been told,
   May be seen in St. Katherine's chapelle;
And scion and heir of the house of St. Clair
   Still love a good hound well.

---

[1] The chapel of St. Katherine-in-the-Hopes, built by Sir William St. Clair, early in the fourteenth century.

[2] This Sir William was slain by the Moors in Spain, while accompanying the heart of Robert Bruce to the Holy Land.

ALICE OF ORMSKIRK

Days and months drag wearily by,
  Scenes and shadows, they haunt me still,
The starlit stream and the wintry sky,
  And the day dying out on the crest of the hill.

And the lights astir in the town below,
  There lived Alice, the frank and free ;
Many a flower could Ormskirk show,
  Alice alone looked kindly on me.

She could whisper, and smile, and sigh,
  Pleading, flattering, so can the rest ;
But oh ! the light in her roving eye
  Would have wiled the babe from its mother's breast.

I freighted my barque with the rich and rare,
  Alice of Ormskirk ! all for thee ;
Little I reckoned of cost or care,
  But I launched her out on a summer sea.

A summer sea, and a smiling sky,
  Never a ripple, and never a frown,
Never a token of shipwreck nigh ;
  What did it matter ?   The barque went down.

For though I was rugged, and wild, and free,
  I had a heart like another man ;
And oh ! had I known how the end would be,
  I would it had broke ere the play began.

SONGS AND VERSES

I would it had broke ere I sued in vain,
  Ere Alice grew cold and cruel to me ;
But though I was dizzy and sick with pain,
  I turned from her bower as haughty as she.

Alice of Ormskirk ! could ye not spare ?
  Never I bore you a thought of ill ;
Alice of Ormskirk, false and fair !
  You have darkened my life ! Must I love you still ?

Oh ! better for me that a blind-born child,
  Never a line I had learned to trace,
Than thus by a look and a laugh beguiled,
  To have read my doom in fair Alice's face.

And better for me to have made my bed
  Under the yews where my fathers sleep,
Calm and weary, at rest with the dead,
  Than have given my heart to fair Alice to keep.

Night by night must I pace the shore,
  Longing, lingering to and fro,
Questioning, " May I not see her once more,
  Alice of Ormskirk ? "—Answering " No ! "

And still the echoing sea-cave rings
  Its one unceasing pitiless strain,
And still the wild wave dashes and sings,
  " Never again love—never again ! "

GRISELDA

For though her smile was sad and faint,
  And though her voice was low,
She never murmured a complaint,
  Nor hinted at her woe;
Nor harboured in her gentle breast
  The lightest thought of ill,
Giving all—forgiving all,
  Pure and perfect still.

Confiding when the world was hard,
  And kind when it was cold,
What wealth of love was stored and barred
  Within that heart of Gold!
Exulting every grief to share,
  And every task fulfil;
Giving all—forgiving all,
  Fond and faithful still.

And when to crush that patient brow
  The storm-cloud broke at last,
And all her pride was shattered now,
  And all her power was past,
She meekly kissed the hand that smote,
  And yielded to its will,
Giving all—forgiving all,
  True and tender still.

LADY MARGARET

"AND grant me his life," Lady Margaret cried,
  "Oh! grant but his life to me,
And I'll give ye my gold and my lands so wide,
  An ye let my love go free.

"And spare me his life!" Lady Margaret prest,
  "As ye hope for pardon above,
And I'll give ye the heart from out of my breast
  For the life of my own true love!"

They led him forth to the silent square,
  In the grey of the morning sky,
And they gave him a cup of the red wine there,
  To drink, and then to die.

Without the gate Lady Margaret stood,
  And she watched for the rising sun,
Till it blushed on the stone-work and gleamed on the
      wood,
  And the headsman's work was done.

Not a limb she stirred ; but when noon-day's glow
  Smote down on her temples bare,
A fiercer sun had not melted the snow
  That streaked Lady Margaret's hair.

VALERIA'S DEATH IN THE COURT OF THE TEMPLE

(FROM "THE GLADIATORS")

THE hand I love hath dealt the blow,
  It is not hard to die like this;
I never thought such joy to know,
That these poor lips to thine should grow,
And all my soul to meet thee flow
  In one impassioned parting kiss.

The hand I love, 'tis mine at last,
  I press it to my sinking breast;
The tide of life is ebbing fast,
The game played out, the lot is cast,
The day gone down, the journey past,
  And nightfall brings eternal rest.

The hand I love, 'twas hardly won,
  Thou canst not prize it, girl, too high;
'Tis freely given, my task is done,
The thread of fate is wound and spun,
The tempest lulls at set of sun,
  And I can lay me down to die.

Dear hand I love, a long farewell!
  Remorse and shame I scorn to own;
Though hard she fought and low she fell,
Pride could not bid her love rebel,
And now her dying gasp shall tell,
  Valeria's heart was thine alone.

"AVE CÆSAR! MORITURI TE SALUTANT!"

WINE in thy visage, roses on thy brow,
   Thine arm begirt with blazing clasp and gem;
Patricians, Commons, eager but to bow
   And kiss thy garment's broad and crimson hem.
Barbarians, Romans, shouting Hail! and thou,
   Th' Imperial lord of earth, and us, and them,
Great patron! hearken to thy swordsmen's cry,
"Good-morrow, Cæsar! we are here to die!"

No Eastern slaves, the dainty fan to hold,
   No satraps we, the jewelled train to bear,
Nor gaudy guards with helm and shield of gold,
   Nor silken eunuchs, plump, and smooth, and fair;
But champions of the arena, firm and bold,
   Men prompt to strike, as they are loth to spare;
Those fiercest fight who have not where to fly:
"Good-morrow, Cæsar! we are here to die!"

A hopeful sight, forsooth! a gallant show!
   Piled to the top in heaps, they sit and stand,
Rank upon rank, and row succeeding row,
   A sea of faces turned to greet our band.
Aloft the canvas awning; and below,
   The dazzling sweep of white and thirsty sand;
Far above all, a blue and laughing sky:
"Good-morrow, Cæsar! we are here to die!"

SONGS AND VERSES

And now the bounds are set, the match is made;
  One shakes the prong across his shoulder bare,
In beaded folds the dangling net is laid;
  Close at his elbow stalks his deadly pair,
Armed with the vizored helm and gleaming blade.
  An hundred more are boasting, jesting there,
Mirth on the lip, defiance in the eye:
"Good-morrow, Cæsar! we are here to die!"

The air is sick and tainted; well I know
  Behind yon boards the Libyan monster lies,
Yawns for his prey and yearns to reach his foe,
  With dripping maw, and sullen, sleepless eyes.
Soon loud applause to dumb suspense shall grow,
  When man and brute are grappling for the prize,
The tiger and the swordsman—he and I:
"Good-morrow, Cæsar! we are here to die!"

The time draws near—even now I seem to feel
  The reeking gash—the torn and dragging limb;
Though to his heart I drive the quivering steel,
  What boots an athlete's arm to cope with *him*?
Beneath that crushing gripe my senses reel,
  White forms and whiter faces round me swim,
Paler and paler, fading ere they fly:
"Good-morrow, Cæsar! we are here to die!"

A goodly lot is ours, in truth, who drive,
  To please a cruel mob, the swordsman's trade;
Resting to drink, and roused again to strive,
  We drop the beaker, but to grasp the blade.
In death derided, pampered when alive,
  To fill the gaps by wanton slaughter made—
Gaps that a later brood must still supply:
"Good-morrow, Cæsar! we are here to die!"

I have a fair young wife at home—and he
   A loving mother ; and Rufellus leaves
Two bright-haired urchins, reaching to his knee ;
   With every stroke some kindred bosom grieves.
'Tis sad to hear the shouts—'tis sad to see
   How few the fallen a Roman crowd reprieves ;
In grim despair the prostrate champions lie :
" Good-morrow, Cæsar ! we are here to die ! "

To-morrow where shall be the long array
   That now defiles so bravely past thy throne—
The victims and the heroes of to-day ?
   Yet comes to-morrow not for us alone.
The bow is bent, nor Jove himself can stay,
   Nor fate recall, the shaft that once had flown ;
And ours hath struck, and thine is hovering nigh :
" Good-morrow, Cæsar ! all are here to die ! "

HERO AND LEANDER

BARE was the shapely form of Hero's love,
    Such form as woke to life the sculptor's art;
Black was the wave and wild the heaven above,
    And chill the fears that curdled round her heart,

As Hero restless turned, and rose to trim
    The friendly radiance of that flickering light,
And still she sighed and trembled still for him,
    Far on the deep beneath the brooding night.

"Yet not so far for *him*, the strong, the brave,
    Whose glad embrace nor time nor tide can bar,
Who boasts his mastery o'er the leaping wave,
    Stout loving heart!   'Tis surely not so far!"

With that she summoned courage, and the flame
    She fed afresh, then turned her to the door,
And starting smiled—and blushed for very shame,
    A blush that left her paler than before.

For no one entered—and the marble stair
    Showed wide and cheerless in her lonely tower,
And something whispered, "Can another fair
    Have lured my false Leander to her bower?"

Ungenerous thought!   "Why tarrieth he so long?"
    Ungenerous thought! half stifled ere it grew;
The gathering waves, the current deep and strong,
    The swimmer's gasping need, too well she knew.

And he was battling on the while as still
  Battles the loving heart, though storms arise,
The loving heart, that strives through good and ill,
  And though it fail at last, unconquered dies.

When first he plunged to meet the opposing wave,
  How comely was that shape, so fresh and bright!
With vigorous strokes, its sidelong way that clave,
  Exulting, godlike, in its youthful might.

The moon shone fitful down in shimmering line;
  Her own Endymion was not half so fair
As he who laughed aloud to lip the brine,
  And shake the sea-drops from his glistening hair.

Sweet was the siren's voice, yet all in vain,
  To lure him back she smote her sounding shell;
And wreathed her snowy arms—unheard the strain,
  Unseen the gesture, and unfelt the spell.

For Hero's glimmering beacon shone to guide,
  And Hero's voice seemed murmuring in his ear;
Though long the watery way, and fierce the tide,
  Ere breath and sinew failed, the goal was near.

But still the wind was freshening, and the deep
  Swelled up in whiter surges, broad and high;
And what could strength 'gainst that resistless
      sweep,
  And what was courage good for, but to die?

Thrice did the choking waters o'er him close,
  Athwart the moon, a driving cloud sped on,
Ere it had passed, a score of bubbles rose
  To spot the wrinkled wave—and he was gone.

SONGS AND VERSES

So Hero woke, and watched, and whiter grew,
　　The beacon fire died out as day drew nigh ;
And on the woman's cheek a paler hue
　　Showed cold and sad beneath the morning sky.

The dawn flushed up.　As sinking to their sleep,
　　In longer curve the waters heaved and rolled ;
While o'er the sobs of a relenting deep,
　　The sunrise drew its sheet of molten gold.

Another morn its shining promise gave,
　　Another day of Light and Life in store ;
And yet a corpse was on the dancing wave,
　　A woman's heart was breaking on the shore.

She saw and stretched her arms ; one stifled moan,
　　One blinding plunge, she reached Leander's side ;
Cold was her darling's sleep, yet not alone,
　　He loved and battled, she but loved and died.

YSONDE WITH THE WHITE HAND

TRISTREM lies desperately wounded. The gangrene becomes daily worse, and can be cured by none but Ysonde of Cornwall. Tristrem despatches Ganhardin to Ysonde, with his ring as a token, directing him to communicate to the queen the extremity of his distress. He desires him to take with him two-sails, one white and the other black; the former to be hoisted on his return in case Ysonde should accompany him to Brittany, and the latter if his embassy should oe unsuccessful. Ysonde of Brittany overhears the conversation, and resolves to be avenged of her husband for his infidelity. Ganhardin goes to England disguised as a merchant. Ysonde disguises herself, and accompanies Ganhardin on board ship to undertake Sir Tristrem's cure. They approach the coast of Brittany displaying the white sail. Ysonde of Brittany perceives the vessel, and knows from the token of the white sail that her rival is on board. Fired with jealousy, she hastens to Sir Tristrem, and tells him the ship is in sight. He conjures her to tell him the colour of the sails. She informs him they are black, on which, concluding himself forsaken by Ysonde, Tristrem sinks back in despair and dies. Ysonde of Cornwall arrives, learns the death of her lover, and expires for grief.

["Sir Tristrem." Abridged from the French metrical romance in the style of "Tomas of Erceldoun," by Sir Walter Scott.]

"YSONDE of Brittany,
  With the white hand,—
Cleaving the western sea,
  Coasting the strand,
Look if a ship there be
  Sailing to land,—
Ysonde of Brittany,
  With the white hand!"

"Red in the western sea,
  Sinketh the sun,   ·

Never a ship to thee
  Saileth but one ;
Love on her deck may be,
  Leechcraft is none :
Husband, so false to me,
  Ill hast thou done !"

"'LOOK IF A SHIP THERE BE
SAILING TO LAND.'"

"Ysonde, my troth and plight,
  Are they not thine?
Wife, lest I die to-night,
  Read me the sign.
Sail hath she black or white
  Dipping the brine?
Read me the truth aright,
  Fair wife of mine !"

" Black as the raven's wing
   Flouting the slain,
Black as the cloud in spring
   Breaking to rain ;
Black as the wrongs that fling
   Shame on us twain,
Flappeth her sail to bring
   Succour in vain ! "

Drooped his unconquered head,
   Paler he grew ;
Death on his marriage-bed
   Held him, he knew.
Word of reproach he said,
   Never but two ;
Breathed, while the spirit fled,
   " Ysonde—untrue ! "

Ysonde of Cornwall, see
   Heart-broken, stand ;
Tristrem was dead ere she
   Leaped to the land.
Lulled may thy vengeance be,
   Deftly 'twas planned ;
Ysonde of Brittany,
   With the white hand !

THE PROUD LADYE

'TIS a cheerless morn for a gallant to swim,
  And the moat shines cold and clear;
Sir Knight, I was never yet baulked of my whim,
And I long for the lilies that float on the brim,
  Go, bring me those blossoms here!"
Then I offered them low on my bended knee,
"They are faded and wet," quoth the Proud Ladye.

"THEN I OFFERED THEM LOW ON MY BENDED KNEE."

A jay screamed out from the topmost pine,
  That waved by the castle wall,
And she vowed if I loved her I'd never decline
To harry his nest for this mistress of mine,
  Though I broke my own neck in the fall;

MISCELLANEOUS VERSE

Then I brought her the eggs and she flouted me,
"You would climb too high," said the Proud Ladye.

The lists were dressed and the lances in rest,
  And the knightly band arrayed ;
'Twas stout Sir Hubert who bore him best,
With a queen's white glove carried high on his crest
  Till I shore it away with my blade.
But I reeled as I laid it before her. "See,
It is soiled with your blood," said the Proud Ladye.

"You have sweet red lips, and an ivory brow,
  But your heart is as cold as a stone,
Though I loved you so fondly and truly, now
I have broken my fetters and cancelled my vow,
  You may sigh at your lattice alone ;
There are women as fair who are kinder to me,
Go look for another, my Proud Ladye!"

Her tears fell fast, she began to rue,
  When she counted the cost of her pride,
Till she played and lost it she never knew
The worth of a heart that is loving and true ;
  And she beckoned me back to her side,
While softly she whispered, "I love but thee!"
So I won her at last, my Proud Ladye.

THE FAIRIES' SPRING

They have stolen the child from his father's hand,
  He is missed from his mother's knee;
They have borne him away to their elfin land,
To ride in the van of a fairy band,
  For a babe of the cross was he;
Fond father, meek mother, ye seek him in vain,
Ye never shall look on your darling again.

To the mountain-side where the flowers grew wild,
  He would wander forth to play;
And the fairies had seen that winsome child,
With his golden curls and blue eyes mild,
  And simple childish way;
So the elf-king caught him, "Come hither," said he;
"Come ride to the land of the fairies with me!"

He thought not once of his mother's woe,
  He forgot his father's home,
For they brought him a steed like the driven snow,
And he smiled as they led him down below,
  Through middle earth to roam;
And they showed him their treasure of jewels and gold,
And they welcomed the boy, for they loved him of old.

But the child soon pined for his mother's care,
  He pined for the light of day,
He pined for the freshness of upper air,
His blue eye ached with the blinding glare
  Of their cavern's magic ray;

For the sign of the cross had been pressed on his brow
And he might not be thrall to the fairy folk now.

But few that have lived with the elfin race
    May visit this earth again ;
No more shall he smile in his mother's face,
For his spirit hath flown to its heavenly place,
    With the fairies it might not remain ;
Though deeply they loved him, and hopeless and wild
Was the elfins' grief for the Christian child.

They buried him down in a cavern lone,
    Deep, deep in the mountain's womb,
And their tears welled up through the hard grey stone,
To the turf above, as they made their moan
    O'er the infant's early tomb ;
And sweet to the thirsting lips of men
Is the spring of tears in the fairies' glen.

CHASTELÂR

As an upland bare and sere
In the waning of the year,
When the golden drops are withered off the broom ;
As a picture when the pride
Of its colouring hath died,
And faded like a phantom into gloom ;

As a night without a star,
Or a ship without a spar,
Or a mist that broods and gathers on the sea :
As a court without a throne,
Or a ring without a stone,
Seems the widowed land of France, bereft of thee !

Our darling pearl and pride,
Our blossom and our bride,
Wilt thou never gladden eyes of ours again ?
Would the waves might rise and drown
Barren Scotland and her crown,
So thou wert back with us in fair Touraine !

CHASTELÂR

WHAT need have we of beacon sheen
  To warn us or to save,
With the star-bright eyes of our lovely queen
  Guiding us o'er the wave?

What need have we of a flowing tide,
  What need of a smiling sky?
'Tis sunshine ever at Mary's side,
  And summer when she is by.

Her glances, like the day-god's light,
  On each and all are thrown;
Like him she shines, impartial, bright,
  Unrivalled, and alone.

Alone! alone! an ice-queen's lot,
  Though dazzling on a throne;
Ah! better to love in the lowliest cot
  Than pine in a palace, alone.

CHASTELÂR

The brightest gems in heaven that glow
  Shine out from midmost sky ;
The whitest pearls of the sea below
  In its lowest caverns lie.
He must stretch afar who would reach a star,
  Dive deep for the pearl, I trow ;
And the fairest rose that in Scotland blows
  Hangs high on the topmost bough.

The stream of the strath runs broad and strong,
  But sweeter the mountain-rill ;
And those who would drink with the fairy throng
  Must climb to the crest of the hill.
For the moonlit ring of the elfin-king
  Is danced on the steepest knowe,
And the bonniest rose that in Scotland blows
  Hangs high on the topmost bough.

The violet peeps from its sheltering brake,
  The lily lies low in the lea,
While the bloom is on ye may touch and take,
  For the humble are frank and free ;
But the garden's pride wears a thorn at her side,
  It has pricked to the bone ere now ;
And the noblest rose that in Scotland blows
  Hangs high on the topmost bough.

MISCELLANEOUS VERSE

'Twere a glorious game to have bartered all
  For the bonniest branch in the bower,
And a man might well be content to fall
  In a leap for its queenliest flower.
To win her indeed were too princely a meed,
  To serve her is guerdon enow,
And the loveliest rose that in Scotland blows
  Hangs high on the topmost bough.

IN solitude the sparks are struck that bid the world
    admire,
Though heart and brain must scorch the while in
    self-consuming fire;
In solitude the sufferer smiles, defiant of his doom,
And madness sits aloof, and waits, and gibbers in the
    gloom.
'Tis dazzling work to weave at will from fancy's brightest
    dyes,
And speed the task, ungrudging all, we have, and hope,
    and prize;
But it must make the devils laugh, to mark how, day by
    day,
The plague-spot widens out and spreads, and eats the web
    away.
In vain the unwilling rebel writhes, so loth defeat to own,
Turns from the day, and scorns to pray, and couches down
    alone.
Oh! better far to wail aloud, on earth and heaven to cry,
Than, like the panther in its lair, to gnash his teeth and
    die.
Then help me, brother, help me! For thy heart is made
    like mine,
The shaft that drains my life away is haply winged for
    thine;
It is not good to stand alone the common cross to bear,
But two or three like one must be, and God shall hear
    their prayer.

MARY HAMILTON

THERE'S a bonny wild-rose on the mountain-side,
      Mary Hamilton.
In the glare of noon she hath drooped and died,
      Mary Hamilton.
Soft and still is the evening shower,
Pattering kindly on brake and bower,
But it falls too late for the perished flower,
      Mary Hamilton.

There's a lamb lies lost at the head of the glen,
      Mary Hamilton.
Lost and missed from sheiling and pen,
      Mary Hamilton.
The shepherd has sought it through toil and heat,
And sore he strove when he heard it bleat,
Ere he wins to the lamb, it lies dead at his feet,
      Mary Hamilton.

The mist is gathering ghostly and chill,
      Mary Hamilton.
And the weary maid cometh down from the hill,
      Mary Hamilton.
The weary maid, but she's home at last,
And she trieth the door, but the door is fast,
For the sun is down and the curfew past,
      Mary Hamilton.

SONGS AND VERSES

Too late for the rose, the evening rain,
>Mary Hamilton.
Too late for the lamb, the shepherd's pain,
>Mary Hamilton.
Too late at the door the maiden's stroke,
Too late the plea when the doom hath been spoke,
Too late the balm when the heart is broke,
>Mary Hamilton.

THE MAIDEN'S VOW

A WOMAN may better her word, I trow;
　　Now lithe and listen, my lords, to me,
And I'll tell ye the tale of the Maiden's Vow,
　　And the roses that bloomed on the bonny rose-tree.

The queen of the cluster, beyond compare,
　　Aloft in the pride of her majesty hung;
Bright and beautiful, fresh and fair,
　　The bevy of blossoms around her clung.

So the winds came wooing from east and west,
　　Wooing and whispering frank and free;
But she folded her petals, quoth she, " I am best
　　On a stalk of my own, at the top of the tree."

And they folded their petals, the rosebuds too,
　　And closer they clung as the wind swept by;
For they vowed a vow, that sisterhood true,
　　Together to fade, and together to die.

" Never a wind shall a rosebud wrest,
　　Never a gallant shall wile us away,
To wear in his bonnet, to wear on his breast,"
　　Rose and rosebuds answering, " Nay."

So staunch were the five to their word of mouth,
　　They baffled the suitors that thronged to the bower;
Till a breeze came murmuring out of the south,
　　And stole home to the heart of the queenliest flower.

SONGS AND VERSES

So she bent her beauty to hear him sigh,
  And ever the brighter and fairer she grew;
What wonder then that each rosebud nigh
  Should open its leaves to the breezes too?

Oh gather the dew while the freshness is on,
  Roses and maidens they fade in a day;
Ere you've tasted the sweetness the morning is gone:
  Love at your leisure, but wed while you may.

Winter is coming and time shall not spare ye,
  Beautiful blossom, so fragrant and sheen;
Joy to the gallants that win ye and wear ye,
  Joy to the roses and joy to their queen!

RETRORSUM

THE dreary fen, from edge to edge,
   Is barren, blank, and sere,
The hoar-frost stiffens in the sedge,
   There's ice upon the mere;
The woodcock in the moon-lit night
   Comes flitting o'er the sea:
What is this phantom, pale and bright,
   That walks with me?

Her eyes are sad, her touch is chill,
   Her voice is soft and low,
Her face is very fair, and still
   Her face is vexed with woe.
She turns her head from side to side,
   And ever looks she back,
Like one who seeks a missing guide,
   Lost on the track.

She lays her quiet hand on mine,
   It freezes to the bone;
Quoth she, " I need no mark nor sign
   To stamp thee for mine own;
Through good and ill, by board and bed,
   With me thy lot is cast,
Me hast thou loved, me didst thou wed;
   I am the Past!

SONGS AND VERSES

" Fair is the Future's shadowy grace,
    She flaunts a tempting prize,
And through the veil that dims her face
    There's promise in her eyes ;
I fear her not—I court the strife ;
    Poor rival must she be,
When all the best of all thy life
    Is bound to me.

" The Present, like a lavish dame,
    Invites thee to her arms,
And looks, and laughs, and bids thee claim
    Her favour and her charms.
That breathing form in act to clasp,
    Oh ! woman to the core !
She melts to nothing in thy grasp,—
    A dream—no more.

" But I am faithful, real, and true,
    From me thou shalt not part :
My wreath of rosemary and rue
    I've wound about thy heart.
I fill thy being, sense, and brain ;
    Mine, while thou drawest breath,
Mine, by the sacrament of pain,
    Even in death !

" Because in life thou didst refuse
    To wince beneath the goad,
Because thy constancy could choose
    The labour and the load ;

Because, like one who scorns defeat
    And falls upon his sword,
Thou didst elect thy fate to meet,—
    Have thy reward.

" Accept the wages, count the cost,
    The toil against the gain ;
Some bitter in the sweet is lost,
    If love be twined with pain ;
If sorrow, like a summer-night,
    Reflect with tender ray
The memory of a vanished light
    That once was day.

" Have thy reward ; I am thy mate,
    Nor wouldst thou barter me
For all that Fancy could create,
    For all that fact could be.
Hereafter in the eternal sphere,
    Where endless ages roll,
Thine, by the bond that bound us here,
    Bride of thy soul.

" Did I not wring from out thy core
    The dross of earthly leaven ?
Assign the task, and teach the lore
    That finds a path to heaven ;
Point where the gate of mercy stands
    Beyond the narrow way,
And force thee down with loving hands
    To kneel and pray ?

"Beneath that moonshine calm and cold,
  Look outward o'er the sea ;
Where shoots a trailing star, behold
  Thy progress but for me !
An upward flash, a feeble light,
  A fleeting, flickering spark,
A little gleam, a downward flight,
  Lost in the dark !

"Quenched by a false and godless glare,
  I nursed the sacred flame,
Cleansed it with penitence and prayer
  From taint of sin and shame.
Thus perfect, purified, and bright,
  This marriage-torch shall cheer
Our watches through the lingering night,
  Till dawn appear.

"Then call me by what name thou wilt,
  Remembrance or Regret,
Repentance, or Remorse for guilt,
  But clasp me closer yet.
Mine is the staff thy steps to stay,
  The hand to hold thee fast,
And mine the lamp that lights the way
  To heaven at last."

THE QUEEN OF THE ROSES

I WATCHED her in the morning hour,
   So pure and fresh and fair,
A blossom bursting into flower,
   That gladdened all the air.

I marked her shedding sweets around
   Beneath the noon-tide ray,
The glory of the garden-ground,
   The pride of the summer's day.

But long before the daylight's close
   The southern blast awoke,
And crushed and tore the queenly rose
   Beneath its pelting stroke.

Alas! her petals strew the bower,
   Yet, mangled though she lie,
The fragrance of that perished flower
   Floats upward to the sky.

I SPIED a sweet moss-rose my garden adorning,
  With a blush at her core like the pink of a shell,
And I wrung from her petals the dew-drop of morning,
  And gathered her gently and tended her well;
For the bee and the butterfly round her were humming,
  To whisper their flattering love-tale and fly,
And too surely I knew that the season was coming
  When the flower must fade and the insect must die.

So deep in the shade of my chamber I brought her,
  And sheltered her safe from the wind and the sun,
And cared for her kindly, and dipped her in water,
  And vowed to preserve her when summer was done.
Though dark was my dwelling, this darling of Flora,
  This spirit of beauty enlivened the gloom:
Was it strange, was it wrong, I should love and adore her?
  Should bathe in her fragrance and bask in her bloom?

But long ere the brightness of summer was shaded,
  My moss-rose was drooping and withering away;
Her perfume had perished, her freshness had faded,
  The very condition of life is decay.
And now more than ever I cherish and prize her,
  For love shall not falter, though beauty depart:
And dearer to me that the others despise her,
  My moss-rose is lying crushed home to my heart.

THE FAIREST FLOWER

The painted pinks are gay and glad,
  The rose is blushing red,
The lady-lily, pale and sad,
  Hangs meekly down her head;
A carpet rich in countless dyes,
  Marred by a single blot,
For seeking still the flower I prize,
Meets but to mock my weary eyes,
  The blank where she is not!

A golden insect hums aloft,
  Nor pauses in its quest;
A wind steals in, and whispers soft
  Of summers in the west;
They search the garden through and through,
  They try each wealthy plot,
The bee to wed, the breeze to woo
That missing flower, and only sue
  The blank where she is not!

And here and there, now low, now high,
  In many a darting ring,
There shoots a shade across the sky,
  The wild bird on the wing;
The wild bird hurries to and fro
  About each well-known spot,
That breathed her fragrance long ago,
That hath not kept one leaf to show
  The blank where she is not!

SONGS AND VERSES

I, too, must wander lonely round
    An unfrequented bower,
And mourn through all the garden ground,
    My early withered flower;
My hopes that foundered, freight and barque,
    My changed and cheerless lot;
For still my life is cold and dark,
And still my heart is sad to mark
    The blank where she is not!

"JOHN ANDERSON"

THINE eyes are meeker, sadder now,
  Though softly still they shine,
And on thy staid and gentle brow
  I trace the thoughtful line.

The voice is dearest of music still,
  Though its tones are hushed and low ;
While deep to my heart those accents thrill,
  As they thrilled to it long ago.

And here and there a silver thread
  Amongst thy locks I spy,
Where the hand of Time on thy dainty head
  Hath but blessed it, and so passed by.

For the golden years have fled to the past,
  And indeed, if truth must be told,
While the wheel spins bravely, the flax wears fast,
  And love, we are growing old.

We are growing old. Oh! the morn was bright,
  And rich was the noontide ray,
But the sunset hour with its fading light
  Is the sweet of the summer's day.

And though spring be so fair with her laughing eyes,
  Like a maid in her early bloom,
There's a holier calm in the autumn skies,
  When the harvest is gathered home.

And a task is in store for the mountain-rill,
　　Though its youth be so fresh and free,
It must fatten the pasture, and feed the mill,
　　Ere it steal to its rest in the sea.

For onward, onward, the river flows,
　　And widens by the way—
And many a noble reach it shows,
　　And many a sunlit bay.

Calmer, and broader, and seaward still,
　　Till headland and cape be past ;
And the stream that was once but a trickling rill,
　　Is lost in the deep at last.

We must all float on with the silent stream,
　　Float out to the silent sea,
Where the soul wakes up from a restless dream,
　　In the hush of eternity !

LOVE'S PEDIGREE

Wild Folly, certain legends tell,
  Was wedded to a maid,
A dusky maid that loved to dwell,
  In drowsy summer shade.

Their offspring is a fairy elf,
  A thing of tricks and wiles,
He plays with hearts to please himself,
  And when they break he smiles.

Unpitied pain, and toil in vain,
  That little tyrant brings ;
And those who fain would slip his chain
  Must cheat him of his wings.

To Cupid's torture, you may guess,
  Each parent lends a part,
The chain, the toil, from Idleness,
  While Folly adds the smart.

ON A SKETCH

*By Augustus Lumley, Esq., of a Cavalier's widow looking
at her husband's portrait*

So bright a gleam, so dear a dream,
So few the happy years !
A loving past, too fair to last,
And nothing left but tears.

"WHAT HAVE I LEFT, OF THEE BEREFT ?"

Melts into space, thy portrait's grace
As daylight into gloom ;

MISCELLANEOUS VERSE

The wreath I braid must droop and fade,
  Ere it can deck thy tomb.

What have I left, of thee bereft?
  My darling bright and brave,
But long lone hours, dead hopes and flowers,
  A picture and a grave!

THE BULLFINCH [1]

My first is the point of an Irishman's tale,
  My second's a tail of its own to disclose ;
But I warn you in time, lest your courage should fail,
  If you're troubled with either the shakes or the slows,
That the longer you look at my whole in the vale,
  The bigger, and blacker, and bitterer it grows !

[1] The reference is not ornithological, but to the thick, high hedges of the Midlands, which hunting men term " bullfinches," because they look as if nothing bigger than a bullfinch could force its way through them.—ED.

THE BONNY BREAST-KNOTS

My first is for my darling's head,
　My second for her hair,
My whole, in loops of white and red,
　I bring her from the fair;
She loves it better sung than said,
　That bonny Scottish air.

FORGET ME NOT

FORGET me not, though I repine
   Because you've found a fresher heart
To give it all that once was mine,
   I'll say farewell, and part!

Because you've found a fairer face,
   A nobler name, a lovelier lot,
I'll meekly bow, and yield my place,
   But oh! forget me not.

For all the world you've been to me,
   And half the world you take away;
The joy of summer from the tree,
   The glory from the day.

To leave a dead year's barren curse,
   A dead leaf whirling on the lawn,
A soulless, starless night, and worse,
   A hopeless, helpless dawn.

Not much I sought.   I had my dream;
   Dear love, your very words I quote,
" A rose, the ripple of a stream,
   A blue sky and a boat."

But roses fade as roses blow,
   And summer skies can lower and frown;
The stream runs deep and dark, and so
   This boat of ours went down.

Hard, hard, to learn the common task!
   Hard, hard, to bear the common lot!
For pity's sake, 'tis all I ask,
   Forget me not, forget me not!

TRUE METAL

For this is love, and this alone,
  Not counting cost nor grudging gain,
That builds its life into a throne,
  And bids the idol reign.

That hopes and fears, yet seldom pleads,
  And for a sorrow weakly borne
(Because it yields not words but deeds)
  Can hide a gentle scorn.

In pride and pique that takes no part,
  Of self and sin that bears no taint,
The homage of a knightly heart
  For a woman and a saint.

Such love will wear through shine and shower,
  Such love can bear to bide its time,
Unwearied at the vesper hour
  As when the matins chime.

Though hate itself be fain to shrink,
  It freely ventures lose or win ;
And friendship shivers on the brink,
  While love leaps boldly in.

And love can strive against a host,
  Can watch and wait and suffer long,
Still daring more, when fearing most,
  In very weakness strong.

Though bruised and sore it never dies,
  Though faint and weary standing fast,
It never fails.   And thus the prize
  Is won by love at last.

ESPÉRANCE

THE vines are thick, the clods are brown,
    Hard is the toil, thy Lord's behest,
And weak the arm, though girt the gown,
    And faint the heart within thy breast;
A noonday sun pours fiercely down,
    My Brother, shall we rest?

Strong is the foe, and sharp the fray,
    With shivered lance and cloven shield
The champions fall, the ranks give way,
    Along the front, across the field,
The stoutest knights are down.   Then say,
    My Brother, shall we yield?

Forbid it, honour, courage, trust!
    Forbid it, all that's brave and wise!
Toil freely on, since toil you must,
    The day of harvest brings the prize;
From black defeat, and crimsoned dust,
    See golden victory rise!

Peace is the end and aim of strife,
    The palms of heaven are earned below;
Earth's vital powers are rich and rife,
    Beneath her winding-sheet of snow;
Death is itself the germ of life,
    And joy the child of woe.

Then Espérance! hope on, the fight
 Is never lost, while fight we may;
At home the hearth is shining bright,
 Though yet unseen along the way
And the darkest hour of all the night
 Is that which brings us day.

LOST

'TWAS yet but May, and here and there
　Pink and white the blossoms fell,
Quivering down through the summer air,
On the shaven sward so trim and bare.
　Oh! I remember well
The very network of the tree,
And its shadows dancing on her and me.
My old love, in the garden chair,
　Looking upward soft and shy,
With her oval face and her rippling hair,
And the rich white dress she used to wear,
　And her work laid idly by.
'Tis strange to think of now, and yet
'Twere stranger, harder, to forget.

Her eyes were deep with the light of love,
　And on her hands, and on her face,
Because the south wind laughed above,
　The blossoms showered apace.
She chid me gently, fondly, when
　Those blossoms to my lips I pressed;
But smiled her own dear smile, and then
　I laid them in my breast.
My old love spoke, the words she said,
　I think she could not deem them true:
"The time shall come when these are dead,
　Our love shall wither too!"
I held my peace, I bowed my head,
　Ah! not for *me*, I knew.

MISCELLANEOUS VERSE

At last I whispered, "Say not so,
　My darling, we are brave and strong;
And love so linked as ours, you know,
　Can strive and suffer long.
Its web may well be warped with woe,
　But never crossed with wrong!"

"MY OLD LOVE, IN THE GARDEN CHAIR."

She plied her work, beneath its modest bands
　Her face was hidden in her fragrant hair,
The tears were falling on her busy hands,
　And thus we parted there.

　.　　　.　　　.　　　.　　　.　　　.　　　.

The blue sea sparkles in the noontide ray,
　The eastern sun is flashing fiercely down,

Here watch the hosts, and yonder, in the bay,
  Lies the beleaguered town.
Hark! the alarum sounds—the French *rappel*
  Collects its eager crowd the trench to fill,
Our drums are beating and our trumpets swell,
  The *thin red line* is mustering on the hill.
    White tents in thousands dot the wasted plain,
      The canvas city, swarming like a fair,
    Wakes up to life, while hungering for the slain,
      A vulture hangs expectant in the air!
But laugh, and jest, and ready cheer,
  And cordial grip of hand in hand,
Would make the game of death appear
But some athletic pastime here,
    In this Crimean land.
  "Fall in!" the way they know too well,
The valley paved with shot and shell,
Accursed as the road to hell,
    That none may travel back.
  "Fall in! attention! steady!" so
The sergeants hurry to and fro,
The ranks are closed, the columns grow,
And winding downwards sure and slow,
    File off to the attack.
While booming out above their measured tread,
  That dull explosion loads the summer air;
It seems a requiem for the noble dead,
  A knell that bids the living brave despair.
It ceaseth not—no respite even when
  The daylight round of blood and strife is gone,
The hours come back, again, and yet again,
  And ever and anon
The death-watch of a hundred thousand men
  Ticks on—ticks on!

Through all the day—through all the night.
  The pale moon rises from the sea,
And sheds a wan and ghostly light
  On him and me.
For I was lying in the trench we made,
Wrapped in my cloak and belted with my blade,
A shattered gabion o'er my slumbers hung,
And down beside me was my comrade flung.
My comrade of a night, 'twas strange how deep,
How calm and moveless seemed that solemn sleep.

Beneath his hand his ready firelock lay,
His coarse red garb denoted common clay ;
A peasant's birth his homely form betrayed,
A peasant's peaceful lot, ere yet he made
His fatal choice—the bayonet for the spade.
I heard the mattock clink, the earthwork fall,
And yet my comrade slumbered through it all.
But hark ! as if to break the spell,
The rush and whistle of a shell
  Divides the midnight air.
The tools are dropped, the muskets ring,
Afoot recumbent figures spring,
From lip to lip the word they fling,
  An oath, a jest, a prayer.
"Stand to your arms, my lads !" 'tis thus we form
The living rampart it is death to storm.

But he alone seemed not to hear,
  My comrade never raised his head,
I bowed me down to scan him near,
  In sorrow rather than in dread ;
  The moon was shining cold and bright,
  My living instincts told me right,

SONGS AND VERSES

His face was fixed—his face was white!
　　Great God! the man was dead!
One stiffened arm was upward thrown, and where,
Beneath the toil-worn hand his wrist was bare,
Blue on the surface of its sallow skin,
A heart, a woman's name was punctured in.
By Heaven! 'twas no unmanly tear I shed,
One common weakness linked me with the dead:
That moment, like a flash I seemed to see
My love's white dress beneath the summer tree;
The next, with steadier pulse and calmer breath,
I took my place to meet or baffle death.

　　.　　　.　　　.　　　.　　　.　　　.　　　.

" Cheer, boys, cheer! "
　　That old familiar strain
No longer mocked the listening ear,
　　Our troops were home again.
An English sun was shining bright,
　　And English meadows green and gold
Were all a-glitter in the light.
　　How could she look so calm and cold?
With wealth of leaves our tree was fair,
It shaded but a cheerless pair;
　　My old love's face was pale and proud,
And I was all unused to bear
A wounded heart, and in despair,
　　My sorrow cried aloud.
" Here, take them back, the tress of hair,
　　The rose, the ring, the glove,
My pride shall never stoop to wear
For emblems but of friendly care
　　The gifts that once were love.
And couldst thou judge me thus unheard,
　　Was that thy faith, is this my due?

Though thousands backed the slanderous word,
  Thou shouldst have *known* me true !
Yes, take them back.   I'll tell thee now,
  All thou hast been to me,
How oft to death I bared my brow,
How pure and strict I kept my vow,
  And all for love of thee !
These very blossoms in my breast,
  That once from here I bore,
Behold them, do they not attest
  The truth of him who served thee best ?
Ay, mark them !"   Then I swore
  Her name from out my heart to wrest,
And care for her no more.
While in the mockery of the gaudy day
I laughed, and flung those withered leaves away.

She kept her eyes from off my face,
  She dared not trust herself to look ;
But stately, in her native grace,
  Though once I thought she shook,
With calm, defiant courtesy, bending low,
She left me, answering only " Be it so."
  .   .   .   .

My old lost love,
  Once more I stand beneath the tree ;
Through branches bleak and bare above,
  The wintry wind is blowing free.
The snow lies white upon the wold,
  The clouds are dark behind the hill,
Around me all is blank and cold ;
  My heart is colder, blanker still.
Ay, mock me in your dreary mirth,
  Ye spectral branches, nod and wave,

SONGS AND VERSES

For I am left alone on earth,
  And she is in her grave.
No more to ask, and plead, and vow,
  Too late for pardon or amends,
I'd give my whole existence now
  We two had only parted friends.
It seems so hard to think for us
  Not even hope can soften woe ;
'Tis cruel to have lost her thus,
  I loved her so !   I loved her so !
Not even hope, yet good men say
  Hope hath no home beneath the sky,
But dwells above, and only they
  Know how to live who live to die.
It must be so, and thus I bear
  My stripes, and bow me to the rod,.
In trust, ere long to follow where
  My darling's feet the path have trod ;
She surely will forgive me there,
  When we have met before our God.

VOID

GONE! wholly gone! How cold and dark,
  A cheerless world of hope bereft,
The beacon quenched, and not a spark,
  In all the dull grey ashes left!

No more, no more a living part
  In life's contending maze to own ;
Dead to its kind, an empty heart
  Feeds on itself, alone! alone!

The present but a blank, and worse,
  No ray along the future cast,
All blighted by the blighting curse,
  Except the past—except the past.

Ay, if the cup be crushed and spilt,
  More than the sin, the loss I rue ;
And if the cloud was black with guilt,
  The silver light of love shone through.

And though the price be maddening pain,
  One half their raptures to restore,
And live but half those hours again,
  I'd pay the cruel price once more.

Dreams! dreams! Not backward flows the tide
  Of life and love. It cannot be.
Well! thine the triumph and the pride,
  The suffering and the shame for me.

NIGHTFALL

LIKE a dream the past hath fled,
All its summer glories shed ;
Hope hath vanished, love is dead ;
　Lonely hours are mine to spend,
　　Watching ever, watching ever,
　Waiting for the end.

Though with promise fair and bright,
Morning rose in golden light,
Ere my noon, came down the night ;
　Welcome to me as a friend,
　　Watching ever, watching ever,
　Waiting for the end.

Sinking with the cruel load,
Sore and smarting to the goad,
Weary, weary of the road ;
　Heaven to me thy respite send !
　　Watching ever, watching ever,
　Waiting for the end.

A DREAM

I KNELT by the grave where my darling was sleeping,
  Cold in its little bed under the stone,
And I prayed that the angels might have it in keeping,
  For the child was in heaven, though I was alone. .

Bowed in the dust with my burden of sorrow,
  Hope had departed, and comfort had fled,
Dreary the vigil and distant the morrow,
  And dark is the hour when we watch by the dead.

Yet deep in my heart came a longing unspoken,
  For Infinite Mercy to grant me my prayer,
And yield to the poor stricken mourner a token
  That He who had taken would hold in His care.

Then round me there grew a great light that was rather
  The glory of God than the lustre of day,
And an angel came down from the·face of his Father,
  And poised o'er the spot where my little one lay.

Too soon he departed, but left me the power
  To gaze on his track when the vision had flown,
And behold in its beauty, fresh gathered, a flower
  From the gardens of heaven lay fair on the stone.

A DIRGE

HILLS of heaven, bright and shining,
  Bid thee welcome, spirits wait,
Thronging down to greet thee, twining
  Garlands at the golden gate;
See! before thee flash and quiver,
  Rising in eternal light,
Daybreak on the crystal river,
  And behind thee night!
Earth hath been wearing thee, now it is past,
    Providence sparing thee,
    Mercy preparing thee,
Angels are bearing thee homeward at last!

Quenched the bitter taste of sorrow,
  Lulled the angry throb of pain,
Glad, yet fearless of the morrow,
  Thine the bliss, without the bane.
Done with earthly trouble, taking
  Thought no more for earthly care,
Spent with earthly travail, waking .
  For its wages there!
Earth hath been wearing thee, now it is past,
    Providence sparing thee,
    Mercy preparing thee,
Angels are bearing thee homeward at last!

Songs of heaven, triumphant singing,
  Rank on rank, in waves of light,

March the immortal legions, bringing
   Crown of gold and robe of white ;
Far above them, lustre streaming
   Round its towers, unbuilt by hands,
Through a mist of glory beaming,
   See, the city stands !
Earth hath been wearing thee, now it is past,
    Providence sparing thee,
    Mercy preparing thee,
Angels are bearing thee homeward at last !

I KNOW I have heard them sing, child, and I know
    that they spoke to me,
With my mother's arms about me, while I sat on my
    mother's knee;
And she told me of love that saved us, and a Father
    we had on high,
And the grave that we need not fear, child, and the
    soul that can never die.
In the gleam of the summer lime-trees, in the glow
    of the summer's day,
And I heard them singing faintly then, for they seemed
    so far away.

Again, when I walked with the loved one; you remember
    the loved one, dear,
And the smile that is gone from among us, and the
    voice we no longer hear,
The voice was so tender and earnest, that joy was too
    deep for mirth,
And the heart was too full for speech, child, and
    heaven had come down on earth.
Not a drop in the cup seemed wanting, the thirst of a
    life to fill,
And farther and fainter the song died out — but I
    heard the angel still.

Then the loved one was taken from me, and I bowed
    my head in my hand,
For my barque was free on a silent sea, and I was alone
    on the strand;

The day had gone down for me, child, the light of my
    life was fled,
And I longed for the sleep of an endless night, and to
    lay me beside the dead.
Then I clung to the arm that smote me, with a prayer
    from a bended knee,
And my heart climbed up to meet the song—and the
    song floated down to me.

I have heard it so often since, child, at church on the
    holy morn
When the music swells, and the praise goes up, that
    "to us a Child is born."
And here in the hush of my home-life, and there
    where the little ones play,
And once in the tremble of twilight at the turn of the
    night and the day;
Each time they sing in a sweeter strain, they call in
    a clearer tone,
And I look for the Reaper to house the grain, and the
    Master to claim His own.

I think it will not be long, child, they are bidding me
    home at last,
To the place where the joy of the future shall be
    linked on the love of the past—
Where the houseless shall seek a shelter, the lonely
    shall find a friend,
Where the heart's desire shall be granted that hath
    trusted and loved to the end;
Where there's fruit in the gardens of heaven from
    hopes that on earth were betrayed,
Where there's rest for the soul life-wearied, that hath
    striven, and suffered, and prayed.

AN ANGEL IN THE WAY

FAIR the downward path is spread,
  Love and light thy coming greet ;
Fruit is blushing o'er thy head,
  Flowers are springing 'neath thy feet ;
Mirth and sin, with tossing hands,
  Wave thee on, a willing prey ;
Yet an instant pause—there stands
  An angel in the way.

Heed the heavenly warning, know
  Fairest flowers the feet may trip ;
Fruits, that like the sunset glow,
  Turn to ashes on the lip.
Though the joys be wild and free,
  Though the paths be pleasant, stay !
Even mortal eye can see
  An angel in the way.

Wilt thou drown in worldly pleasure ?
  Wilt thou have, like him of old,
Length of days and store of treasure,
  Wisdom, glory, power, and gold ?
Life and limb, shall sickness waste,
  Want shall grind thee day by day,
Still to win thee, God hath placed
  An angel in the way.

Trusting all on things that perish,
  Shall a hopeless faith be thine ?

Earthly idol wilt thou cherish?
  Bow before an earthly shrine?
Meet rebuke to mortal love
  Yearning for a child of clay,
Death shall cross thy path and prove
  An angel in the way.

When the prophet thought to sin,
  Tempted by his heathen guide;
When a prince's grace to win,
  Prophet-lips would fain have lied,—
Even the brute the sage controlled
  Found a human voice, to say
" Master, smite me not—Behold
  An angel in the way!"

So, when vice, to lure her slave,
  Woos him down the shining track,
Spirit-hands are stretched to save,
  Spirit-voices warn him back.
Heart of man! to evil prone,
  Chafe not at thy sin's delay;
Bow thee humbly down, and own
  An angel in the way.

R. I. P.

REST thee, proud peerless face!
   · Rest thee, fair head!
There, in that other place,
Wearing each living trace,
Beauty, and scornful grace,
    Peace to the dead!

Rest thee, fond wilful heart!
   Where thou art fled!
Clear of the strife thou art,
Ours is the living smart,
Thine is the better part,
    Peace to the dead!

Rest thee, beloved one!
   Well hast thou sped!
Sand of thy glass is run,
Trouble and toil are done,
Sorrow to vex thee none,
    Peace to the dead!

Rest, where we lay thee deep
   In thy lone bed ;
Tears never more to weep,
Vigil nor ward to keep,
Folded at last to sleep,
    Peace to the dead!

BONES AND I

BONES AND I

BONES AND I

THE SKELETON AT HOME

———+———

INTRODUCTION

ONG ago, visiting the monastery of La Trappe, I was struck with the very discontented appearance of its inmates. In some of their faces, indeed, I detected no expression whatever, but on none could I perceive the slightest gleam of satisfaction with their lot. No wonder; few men are of the stuff that makes a good recluse. The human animal is naturally gregarious, like the solan goose, the buffalo, the monkey, or the mackerel. Put him by himself, he pines for lack of mental aliment, just as a flower fades for want of daylight in the dark. A multitude of fools forms an inspiriting spectacle, a solitary specimen becomes a sad and solemn warning. If the Trappists, who are not entirely isolated from their kind, thus wither under the rigour of those repressive rules enjoined by the Order, what must have been the condition of such hermits and anchorites as passed whole months, and even years together, in the wilderness, unvisited by anything more human than the distempered phantoms of their dreams? No shave, no wash, no morning greeting, and no evening wine. How many, I wonder, preserved their sanity in the ordeal? how many, returning dazed and bewildered to the haunts of men, tottered about in helpless, wandering, maundering imbecility? Were there not some hard, boisterous natures who plunged wildly into the excesses of a world so long forsworn, with all the appetite of abstinence, all the reckless self-abandonment of the paid-off man-of-war's man on a spree? No; few people are qualified for recluses. I am proud to be amongst the number.

I live in a desert, but my desert is in the very heart of London. The waste is all round me, though; I have taken good care of that. Once, indeed, it blossomed like the rose, for a thousand fertilising streams trickled through its bright expanse. Do not you as I did. I turned all the streams into one channel, "in the sweet summer-time long ago," and "sat by the river," like those poor fools in the song, and said, "Go to! Now I shall never thirst again!" But in the night there came a landslip from the upper level, and choked the river, turning its course through my neighbour's pastures, so that the meadows, once so green and fresh, are bare and barren now for evermore. I speak in parables, of course ; and the value of " this here obserwation," like those of Captain Bunsby, "lies in the application of it." I need not observe, the street in which I hide myself is a *cul de sac*. A man who sells chick-weed, perhaps I should say, who would sell chickweed if he could, is the only passenger. Of the houses on each side of me, one is un-finished, the other untenanted. Over the way, I confront the dead wall at the back of an hospital. Towards dusk in the late autumn, when the weather is breaking, I must admit the situation is little calculated to generate over - exuberance of animal spirits. Sequestered, no doubt, shady too, particularly in the short days, and as remote from the noise or traffic of the town as John o' Groat's House, but enlivening—No.

On first beginning to reside here, I confess I felt at times a little lonely and depressed. There-fore I brought home " Bones " to come and live with me. And who *is* Bones ? Ah! that is exactly what I have never been able to find out. Contemplative, affable, easily pleased, and an admirable listener, he is yet on some points re-served to a degree that might almost be termed morose ; while in his personal appearance there is a dignity of bearing, an imposing presence, which forbids the most intimate associate to attempt a liberty.

I will describe him, as I see him at this moment, reclining in an easy attitude on the cushions of my favourite arm-chair, benevolently interested, it would seem, in my lightest movements, while I sit smoking silently by the fire. Neither of us is a great talker quite so early in the evening.

He is a well-formed and very complete skeleton of middle height—perfect in every respect, and in all his articulations, with the exception of two double teeth absent from the upper jaw. The arch of his lower ribs is peculiarly symmetrical, and his vertebræ are put in with a singular combination of flexibility and strength. As I look at him now leaning back in a graceful attitude, with one thigh-bone thrown carelessly over the other, he reminds me of so many people I knew when I lived in the world, that I seem to fancy myself once more a denizen of that revolving purgatory which goes by the name of general society. Poor A—— was almost as fleshless, B—— much more taciturn, and C—— decidedly not so good-looking. Bones, however, possesses a quality that I have never found in any other companion. His tact is beyond praise. Under no circumstances does he become a bore—that is why we get on so admirably together. Like a ghost, he speaks only when spoken to. Unlike a wife, refrains from monopolising the last word. If he didn't rattle so on the slightest movement—a fault of anatomy, indeed, rather than temper—as a companion he would be—perfection.

It is a dull, close evening. Were it not so near winter one might predict a thunderstorm. The smoke from my meerschaum winds upwards in thin blue wreaths, uninfluenced by a breath of outward air, though the windows are open to the deserted street, black and silent as the grave. My lamp is not yet lit (we both affect a congenial gloom), the fire is burning out, but there is a dull red glow like a fever - spot lowering under a volcanic arch of cinders ; and looking into it with unwinking eyes, I see the long - drawn, weary, beaten road that leads backward through a life. I see a child set down to run alone, half-frightened, laughing, trusting, almost happy, and altogether gay. I see a youth bold, healthful, courageous, full of an impossible chivalry, a romantic generosity that delights to lavish no matter what—money, love, hope, happiness, coining heart and intellect into gold that he may squander it on the passersby. I see a strong man crushed—a proud head grovelling in the dust, a high spirit broken, a cowering wretch imploring that his punishment may be lightened ever such a little, trembling and wincing like a slave beneath the scourge. At this moment the fire falls in with a crash, while a pale yellow flame leaps flickering out of the midst, and starting from my seat to light our lamp for the rest of the evening, I demand aloud, " What then is the purpose of Creation ? From a quenched rushlight to an extinct volcano, from the squeak of a mouse to yesterday's leading article, from a mite smothered in a cheese to an emperor murdered in Mexico, is the march of Time but the destructive progress of a bull in a china-shop ? Are the recurring centuries but so many ciphers added to the sum of a thriftless, objectless expenditure ? Is the so-called economy of the universe but an unbridled, haphazard course of boundless and incalculable waste ?"

His backbone creaks uncomfortably while he moves in his chair. " Waste ?" he repeats in the hushed, placid tones that make him so invaluable as a companion—"Waste ? The subject is by no means limited. I have some experience in it of my own. Would you favour me with your ideas ?" and I go off at score with—

CHAPTER I

WHY are these things so?" I exclaim, plumping down again into my seat. "Why have the times been out of joint ever since Hamlet's first appearance on the stage, with black tights and rosettes on his shoes? Why is the whole world still at sixes and sevens? What is the object of it all? *Cui bono? cui bono? cui bono?* Is there the slightest appearance of a result? any tendency towards a goal? Shall we ever get *anywhere*, or are we travelling perpetually in a circle, like squirrels in a cage, convicted pickpockets on the treadmill? By the way, who convicted the pickpockets, and sentenced them? The sitting magistrate, of course; and do the awards of that worthy functionary produce any definite result in the direction of good order and morality, or must his daily incubation too be wasted upon addled eggs? Do you remember the story of the man who cut his throat because he was so tired of dressing and undressing every day? Don't shake your head—I beg pardon, your skull—you told it me yourself. I can appreciate his prejudices, but how did he know there might not be buttons and buttonholes where he was going? That is, supposing he went anywhere—if he didn't, he was wasted altogether. If he did, perhaps he was of no use when he got there. Wasted again—only a human life, after all. Not much when you think of it amongst the millions that cling about this old globe of ours, rising, swarming, disappearing like the maggots on a dead horse, but of no light importance to the bearer when you remember its weight of sorrows, anxieties, disappointments, and responsibilities, not to mention the Black Care sitting heavily at the top to keep the whole burden in its place. Life is a bubble, they say. Very well— but is it blown from a soap-dish by a schoolboy, rising heavenward, tinted with rainbow hues, to burst only when at its most beautiful and its best : or is it not rather a bubble gurgling to the surface from the agonised lungs of some struggling wretch drowning far below in the dark, pitiless water,

Unknell'd, uncoffin'd, and unknown?

ON WASTE

—Wasted, too, unless the fish eat him, and then who knows? none of us perhaps may ever eat the fish.

" Listen to me. I won't make your flesh creep, for unanswerable reasons. I don't even think I shall freeze the marrow in your bones. I could tell you some strange stories, but I daresay your own experiences are more remarkable than mine. I will only ask you to reflect on the amount of suffering that came under our daïly notice when we lived in the world, and say whether every pang of mind or body, every tear shed or swallowed down, every groan indulged or re-pressed, were anything but sheer waste. Can you not recall a hundred instances of strength sapped by drink, of intellect warped by madness, of beauty fading under neglect, or withered by disappointment? Here a pair of lives are wasted because they must needs run out their course in different grooves — there two more are utterly thrown away, because, encompassed in a golden link, they can by no means shake themselves free. The fairest of all, it may be, and the most promis-ing, never blooms into perfection for want of its congenial comrade (wasted too, perhaps, at the antipodes), and failing thus to reach maturity, dwindles, dwarfed and unmated, to the grave. Think of Beauty wasted on the Beast—the Beast, too, utterly out of his element, that he must roll on the garden sward rather than labour in the teeming furrow. Look at Hercules spellbound in the lap of Omphale, broad-fronted Antony enervated by black-browed Cleopatra. Consider the many Messrs. Caudle who lavish as much good-humour as would set up a dozen households on their legal nightmares, and do not forget poor Miss Prettyman pining in lonely spinsterhood over the way. See the mother training up her child, impressing on him, far more forcibly than she feels them for herself, lessons of honour, truth, probity, and the unspeakable blessing of faith—praying her heart out for that wilful little urchin, night and morning, on her knees. A good Christian with humble hopes of heaven, does she know that, far more lavishly than those heathen termagants in hell, she is pouring water in a sieve? Does she know she may live to see that smooth, soft, wondering brow scored deep with sorrow, or lowering black with sin—that round rosy cheek hollowed by depravity, or bloated with excess? Worst of all, the merry, guileless heart embittered by falsehood, and hardened with ill-usage till it has ceased to feel for others, even for itself! Great Heaven! have we not seen them—these simple, honest, manly hearts, taken by some soft-eyed demon with loving ways, and sweet, angelic smile, to be kept carefully, to be watched jealously, till their fabric has been thoroughly studied, then broken deftly and delicately, yet with such nice art that they can never mend again, and so, politely 'returned, with thanks'?

"Forgive me: on such anatomical outrages I have no right to expect you should feel so warmly as myself.

"Millions of creatures, beautiful exceedingly, scour over the desert plains of explored Africa; in its unknown regions, millions more may be supposed to feed, and gambol, and die. What is the use of them? If you come to that, what was the use of the Emperor Theodore, or the King of the Cannibal Islands, or any other potentate who remains utterly unimpressed when we threaten 'to break off diplomatic relations'?

"Myriads of insects wheel about us in the sun's declining rays every summer's evening. Again, what is the use of them? What is the use of the dragon-fly, the bumble-bee, the speckled toad, the blue-nosed monkey, the unicorn, the wild elephant, or, indeed, the Ojibbeway Indians?"

Here, contrary to his custom, Bones interrupted me in full career.

"One moment," said he, with his courteous grin. "Allow me to point out that yours is inadmissible, as being simply an *argumentum ad absurdum*. It would hold equally good with Léotard, Mr. Beales, or any other public exhibitor—nay, you might advance it for suppression of the Lord Mayor or the Archbishop of Canterbury."

BONES AND I

He bowed reverentially while he mentioned the last-named dignitary ; and I confess I was inclined to admit the truth of his remark.

" Then I waive the question," I replied, "as regards the brute ·creation, though I think I could find something to say, too, about the weasel sucking rabbits, the heron gobbling fish, the hawk striking its quarry, or the hounds running into their·fox. But we will suppose that the whole animal world, from the angler's lob-worm to the costermonger's donkey, is enjoying its paradise *here*, and return to our own kind, their sorrows, their sufferings, and natural consequence of sorrow and suffering, their sins."

He shook his skull gently, and muttered something in his spinal vertebræ about a cart and a horse, but I took no notice, and proceeded with dignity—

" I have learnt my Latin Grammar, and almost the only one of its precepts I have not forgotten impresses on me that—

Spades turn up wealth, the stimulant of crime.

I suppose you will not dispute that the root of all evil is money ? "

" Most emphatically," he exclaimed, and his articulations rattled with startling vehemence, "most emphatically I deny the position. A man may roll in wealth and be none the worse for it. On the contrary, poverty, but for the unremitting labour it demands, would be far more conducive to crime than a sufficiency, or even a superfluity of means.   No ; the real enemy with whom every man has to contend confronts him in the morning at his glass, and sticks persistently to him throughout the day.   The source of most unhappiness, the cause of all ill-doing, the universal origin of evil, is *not* money, but self "—

" You mean selfishness," I retorted ; "and I am surprised to hear a man of the world—I mean of the *other* world, or, indeed, of any world whatever—assert so obvious a fallacy.   Just as the liver, and not the heart, is the seat of our real well-being, so I maintain that self-indulgence, and not self-sacrifice, is the origin, the main-spring, the motive-power of all effort, progress, improvement, moral, social, and physical.   Researches of science, triumphs of art, masterpieces of genius—what are these but results of the same instinct that directs the bee to the flower-garden, the vulture to the carcase?   To eat is the first necessity of man.   He labours that he may live. Grant this, as you cannot but concede the position to be unassailable, and you talk to me in vain of sentiment, philanthropy, benevolence, all the loathsome affectations of sympathy with which the earth-worm tries to impose upon its kind. A man begins by being honest.   Why?   Because without honesty, down the particular groove in which he spins, he cannot earn his daily bread.

When he has enough of this and to spare, he turns his attention to decent apparel, a commodious house, a general appearance of respectability ; that is, he aims at being respectable—in other words, at imposing on those who have been less successful in the universal scramble than himself. Soon he buys a warming-pan, a Dutch oven, china ornaments for his chimney-piece, and the History of the Prodigal to hang about his walls. By degrees, as wealth increases, he moves into a larger residence, he rolls upon wheels, he replaces the china ornaments with a French clock ; the Prodigal Son with modern oil-paintings, and hides the warming-pan in the housemaid's closet upstairs. About this period he begins to subscribe to charitable institutions, to give away what he does not want, to throw little pellets of bread at the monster who is always famished and always roaring out of doors, lest it should come in and snatch the roast-beef off his table. Some day a team of black horses with nodding plumes, and a red-nosed driver, come to take him away, 'very much respected,' and, forgive the personality, there is an end of him, as far as we are concerned. Will you tell me the man's life has not been a continual concession to self?—waste, waste, utter waste, from the pap - boat that preserved his infancy, to the brass-nailed coffin that protects his putridity from contact with the earth to which he returns? Why, his very virtues, as he called them, were but payments, so to speak, keeping up the insurance for his own benefit, which he persuaded himself he had effected on the other world.

"Now, supposing the pap-boat had been withheld, or the nurse had tucked him into his cradle upside down, or — thus saving some harmless woman a deal of inconvenience and trouble—supposing he had never been born at all, would he have been missed, or wanted? Would not the world have gone on just as well without him? Has not his whole existence been a mistake? The food he ate, the clothes he wore, the house he lived in—were not these simply wasted? His efforts were waste, his wear-and-tear of body and mind were waste, above all, his sorrows and his sufferings were sheer, unpardonable waste. Yes; here I take my stand. I leave you every enjoyment to be found in creation, physical, moral, and intellectual. I make you a present of the elephant wallowing in his mud-bath, and the midge wheeling in the sun; I give you Juliet at her window, and Archimedes in his study; but I reserve the whale in her death-flurry, and the worm on its hook. I appeal to Jephthah sorrowing for his darling, and Rachel weeping for her children. I repeat, if that self-care, which indeed constitutes our very identity, be the object of existence, then all those tearful eyes that blur the light of every rising sun—all those aching hearts that long only for night to be eternal—are but so many witnesses to the predominance in creation of a lavish and unaccountable waste."

Like many thoughtful and deliberate natures, I am persuaded that in early life Bones must have been a snuff-taker. He affects a trick of holding his fleshless finger and thumb pressed together and suspended in air, before he delivers himself of an opinion, that can only have originated in a practice he has since been compelled, for obvious reasons, to forego. Pausing during several seconds in this favourite attitude, he sank gravely back in his chair, and replied—

"False logic, my good friend. False premises, and a false conclusion. I deny them all; but the weather, even in *my* light attire, feels somewhat too close for wordy warfare. Besides, I hold with you, that an ounce of illustration is worth a pound of argument; I will ask you, therefore, as I know you have been in Cheshire, High Leicestershire, and other cattle-feeding countries, whether you ever watched a dairymaid making a cheese? If so, you must have observed how strong and pitiless a pressure is required to wring the moisture out of its very core. My friend, the human heart is like a cheese! To be good for anything, the black drop must be wrung out of it, however tight the squeeze required, however exquisite the pain. Therefore it is, that we so often see the parable of the poor man's ewe lamb enacted in daily life. One, having everything the world can bestow, is nevertheless further endowed with that which his needy brother would give all the rest of the world to possess. For the first, the pressure has not yet been put on, though his time, too, may come by and by. For the second, that one darling hope, it may be, represents the little black drop left, and so it must be wrung out, though the heart be crushed into agony in the process. You talk of suffering being pure waste; I tell you it is all pure gain. You talk of self as the motive to exertion; I tell you it is the abnegation of self which has wrought out all that is noble, all that is good, all that is useful, nearly all that is ornamental in the world. Shut the house-door on him, and the man must needs go forth to work in the fields. It is not the dreamer wrapped in his fancied bliss, from whom you are to expect heroic efforts, either of mind or body. You must dig your goad into the ox to make him use his latent strength; you must drive your spurs into the horse to get out of him his utmost speed. Wake the dreamer roughly —drive spurs and goad into his heart. He will wince and writhe, and roll and gnash his teeth, but I defy him to lie still. He must up and be doing, from sheer torture, flying to one remedy after another till he gets to work, and so finds distraction, solace, presently comfort, and, after a while, looking yet higher, hope, happiness, and reward.

BONES AND I

" Self, indeed!   He is fain to forget self because
that therewith is bound up so much it would
drive him mad to remember ; and thus sorrow-
taught, he merges his own identity in the com-
munity of which he is but an atom, taking his
first step, though at a humble and immeasurable
distance, in the sacred track of self-sacrifice, on
which, after more than eighteen hundred years,
the footprints are still fresh, still ineffaceable.
Waste, forsooth!   Let him weep his heart out
if he will!   I tell you that the deeper the furrows
are scored, the heavier shall be the harvest, the
richer the garnered grain.   I tell you, not a tear
falls but it fertilises some barren spot,[1] from which
hereafter shall come up the fresh verdure of an
eternal spring in that region

Where there's fruit in the gardens of heaven, from the hope
    that on earth was betrayed ;
Where there's rest for the soul, life-wearied that hath striven,
    and suffered, and prayed.

" I'm rather tired.   I won't discuss the question
any further.   I'll go back into my cupboard, if
you please.   Good-night!"

[1] Alfred de Musset sounds much the same strain—

    " Les moissons pour mûrir ont besoin de rosée ;
      Pour vivre et pour sentir l'homme a besoin de pleurs,
      La joie a pour symbole une plante brisée
      Humide encore de pluie et couverte de fleurs."—ED.

CHAPTER II

THROUGH THE MILL

MOST people are ashamed of their skeletons, hiding them up in their respective cupboards as though the very ownership were a degradation—alluding to them, perhaps, occasionally in the domestic circle, but ignoring them utterly before the world—a world that knows all about them the while,—that has weighed their skulls, counted their ribs, and can tell the very recesses in which they are kept. Now, in my opinion, to take your skeleton out and air him on occasion, is very good for both of you. It brings him to his proper dimensions, which are apt to become gigantic if he is hidden too scrupulously in the dark, and it affords opportunities for comparison with other specimens of the same nature entertained by rival proprietors in the line. If I kept mine, as some do, in close confinement, I should be in a continual fidget about his safety; above all, I should dread his breaking out at untoward seasons, when he was

least expected, and least desired.   But Bones
and I have no cause to be ashamed of each other.
There is no disgrace nor discomfort attached to
either of us in our cheerful companionship. He
is good enough to express satisfaction with his
present lodging, and even affirms that he finds
it airy and commodious, as compared with his
last; while it is a real pleasure to me, living as
I do so much alone, to have a quiet, intelligent
companion, with whom I can discuss the different
phases of existence, speculative and real,—the
sower who never reaps—the fools who are full
of bread, roses for one, thorns for another; here
over-ripe fruit, there grapes sour, though by no
means out of reach; successful bows drawn at a
venture, well-aimed shafts that never attain the
mark, impossible hopes, unavailing regrets—the
baseless mirage of the Future, and the barren
reality of the Past.

It was colder last night.   The wind was getting
up in those fitful howls which denote the com-
mencement of a two-days' gale; veering besides
from east by north to east-north-east.   So we
made fast the shutters, stirred the fire, and drew
our chairs in for a comfortable chat.   Something
in the sound of that waking blusterer out of
doors recalled to me, I know not why, the image
of a good ship, many long years ago, beating
on the wide Atlantic against a head-wind, that
seemed to baffle her the more for every plunge

she made.   No steam had she to help her struggle against the elements; tough hemp, patched canvas, and spars as yet unsprung, were all her reliance; and these strained, flapped, and creaked to some purpose while she battled foot by foot to lie her course.   Again I seemed to watch the dark wave race by our quarter, with its leaping crest of foam, the trickling deck, the battened hold, the diving bowsprit, the dripping spars, the soaking canvas, with its row of reef-points like the notes on a music score.   And the grey, sullen curtain of mist and rain, walking on the waters, nearer, nearer, till it dashed its needle-pointed drops into my face.   Again I looked admiringly on the men at the wheel, with their pea-jackets, glazed hats, sea-going mits, keen, wary glances, and minute wrinkles about the eyes.   Again I heard the pleasant voice of the bravest, cheeriest skipper that ever stood five feet two, and weighed fifteen stone, while he accosted me with his " Dirty weather, sir, and looks sulky to windward still.   Makes her drive piles, as we say, and speak Spanish about the bows; but she behaves beautifully!   Bless you, she likes it! Yes, I expect we shall have it hotter and heavier too, after sundown.   A head-wind, no doubt. I've just been jotting off the reckoning; you'll find the chart below, in my cabin.   We've made a longer leg than common on the starboard tack. I've left a pencil-mark at the exact spot where we went about. Steady, men (this to the glazed hats)! Luff, and be d——d to you! Can't ye see it coming?"

So I went below and conned the captain's chart thoughtfully enough, comparing our great expenditure of energy with the small results attained, and wondering how we were ever to make our port at last.

The scene thus conjured up awoke its corresponding fancies.

"Have you never reflected," said I, "on the utter fallacy of that French proverb which affirms, 'Ce n'est que le premier pas qui coûte'? unless indeed it refers to immorality, the downward career of which beats the rolling stone of Sisyphus in a canter. But on all other journeys through life, it seems to me that not only the first steps, but the first leagues, are intensely laborious and unsatisfactory. Disappointment lies in wait at every milestone, and the traveller feels tired already ere he has reached the crest of the first hill. All crowns, I grant you, like those of the Isthmian Games, are mere parsley at best; but in these days no competitor ever wins that worthless headdress till he is so bald that common decency demands a covering. Where are the heaven-born statesmen now, to rule the destinies of continents at twenty-six? the generals and admirals, who became world-wide heroes within ten years of corporal punishment at school? the poets full‑fledged in immortality before their whiskers were grown? Where, in short, will you point me out a single instance of any individual attaining fame until his zest for it has passed away—winning his pedestal till his poor legs are too tired to stand straight thereon—making his fortune till he is too old to enjoy it; or, indeed, getting anything he wants *when* he wants it? Lazarus has no dinner—Dives has no appetite— Struggler, who thinks he has both, is sure to be kept waiting that extra half-hour, which sickens him, and finds he can't eat his soup when it comes!

"What uphill work it is, that beginning of the pilgrimage. And how confidently we start in the glorious ignorance of youth, heads erect, backs straightened, footsteps springing like a deer, with an utter disregard of warning, a sovereign con- tempt for advice. Like myself, I doubt not you have scaled many a hill, even when you carried more flesh than you do now. Don't you re- member, in the clear, pure mountain air, how near the top looked from the valley down below? Don't you remember how, about noonday, still full of strength and spirit, though having done a stalwart spell of work, you spied the ridge that you were convinced must be your goal, and strained on, panting, heated, labouring, yet exultant, because success was so nearly within your grasp? A few more strides—hurrah! your chin is level with the ridge, and lo! there is another precisely similar to be surmounted at about the same angle and the same distance. Not yet discouraged, only a little startled and annoyed, till another and another have been gained, and so surprise becomes disappointment, vexation, misgiving, discomfiture, and lastly, but to the strongest natures, despair! Even with these, when the real summit has been at length attained, all their long - looked - for enjoyment resolves itself into the negative satisfaction of rest; and for one who thus arrives exhausted at his destination, think how many a footsore, quivering, way - wearied wanderer must lie out all night shelterless, on the barren, wind-swept hill.

"It seems that the process, termed at Newmarket, 'putting a race-horse through the mill,' is practised with the human subject till he has learned the disheartening lesson that labour pushed to exhaustion borders on pain — that heartbreaking efforts, while they lower the tone of our whole system, are apt to destroy the very efficiency they are intended to enhance. I have heard good judges affirm that even at Newmarket they are apt to over - train their horses. Do you not think that we, too, should run the race of life on better terms were we not put so pitilessly 'through the mill'?"

Here my companion allowed himself a mild

gesture of dissent, clasping his bony fingers over his knotted knees, as if prepared to go into the subject at length. "You are one of those people," said he, "who seem to think the world is intended for a place of uninterrupted rest and enjoyment—a sort of Fiddler's Green, as sailors term their paradise, where it is to be beer and skittles every day and all day long. You would have no 'small end to the horn,' as my friends over the water say; and what sort of music do you think you could blow out of it? You would have food without hunger, rest without labour, energy without effort. You would be always going downhill, instead of up. And think where your journey would end at last! You object to the mill, you say, and yet it is that same process of grinding which converts the grain into flour fit for bread. Look at the untried man, the youth embarking on his career, vain, ignorant, sanguine, over-confident, prejudiced. How is he to learn his own powers, his capabilities of endurance, his energy under difficulties, above all, his readiness of resource, save by repeated disappointment and reverse? You have alluded to statesmen, commanders, and poets, who, in seven-leagued boots as it were, reached the top of the hill at one stride. But Pitt's was an abnormal temperament—a grey head upon green shoulders—an old man's heart beating its regular pulsations within the slender compass of a young man's waistcoat. Nelson's chivalrous and romantic disposition preserved him from the overweening vanity and self-esteem that might have been looked for as the result of such brilliant achievements at so early an age. His mad, absorbing passion, too, may have scored many a furrow in the hero's heart, while his young brow remained smooth and fair as marble. 'On vieillit bientôt sur le champ de bataille!' and the first Napoleon's aphorism holds good no surer on the field of honour than in the lists of love. Shelley's fate was scarcely an enviable one; and did you like Byron any better after you had read his letters and learned the demoralising effects, even on such genius as his, of temples crowned by an immortal Fame, ere yet the beard had sprouted on his chin?

"Alexander of Macedon, indeed, conquered the world before he was thirty, and — drank himself to death ere he had reached his prime!

"The fact that he does not care one straw about it, is the very antidote to preserve a man from the subtle poison of success. He who has been long climbing the ladder finds that when he looks over the parapet all sense of elevation and consequent giddiness is gone. Whatever others may think, to his own perceptions he is on a level with the rest of his kind—can judge of them, and for them, from the same point of view; and, more important still, experiences no misgivings that he may topple down and break his neck. Ambition is a glorious lure, no doubt tempting the climber to noble efforts, skilful, vigorous, and well-sustained. But when he has reached the fancied resting - place so ardently desired, what does he find? A keener air, a scantier foothold, a sentry - box instead of a feather-bed, a stern necessity for further exertion, where he expected indulgence and enjoyment and repose.

" Duty is a cold - eyed monitress, reserved, inflexible, severe; Ambition, a high - born lady, haughty, capricious, unfeeling, like those dainty dames of old patrician Rome,

> Who in Corinthian mirrors their own proud smiles behold ;
> Who breathe of Capuan odours, and shine in Spanish gold ;

Pleasure, a laughing, lavish courtesan, gay, gaudy, thoughtless, slave to the impression of the hour. This last you may buy at your will for a handful of silver, or, at most, a talent of gold; and there are few, alas! who have not learned how soon her false smile palls upon the fancy, her painted cheek grows irksome to the eye. The second you must woo, with many a stealthy footstep, many a cringing bow, offering at her shrine truth, honour, self-respect, to find, if you are so fortunate as not to be discarded like a pair of worn-out gloves, that you have only gathered a nut without a kernel, after all. For the first, you must serve as Jacob served, through long years of labour, patience, and self-denial; but when you have won your Rachel at last, she discloses for you all her glorious, unfading beauty, cleaving to you, true and constant through good and evil, the warmth and comfort of your hearth, the light of your happy home.

"When the courtesan has been paid off and dismissed in early youth, the haughty lady wooed through long years of manhood, and won, to be despised, in middle life, this is the goddess you claim to be your bride, and once wedded, you will never leave her till you die.

"The Isthmian crown was indeed woven from humble parsley, but do you think it could have borne a higher value had every leaf consisted of beaten gold? Which would you rather wear, the bronze Victoria Cross, or the Star and Ribbon of the Garter? Depend upon it, that to the young champion of the games, flushed, exulting, treading upon air, that vegetable coronal represented everything most desirable and precious in earth or heaven. No; it is the old experienced athlete, the winner of a thousand prizes, who has learned the intrinsic value of the article, and who knows that its worth consists not in itself, nor even in the victory it represents, but in the strength of frame, the speed of foot attained by training for its pursuit. From many a long summer's day of toil and abstinence, from panting lungs and aching muscles, from brows covered with sweat, and feet with dust, he has wrested the endurance of the camel, the strength of the ox, and the footfall of the deer. Does he grudge his past labour? Not he, thankful that he has been 'through the mill.'

"I grant you the process is not entirely pleasant; I grant you that effort is with many men a sensation of discomfort almost amounting to pain; that self-denial is very difficult to most, disappointment simply disgusting to all. When the body feels weary, the brain overtasked, we are apt to think the meal is being bolted too fine, the grinding becoming unnecessarily severe; above all, when that pitiless millstone comes crushing down upon the heart, and pounds it to powder, we cry aloud in our agony, and protest that no sorrow was ever so unbearable as ours. What mole working underground is so blind as humanity to its own good? Why, that same grinding to powder is the only means by which the daintiest flour can be obtained. The finest nature, like the truest steel, must be tempered in the hottest furnace; so much caloric would be thrown away on an inferior metal. Capacity for suffering infers also capacity for achievement; and who would grudge the pain about his brows, when it reminded him he was wearing an imperial crown?

"Sooner or later the process must be undergone by all. With some it goes on through a lifetime ; others get the worst of it over in a few years. One man may have done with it altogether before his strength of mind or body has failed with declining age—

Dum nova canities—dum prima et recta senectus.[1]

" His neighbour may have one foot in the grave before the grain has been thoroughly purged and sifted, and refined to its purest quality, but through the mill he must pass. It is just as much a necessity of humanity as hunger or thirst, or sorrow or decay. There is no escape. However long protracted, it is inexorable, unavoidable, and effectual, for

Though the mills of God grind slowly,
Yet they grind exceeding small."

---

[1] While the good grey head is still erect—before old age has lost its freshness and vigour.

CHAPTER III

GOURDS

SO Jonah was exceeding glad of the gourd. I can understand his feelings perfectly. Does it not happen to most of us, at least once in a lifetime, thus to be 'exceeding glad of the gourd,' and in ninety-nine cases out of a hundred with the same result? *Nil violentum est perpetuum.*[1] So surely as it comes up in a night, so surely must it wither in a day. You have been in a hot climate? I don't intend any disagreeable allusion, I mean the tropics, I give you my honour! Do you not remember the delight of getting out of your tent, or 'booth' as we still call them at our village merry-makings, to sit under anything like a tree or shrub, where, shaded from the sun, you could catch the welcome breath of every breeze that

[1] Nothing violent lasts long.

blew? The French officers in the Crimea used to build for themselves trellised out-houses of branches interlaced, swearing volubly the while, and appearing to derive from these bowers no small comfort and refreshment. I can imagine the astonishment of *mon lieutenant* when, on waking in his tent, he should have discovered, like Jack and the Beanstalk, that one of these had sprung up for him, unsolicited, in a night. How he would have stared, and shrugged, and gesticulated, and cursed his star with less asperity, and been ' exceeding glad of the gourd'!

"They are of many kinds, these excrescences that grow up with such marvellous celerity to afford us an intense and illusive delight ; but they all resemble their prototype at Nineveh, in so far that, ere the seed has yet germinated, the worm is already prepared which shall smite the gourd, and cause it to wither away. There were hundreds of them shot to gigantic dimensions and exploded with the South Sea Bubble of the last century. Thousands owed their birth and disappearance to the railway fever of five-and-twenty years ago. Not a few were called into existence by a blockade of the Southern ports, during the late war of opinion in the United States, and destroyed by its suspension at the peace. It seems to be a law in the moral as in the physical world that the endurance of things must be in proportion to the length of time required to bring them to maturity. The oak is said to be three hundred years in arriving at its prime, and that its vigour is still unimpaired after a thousand changes of foliage we have ocular demonstration in many parts of England; while the mustard-and-cress, which can be raised in twenty minutes on a square of flannel dipped in hot water, wastes and withers away in an hour.

"The same in the animal creation. Like Minerva from the brain of Jove, the butterfly springs into its sunny existence, winged, armed, and clothed in gorgeous apparel, all at once; but when the night-breeze shakes the perfume from your garden - flowers, and the evening - bank of clouds is coming up from the west, you look for that ephemeral masterpiece in vain. Now the elephant only attains his majority, so to speak, when between forty and fifty years of age; therefore he has hardly become an "old rogue" at two hundred, and the identical proboscis that saluted Clyde, or curled round the crushed remains of Tippoo Sahib's victims, is to-day lowered in honour of our own *jeunesse dorée*, with whom a run through British India is considered little more of an expedition than a jaunt into Welsh Wales.

"Cornaro, if I remember right, fixes the normal duration of life, in the Mammalia, at a term of five times the number of years required to reach their prime. Thus a dog, he says, comes to maturity at two, and lives till ten ; a horse at five, and lives till five-and-twenty ; and arguing by analogy, a man, who only attains his full strength at twenty-three or four, should not, therefore, if he led a natural and rational life, succumb till he had arrived at a hundred and fifteen or twenty years.

" Forbid it, Atropos ! for their sakes as well as ours. Think of the old fogies, now sufficiently numerous, who would overflow the clubs ! Think, when it came to our own turn, of the numbers of gourds we should have raised, outlived, buried, but, alas ! not forgotten.

" 'A fine old man, sir !' said one of the best judges of human nature that ever fathered a proverb. 'There's no such thing. If his head or his heart had been worth anything, they would have worn him out years ago ! ' "

" You have got off the subject as usual," objected Bones, " and are trenching on a topic of which you are far less qualified to speak than myself. What do you know about the duration of life, the ceaseless wear-and-tear, the gradual decay, the last flickers of the candle, leaping up, time after time, with delusive strength, until it goes out once for all ? You can tell where Noah was, but do you know where the candle went to when it left the great sea-captain in the dark ? Not you ! Never mind, don't fret, you will find out some day sure enough, and be as wise as Tullus, Ancus, good Æneas, and the rest of us![1] In the meantime stick to your text. The morbid spirit possesses you, and well I know it will only come out of the man with much talking. If it does you any good, never mind *me*—fire away! Tell us something more about the gourd, and the worm that smote it. That is what you are driving at, I feel sure."

"'Morbid!'" I repeated, somewhat indignantly. "And why *morbid*, I should like to know? A man takes his stand, as you and I do, outside of, and apart from, the circling, shifting mass of his fellow-creatures, and makes his own observations, uninfluenced by their clamour, their customs, their ridiculous prejudices and opinions, confiding those observations unreservedly to one who should, *ex officio* indeed, be entirely free from the earthly trammels that cumber liberal discussion in general society, and he is to be called *morbid*, forsooth! It was only one of your ghastly jests, was it? Enough! I am satisfied. There can be no bone of contention—I mean no subject of dispute—between you and me—we have not the ghost of a reason—I mean the shadow of a cause —for disagreement. I confess my weakness:

[1] Cui deinde subibit,
Otia qui rumpet patriæ, residesque movebit
Tullus in arma viros, et jam desueta triumphis
Agmina. Quem juxta sequitur jactantior Ancus.
Virgil. *Æneid*, vi. 813.

BONES AND I

I own to a fatal tendency to digression. One thought leads to another, and they follow in a string, like wild geese, or heirs of entail, *velut unda supervenit undam.* By the way, this very subject, the association of ideas, opens up a boundless field for speculation. But I refrain— I return to my gourd—I am back in Nineveh with the prophet once more. Nineveh, in its imperial splendour, gorgeous in Eastern colouring, sublime with Eastern magnificence, glittering with Eastern decorations—solemn, gloomy, and gigantic, grand in the massive dignity of size, winged bulls hewn from the solid rock guard the long perspective of a thousand avenues, leading to palaces that rise, tier upon tier, into the glowing sky. Lavish profusion—marble, and bronze, and gold — gleams and dazzles and flashes in the streets. The palm-tree bends her graceful head earthward; the aloe aims her angry spikes at heaven ; the camel, with meek, appealing eyes, seems to protest against the bales of costly merchandise with which its back is piled ; the white elephant in scarlet trappings, stolid and sagacious, stands patient, waiting for its lord ; throngs of dusky, half-naked Asiatics pass to and fro along the baking causeways ; loud bleatings of sheep, lowings of oxen, cries of parched, thirsty animals resound in the suburbs ; while over all a Southern sun blazes down with scorching fury, and an east wind off the Desert comes blustering in, hot and stifling, like a blast from hell.

"So the prophet is 'exceeding glad of his gourd.' He will rest in its shade; he will look pitifully on the broiling passers-by; he will hug himself in that sense of comfort which human nature, alas! is too apt to experience from the very fact that others are in a worse condition than its own; but even while he thus rejoices, the worm has done its work—the gourd is withered up, the sirocco suffocates his lungs, the sun beats on his head, and, like the rest of us when we lose that which we choose to consider the one thing essential to our happiness, he shows the white feather on the spot, and says, 'It is better for me to die than to live.'

"Death never seems to come for those who wish it—though perhaps if the Great Liberator felt bound to appear every time he was invoked, the cry might not be raised quite so often. Who is there that has not bowed his head in misery, and wondered whether he could be so wretched anywhere else as here, in the mocking sunlight, with his gourd withered before his face? It is gone—gone. See! There is the very spot on which it stood but yesterday, so green, so fresh, so full of life, so rich in promise! And to-day— a blank! It seems impossible! Ay, that is perhaps the worst of the suffering—that numbed, stupefied state, which refuses for a time to grasp the extent of its affliction — that perverse and cowardly instinct which clings to a thread that it yet knows is wholly severed—which turns even Hope to a curse, because it makes her a bar to resignation. Few of us can boast more courage than Jonah when the gourd is fairly withered away.

"For one it has been riches, perhaps, comprising luxury, position, variety—all the advantages that spring from an abundance of worldly goods. Some fine morning, Fortune, *ludem insolentem ludere pertinax,*[1] gives her wings a shake, spreads them, and flits away ; leaving in her place haggard Want, gaunt Ruin, bailiffs in the drawing-room, furniture ticketed for sale upstairs. The children's rocking-horse, the wife's pianoforte, all the well-known trifles of daily use and ornament, must be cast into the chasm, as the Romans threw their effects into that awkward rent in the Forum. And the master of the household is fortunate if he be not compelled, like Curtius, to leap in after his goods. His friends are astonished, and bless themselves. His relations had predicted the catastrophe long ago. These, of course, turn their backs on him, incontinently, from motives of self-respect, no doubt, but a few of the former, such as had professed to love him least, lend a helping hand. Nevertheless, the gourd is withered, and the man, faint and sick unto death,

[1] Intent upon playing her insolent game.

only wishes his hour was come and he might lie down to be at rest.

"Or it has been a child—God forbid it should have been an only one! Some golden-headed darling that used to patter downstairs with you every morning to breakfast, and stand at your elbow every night after dinner. Whose dancing eyes never met your own but with the merry, saucy, confiding glances that seldom outlast a fifth birthday, and to whom you could no more have said an unkind word than you could cut off your right hand. Yesterday it was chasing butterflies across the lawn, and you carried it yourself with laughing triumph, rosy, happy, and hungry, in to tea. But the worm had begun its work, even then. This morning you missed the glad little voice at breakfast, and looking at the jam on the table a sad misgiving, stifled as soon as born, shot through you like a knife. It was pitiful to watch all day, in the nursery, by the little bed, — to see the golden head lying so listless, the chubby hands so waxen and still, the heavy lids drooping so wearily over the blue eyes that yet shone with a light you never saw in them before. There rose a mist to dim your own when the patient little voice asked gently, 'Is that papa?'—and noticing two or three neglected playthings on the counterpane, you walked to the window and wept.

"So the afternoon wore on, and the doctor

came, and there was cruel hope and torturing suspense, and a wrench that so stupefied you, it is difficult to remember anything clearly afterwards, though you have a dim perception of a pair of scissors severing some golden curls while nurse went down on her knees to pray.

"And at sundown you walk out into your garden along the very path that brought you both home yesterday, but you walk like a man in a dream, for ringing in your ears is the wail that was heard of old in Ramah, and you know your darling is with the angels, wondering feebly why that knowledge cannot console you more.

"Or perhaps your gourd was only a woman's love!—not a growth, certainly, however exuberant, on which a wise man should place so much dependence as on lignum vitæ, for instance, or heart-of-oak. But, so far as I can see, either wise men do not fall in love, or they allow wisdom to slip out of their grasp in the very act of making that fatal stumble. So, in defiance of all theory, warning, and practical experience, you may have congratulated yourself with insane vehemence on the upspringing of this delicate exotic, and looked forward to the passing of many happy hours under its shade. You shut your eyes wilfully, of course, to the obvious fact that you never *are* happy, even when in full accomplishment of your wishes you stretch your lazy length at the feet of your gourd. There is sure to be an insect that stings, or a sunbeam that dazzles, or a cold wind in the nape of your neck. Nevertheless, the vegetable, so long as it exists, is not only the delight of your heart, but the very sustenance of your brain. That is the fatal part of the disease. Your gourd connects itself with everything you think, or do, or say, spreading her roots, as it were, over every foot of land you possess, shutting out earth's horizon with her slender stem, and, worse than all, poking her dainty head between you and heaven.

"Then, when she withers up—a disappointment which, to do her justice, she is capable of inflicting in the loveliest weather and at the shortest notice—you find to your dismay that, with her, all the fair side of creation has withered too. There is no more freshness in the meadows, no more promise in the smile of spring. The scent is gone from the garden-flowers, the music from the song of birds. Summer's vivid glow has faded, and the russet of autumn is no longer edged with gold. Hope's rosy hues have ceased to tinge the morning, and the glory has departed from noonday.

"Like Jonah, you 'do well to be angry,' and it is well for you if you can be very angry indeed. That stimulant will do more to heal your wound over than any other remedy I can think of, except the planting of a fresh seedling to await another failure; but God help you if yours is a nature less susceptible of wrath than of sorrow! If you are brave, generous, forgiving, confiding, 'Je vous en fais mon compliment!' There is no more to be said. Where your gourd grew, nothing green will ever spring up again! What say you, Bones? I think you and I are well out of the whole thing!"

He waved his fleshless hand gently, with the gesture of one who puts from him some dim and distant recollection.

"There is a bitter flavour," said he, "about that remark which I should hardly have expected, and which is by no means to my taste. You and I can surely afford to look at these things from a comprehensive, philosophical, and indulgent point of view. No more gourds are likely to grow for either of us; and although your style of figure is, perhaps, less entitled to defy the worm than mine, yet I think you have but little to fear from the kind which caused such an outbreak of temper in the disgusted prophet. The whole story of the gourd, I need not point out to you, is a lesson. It was intended as a lesson for Jonah, it is intended as a lesson for ourselves. Forgive me for observing that you seem to have entirely lost the point of it, and, as usual in our discussions, you have sacrificed argument to declamation. It is weak, of course, to be too much delighted with the gourd, it is cowardly to be too much afraid of the worm, but "—

"There is one kind of worm I am horribly afraid of," I interrupted, for I admit I was a little nettled and out of temper.

"And that?" he asked, with the courtesy which distinguishes his manner under all circumstances.

"Is the borer-worm!" I replied, brutally enough; and I am afraid he was a little hurt, for he rose at once and went into his cupboard, while I walked off moodily to bed.

CHAPTER IV

A VAMPIRE

LEANING idly against the chimneypiece the other night, contemplating my companion in his usual attitude, my elbow happened to brush off the slab a Turkish coin of small value and utterly illegible inscription. How strangely things come back to one! I fancied myself once more on the yellow wave of the broad Danube; once more threading those interminable green hills that fringe its banks; once more wondering whether the forest of Belgrade had been vouchsafed to Eastern Europe as a type of Infinity, while its massive fortress, with frowning rampart and lethargic Turkish sentries, was intended to represent the combination of courage and sloth, of recklessness and imperturbability, of apparent strength and real inefficiency, which distinguishes most arrangements of the Ottoman Empire.

"Bakaloum" and "Bismillah!" "Take your chance!" and "Don't care a d——n," seemed to be the watchwords of this improvident Government. It lets the ship steer herself; and she makes, I belief, as bad weather of it as might be expected under such seamanship.

Engrossed far less, I admit, with political considerations than with the picturesque appearance of a Servian population attending their market, I rather startled my friend with the abruptness of the following question :—

" Do you believe there is such a thing as a Vampire? "

He rattled a little and almost rose to his feet, but reseating himself, only rejoined—

" Why do you ask? "

" I was thinking," I replied, " of that romantic-looking peasantry I used to see thronging the market-place of Belgrade. Of those tall, handsome men, with the scowl never off their brows, their hands never straying far from the bellyful of weapons they carried in their shawls. Of those swarthy wild-eyed women, with their shrill, rapid voices, their graceful, impatient gestures, carrying each of them the available capital of herself and family strung in coins about her raven hair, while on every tenth face at least, of both sexes, could not fail to be observed the wan traces of that wasting disease which seems to sap strength and vitality, gradually, and almost surely, as consumption itself. Yes, I think for every score of peasants I could have counted two of these 'fever-faces,' as the people themselves call their ague - ridden companions, though I ascertained after a while, when I came to know them better, that they attributed this decimation of their numbers, and faded appearance of the victims, rather to supernatural visitation than epidemic disease. They believe that in certain cases, where life has been unusually irregular, or the rites of religion reprehensibly neglected, the soul returns after death to its original tenement, and the corpse becomes revivified under certain ghastly conditions of a periodical return to the tomb and a continual warfare against its kind. An intermittent existence is only to be preserved at the expense of others, for the compact, while it permits reanimation, withholds the blood, 'which is the life thereof.' The stream must therefore be drained from friends, neighbours, early companions, nay, is most nourishing and efficacious when abstracted from the veins of those heretofore best beloved. So the Vampire, as this weird being is called, must steal from its grave in the dead of night, to sit by some familiar bedside till the sleeper shall be steeped in the unconsciousness of complete repose, and then puncturing a minute orifice in the throat, will suck its fill till driven back to its resting-place by the crimson streaks of day. Night after night the visits must be repeated ; and so, week by week, the victim pines and droops and withers gradually away.   There is no apparent illness, no ostensible injury, but the frame dwindles, the muscles fall, the limbs fail, the cheek fades, and the death-look, never to be mistaken, comes into the great haggard, hollow, wistful eyes.   I have repeatedly asked the peasants whether they had ever met any of these supernatural visitants, for they spoke of them so confidently, one might have supposed the famished ghouls were flitting about the villages nightly ; but though presumptive evidence was forthcoming in volumes, I was never fortunate enough to find an actual eye-witness.   The sister of one had been frightened by them repeatedly ; the cousin of another he had himself carried to her tomb, drained of her last life-drops by a relative buried some weeks before ; and the grandmother of a third had not only met and talked with this inconvenient con-nection, expostulating with it on its depraved appetites, and generally arguing the point on moral as well as sanitary grounds, but had induced it by her persuasions, and the power of a certain amulet she wore, to abstain from persecuting a damsel in the neighbouring village for the same ghastly purpose, or, at least, to put off its visits till the horrid craving should be no longer endurable. Still I could meet nobody who had actually seen one in person ; and that is why I asked you just now if you believed there was such a thing as a Vampire?"

He nodded gravely. "They are rare," said he; "but I believe in such beings, because I have not only seen one, but had the advantage of its personal notice, and a very pretty, pleasing acquaintance it was! You would like to know something more? Well, it compromises nobody. You will not quote me, of course. Indeed I don't see how you can, for I still mention no real names. I don't mind telling you the story of a life, such as I knew it; a life that by some fatality seemed to drag down every other that came within the sphere of its attractions to sorrow, humiliation, and disgrace. I have no brain to swim, no pulses to leap, no heart to ache left, and yet the memory stirs me painfully even now.

"In early manhood," he continued, bending down as though to scan his own fleshless proportions with an air of consciousness that was almost grotesque, "I paid as much heed to my personal appearance, and flourished it about in public places as persistently as others of like age and pursuits. Whether I should do so if I had my time to come again, is a different question, but we will let that pass. Being then young, tolerably good-looking, sufficiently conceited, and exceedingly well-dressed, I had betaken myself one evening to your Italian Opera, the best, and I may add the dearest, in Europe. I was fond of music and knew something about it, but I

was fonder still of pretty women, though concerning these I enjoyed my full share of that
ignorance which causes men so to exaggerate
their qualities both good and bad; an ignorance
it is worth while to preserve with as much care
as in other matters we take to acquire knowledge,
for there is no denying, alas! that those who
know them best always seem to respect them
least.

"I rose, therefore, from my stall at the first
opportunity and turned round to survey the
house. Ere I had inspected a quarter of it,
my glasses were up, and I will tell you what
they showed me—the most perfect face I ever
saw. Straight nose, thin and delicately cut,
large black eyes, regular eyebrows, faultless chin,
terminating a complete oval, the whole set in a
frame of jet-black hair. Even my next neighbour,
who, from an observation he let fall to a friend,
belonged apparently to the Household Troops,
could not refrain from ejaculating 'By Jove,
she's a ripper!' the moment he caught sight of
the object on which my gaze was fixed.

"I saw something else too. I saw that the
lady by her side was a foreigner with whom I had
long been acquainted ; so edging my way into the
passages, in two minutes I was tapping at their
box-door like a man who felt pretty sure of being
let in.

"The foreigner introduced me to her friend,

and as the second act of the opera was already in progress, told me to sit down and hold my tongue. We were four in the box. Another gentleman was placed close behind the lady who first attracted my attention. I had only eyes just then, however, for the wild, unearthly beauty of my new acquaintance.

"I have seen hundreds of pretty women, and even in youth my heart, from temperament, perhaps, rather than reflection, was as hard as my ribs ; but this face fascinated me—I can use no other word. My sensations were so strangely compounded of admiration, horror, interest, curiosity, attraction, and dislike. The eyes were deep and dark, yet with the glitter in them of a hawk's, the cheek deadly pale, the lips bright red. She was different from anything I had ever seen, and yet so wonderfully beautiful! I longed to hear her speak. Presently she whispered a few words to the man behind her, and I felt my flesh creep. Low as they were modulated, there was in every syllable a tone of such utter hopelessness, such abiding sorrow, regret, even remorse, always present, always kept down, that I could have imagined her one of those lost spirits for whom is fixed the punishment of all most cruel, most intolerable, that they can never forget they are formed for better things. Her gestures, too, were in accordance with the sad, suggestive music of her voice—quiet, graceful, and somewhat listless in the repose, as it seemed, rather of unhappiness than of indolence. I tell you I was not susceptible ; I don't think boys generally are. In love, more than in any other extravagance, ' there is no fool like an old one.'

" I was as little given to romance as a ladies' doctor ; and yet, sitting in that box watching the turn of her beautiful head as she looked towards the stage, I said to myself, ' I'll take good care she never gets the upper hand of *me*. If a man once allowed himself to like her at all, she is just the sort of woman who would blight his whole life for him, and hunt the poor devil down to his grave !' Somebody else seemed to have no such misgivings, or to have arrived at a stage of infatuation when all personal considerations had gone by the board. If ever I saw a calf led to the slaughter it was Count V——, a calf, too, whose throat few women could have cut without compunction. Handsome, manly, rich, affectionate, and sincere, worshipping his deity with all the reckless devotion, all the unscrupulous generosity of his brave Hungarian heart, I saw his very lip quiver under its heavy moustache when she turned her glittering eyes on him with some allusion called up by the business of the stage, and the proud, manly face that had never quailed before an enemy, grew white in the intensity of its emotion. What made me think of a stag I once found lying dead in a Styrian pass, and a golden eagle feasting on him with her talons buried in his heart?

"The Gräfinn, to whom the box belonged, noticed my abstraction. 'Don't fall in love with her,' she whispered; 'I can't spare you just yet. Isn't she beautiful?'

"'You introduced me,' was my answer, 'but you never told me her name.'"

"'How stupid!' said the Gräfinn. 'At present she is a Madame *de* St. Croix, an Englishwoman nevertheless, and a widow, but not likely to remain so long.' And with a mischievous laugh she gave me her hand as I left the box, bowing to Madame *de* St. Croix and also to the Hungarian, who in his happy preoccupation was perfectly unconscious of my politeness.

"I saw them again in the crush-room. The Gräfinn had picked up an *attaché* to some lega-tion, who put her dutifully into her carriage. The Hungarian was still completely engrossed with Madame *de* St. Croix. I have not yet forgotten the look on his handsome face when she drove off with her friend. 'He's a fool,' I said to myself; 'and yet a woman might well be proud to make a fool of such a man as that.'

"I left London in the middle of the season, and thought no more of Madame *de* St. Croix. I had seen a pretty picture, I had heard a strain of sweet music, I had turned over the page of an amusing romance—there was an end of it.

"The following winter I happened to spend in Vienna. Of course I went to one of the masked balls of the *Redouten-Saal.* I had not been ten minutes in the room when my ears thrilled to the low, seductive accents of that well-remembered voice. There she was again, masked of course, but it was impossible to mistake the slim, pliant figure, the graceful gestures, the turn of the beautiful head, and the quiet energy that betrayed itself, even in the small gloved hand. She was talking to a well-known Russian magnate less remarkable for purity of morals than diplomatic celebrity, boundless extravagance, and devotion to the other sex. To be on terms of common friendship with such a man was at least compromising to any lady under sixty years of age; and it is needless to say that his society was courted and appreciated accordingly.

"Madame *de* St. Croix seemed well satisfied with her neighbour; and though in her outward manner the least demonstrative of women, I could detect through her mask the same cruel glitter in her dark eyes that had so fascinated me, six months before, in the Gräfinn's opera-box. The Russian talked volubly, and she leaned towards him, as those do who are willing to hear more. *Château qui parle* furls its banner, *femme qui écoute* droops her head. Directly opposite, looking very tall and fierce as he reared himself against the doorway, stood Count V——. The

Hungarian was pale as death. On his face, so worn and haggard, so cruelly altered since I saw it last, was set the stamp of physical pain, and he gnawed the corner of his brown moustache with that tension of the muscles about the mouth which denotes a paroxysm bravely kept down. As friends accosted him in passing, he bowed his head kindly and courteously while his whole face softened, but it was sad to see how soon the gleam passed away and the cloud came back, darker and heavier than before. The man's heart, you see, was generous, kindly, and full of trust—such a heart as women like Madame *de* St. Croix find it an interesting amusement to break.

"I think he must have made her some kind of appeal; for later in the evening I observed them together, and he was talking earnestly in German, with a low pleading murmur, to which I thought few women could have listened unmoved. She answered in French; and I was sorry for him when she broke up the colloquy with a little scornful shrug of her shoulders, observing in a hard, unfeeling tone, not like her usual voice, 'Que voulez-vous? Enfin, c'est plus fort que moi!'

"The Russian put her into her sledge, for there was a foot of snow in the streets, and Count V—— walked home through it, with a smile on his face and his head up, looking strangely elated, I thought, for a man the last strand of whose moorings had lately parted and left him adrift.

"I had not then learned there is no temporary stimulant so powerful as despair, no tonic so reviving as a *parti pris*.

"Next day, lounging into the *Chancellerie* of the Embassy for my usual gossip, I found little Hughes, an unpaid *attaché* (who earned, indeed, just as much as he received), holding forth with considerable spirit and energy.

"'Curse him!' said this indomitable young Briton. 'If it had been swords, I should like to have fought him myself. I hate him! I tell you. Everybody hates him. And V—— was the best chap between here and Orsova. He was almost like an Englishman. Wouldn't he just have polished him off if they'd had swords. That old muff, Bergheimer of the Cuirassiers, ought to be hanged. Do you think, if *I'd* been his second, I'd have put him up with pistols against the best shot in Europe?—and at the barrier too! It's not like at home, you know. I never knew such a mull as they made of it amongst them. This cursed Calmuck gets the pull all through, and poor V——, who had lost his fortune already, loses his lady-love and his life. What a rum world it is!'

"Here the orator rolled and lit a cigarette, thus affording me a moment to inquire into the cause of his indignation. I then learned that, in consequence of a trifling dispute after last night's ball, a duel had been fought at daybreak, in the snow, between Count V—— and a Russian noble-man, in which the former was shot through the heart.

"'Never got *one* in at all!' said Hughes, again waxing eloquent on his friend's wrongs. 'I've seen both the seconds since. They were to walk up to a handkerchief, and the Russian potted him at forty yards the first step he made. They may say what they like about the row originating in politics—I know better. They quarrelled because Madame *de* St. Croix had left V——and taken up with this snub-nosed Tartar. First, she ruined my poor friend. I know all about it. He hadn't a rap left; for if she'd asked him for the shirt off his back, he'd have stripped like beans! Then she broke his heart — the cheeriest, jolliest, kindest fellow in Europe—to finish up by leaving him for another man, who kills him before breakfast without a scruple ; and if the devil don't get hold of *her* some fine day, why he's a disgrace to his appointment, that's all! and they ought to make him Secretary of Legation here, or pension him off somewhere and put him out of the way! Have another cigarette!'

"Ten years afterwards I was sitting in the gardens of the Tuileries, one fine morning towards the middle of May, wondering, as English people always do wonder, on a variety of subjects—why the cigars were so bad in Paris, and the air so exhilarating — why the tender green leaves quivering over those deep alleys should have a sunshine of their own besides that which they reflected from above—why the *bonnes* and nursery-maids wore clean caps every day— why the railings always looked as if they had been regilt the same morning, and why the sentry at the gate should think it part of his duty to leer at every woman who passed, like a satyr.

" Indeed I believe I was almost asleep, when I started in my chair, and rubbed my eyes to make sure it was not a dream. There, within ten paces of me, sat Madame *de* St. Croix, if I was still to call her so, apparently not an hour older than the first time we met. The face was even paler, the lips redder, the cruel eyes deeper and darker, but in that flickering light the woman looked more beautiful than ever. She was listening quietly and indolently, as of old, to a gentleman who sat with his back to me, telling his own story, whatever it might be, in a low, earnest, impressive voice. I raised my hat when I caught her eye, and she bowed in return politely enough, but obviously without recognition. The movement caused her companion to turn round, and in two strides he was by my chair, grasping me cordially by the hand. He was an old and intimate friend, a colonel in the French army, by whose side I had experienced more than one strange adventure, both in Eastern Europe and

Asia Minor—a man who had served with distinction, of middle age, a widower, fond of society,
field-sports, speculation, and travelling ; essentially
bon camarade, but thoroughly French in his reflections and opinions. The last man in the world,
I should have thought, to be made a fool of by a
woman. Well, there he was, her bounden slave !
Absurdly happy if she smiled, miserable when she
frowned, ready to fetch and carry like a poodle,
perfectly childish about her, and utterly contemptible. If she had really cared for him, the
temptation must have been irresistible, and she
would have bullied him frightfully. But no,
there was always the same repose of manner,
the same careless kindness, the same melancholy,
the same consciousness of an unquestionable
superiority. One of his reasons, he soon confided
to me, for being so fond of her was that they
never had an angry word ! For a week or two
I saw a good deal of them. Paris was already
empty, and we did our plays, our Opéra Comique,
and our little dinners pleasantly enough. She
was always the same, and I found myself, day by
day, becoming more conscious of that nameless
charm about her, which I should despair of being
able to describe. Yet as often as I met the glance
of those deep, dark, unearthly eyes, a shudder
crept over me, such as chills you when you come
face to face with a ghost in your dreams. The
colonel, I have said, was devoted to her. He

was rarely absent from her side, but if by chance alone with me, would talk of her by the hour.

" He had found, he declared, fortunately before he was too old to appreciate it, the one inestimable treasure the earth contained. He had cherished his fancies, committed his follies, of course, *tout comme un autre*, but he had never experienced anything like this. It was his haven, his anchorage, his resting-place, and he might glide down into old age, and on to death, perfectly happy, because confident, that with *her* heart and *her* force of character, she would never change. He could not be jealous of her. Oh no! She was so frank, so confiding, so sincere. She, too, *passé par là*, had told him so; unlike other women, had confessed to him not only her last, but her many former attachments. He knew all about poor V——, who was shot in a duel, and the Russian general, banished to Siberia. How fortunate she had broken with him before his disgrace, because, in the loyalty of her nature, she would surely have followed him into exile, although she never cared for him in her heart, never. No, nor for any of the others; never had been fairly touched till now. Him, the colonel, she really *did* love. He had proved his devotion so thoroughly (I found out afterwards, though not from him, that my friend had been fool enough to sacrifice both fortune and profession for her sake), he was so reliable, she said, so kind, and so *good.* In short, he was perfectly happy, and could see no cloud in his horizon, look which way he would.

"When I left Paris they accompanied me to the railway station ; and the last I saw of them was their two heads very close over a railway guide, projecting a trip into a lonely part of Switzerland, where they would have no society but their own.

"Six months afterwards *Galignani* informed me that my friend the colonel had been reinstated in the French army and appointed to a regiment of Chasseurs d'Afrique then serving in Algeria, where, before the Tuileries Gardens were again green, I learned from the same source he had already solved the great problem in an affair of outposts with the Khabyles. Long years elapsed, and there were streaks of grey in my hair and whiskers ere I saw Madame *de* St. Croix again. I had heard of her, indeed, at intervals both in London and Paris. I am bound to say her name was always coupled with those who were distinguished by birth, talent, or success. She was very choice, I believe, in the selection of her victims, despising equally an easy conquest and one of which the ravages could be readily repaired. The women hated her, the men said she was charming. For my part I kept out of her way ; we were destined to meet nevertheless. I had embarked in a Peninsular and Oriental steamer at Marseilles very much indisposed, and retiring at once to my berth never quitted it till we were entering the Straits of Bonifacio. Here I came on deck, weak, exhausted, but convalescent, drinking in the sunshine and the scenery with that thirst for the beautiful which becomes so fierce after the confinement of recent illness. I literally revelled in the Mediterranean air, and basked in the warmth of those bright colours so peculiar to the shores of that summer-sea. I was approaching middle age; I had ventured body and mind freely enough in the great conflict; and yet, I thank Heaven, had hitherto been spared the crushing sorrow that makes a mockery of the noblest and purest enjoyments of earth, causing a man to turn from all that is fairest in sight and sense and sound with the sickness of a dead hope curdling at his heart. But then I had kept clear of Madame *de* St. Croix.

"When my eyes were at last sated with the gaudy hues of the coast and the golden glitter of the water, I was a little surprised to see that lady sitting within three paces of me reading a yellow-bound French novel. Great Heaven! what was the woman's secret? She looked younger than ever! Even in the searching glare of a Southern noon not a line could be detected on the pure, pale forehead, not a crease about the large, wistful, glittering eyes. That she was gifted with perennial youth I could see for myself; that she was dangerous even to the peace of a grey-haired man, I might have found out to my cost had our voyage been retarded by contrary winds or any such unavoidable delay, for she was good enough to recognise me on this occasion, and to give me a large share of her conversation and companionship. Thus it was I learned to own the spell under which so many had succumbed, to appreciate its power, not to understand, far less describe, its nature. Fortunately for me, ere its work could be completed we arrived at Athens, and at Athens lay a trim, rakish-looking English yacht, with her ensign flying and her fore-topsail loosed, waiting only the steamer's arrival to spread her wings and bear off this seductive sorceress to some garden of paradise in the Ægean Sea.

" The owner of the yacht I had often heard of. He was a man remarkable for his enterprise and unfailing success in commerce as for his liberality, and indeed extravagance, in expenditure. He chose to have houses, pictures, horses, plate, everything of the best, was justly popular in society, and enormously rich.

" I never asked and never knew the port to which that yacht was bound. When we steamed out of the harbour she was already hull-down in the wake of a crimson sunset that seemed to stain the waters with a broad track of blood; but I saw her sold within eighteen months at South-ampton, for her late owner's name had appeared in the *Gazette*, and the man himself, I was told, might be found, looking very old and careworn, setting cabbages at Hanwell, watching eagerly for the arrival of a lady who never came.

"You may believe I thought more than once of the woman whose strange destiny it had been thus to enslave generation after generation of fools, and to love whom seemed as fatal as to be a priest of Aricia or a favourite of Catharine II. Nevertheless, while time wore on, I gradually ceased to think of her beauty, her heartlessness, her mysterious youth, or her magic influence over mankind. Presently, amongst a thousand engrossing occupations and interests, I forgot her as if she had never been.

"I have driven a good many vehicles in my time, drags, phaetons, dogcarts, down to a basket-carriage drawn by a piebald pony with a hog-mane. Nay, I once steered a hansom cab up Bond Street in the early morning, freighted with more subalterns than I should like to specify of Her Majesty's Household Troops, but I never thought I should come to a Bath chair!

"Nevertheless I found myself at last an inside passenger of one of these locomotive couches, enjoying the quiet and the air of the gardens at Hampton Court in complete and uninterrupted solitude. The man who dragged me to this pleasant spot having gone to 'get his dinner,' as he called it, and the nursery-maids, with their

interesting charges, having retired from their
morning, and not yet emerged for their afternoon stroll, I lay back, and thought of so many
things—of the strength and manhood that had
departed from me for ever; of the strange, dull
calm that comes on with the evening of life, and
contents us so well we would not have its morning
back if we could; of the *gradual clairvoyance* that
shows us everything in its true colours and at its
real value; of the days, and months, and years
so cruelly wasted, but that their pleasures, their
excitements, their sins, their sorrows, and their
sufferings were indispensable for the great lesson
which teaches us *to see.* Of these things I thought,
and through them still, as at all times, moved the
pale presence of an unforgotten face, passing like
a spirit, dim and distant, yet dear as ever, across
the gulf of years—a presence that, for good or
evil, was to haunt me to the end.

"Something in the association of ideas reminded me of Madame *de* St. Croix, and I said
to myself, 'At last age must have overtaken that
marvellous beauty, and time brought the indomitable spirit to remorse, repentance, perhaps
even amendment. What can have made me
think of her in a quiet, peaceful scene like this?'

"Just then a lady and gentleman crossed the
gravel walk in front of me, and took their places
on a seat under an old tree not a dozen yards off.
It was a lovely day in early autumn; the flowers

were still ablaze with the gaudiest of their summer beauty, the sky was all dappled grey and gold, earth had put on the richest dress she wears throughout the year; but here and there a leaf fell noiseless on the sward, as if to testify that she too must shed all her glories in due season, and yield, like other beauties, her unwilling tribute to decay.

"But there was nothing of autumn in the pair who now sat opposite my couch, chatting, laughing, flirting, apparently either ignoring or disregarding my proximity. The man was in all the bloom and beauty of youth; the woman, though looking a few years older, did not yet seem to have attained her prime. I could scarcely believe my eyes! Yes, if ever I beheld Madame *de* St. Croix, there she sat with her fatal gaze turned on this infatuated boy, leading him gradually, steadily, surely, to the edge of that chasm, into which those who plunged came to the surface nevermore. It was the old story over again. How well I remembered, even after such an interval, the tender droop of the head, the veiling eyelashes, the glance so quickly averted, yet, like a snapshot, telling with such deadly effect; the mournful smile, the gentle whisper, the quiet, confiding gesture of the slender hand, all the by-play of the most accomplished and most unscrupulous of actresses. There was no more chance of escape for her companion than for a fisherman of the

North Sea, whose skiff has been sucked into the Maëlstrohm, with mast unshipped and oars adrift half a mile astern. By sight, if not personally, I then knew most of the notabilities of the day. The boy, for such I might well call him in comparison with myself, seemed too good for his fate, and yet I saw well enough it was inevitable. He had already made himself a name as a poet of no mean pretensions, and held besides the character of a high-spirited, agreeable, and unaffected member of society. Add to this, that he was manly, good-looking, and well-born ; nothing more seemed wanting to render him a fit victim for the altar at which he was to be offered up. Like his predecessors, he was fascinated. The snake held him in her eye. The poor bird's wings were fluttering, its volition was gone, its doom sealed. Could nothing save it from the destroyer? I longed to have back, if only for a day, the powers which I had regretted so little half an hour ago. Weak, helpless, weary, and worn-out, I yet determined to make an effort, and save him if I could.

"They rose to go, but found the gate locked through which they had intended to pass. She had a way of affecting a pretty wilfulness in trifles, and sent him to fetch the key. Prompt to obey her lightest wish, he bounded off in search of it, and following slowly, she passed within two paces of my chair, bending on its helpless invalid a look

that seemed to express far less pity for his condition than a grudging envy of his lot. I stopped
her with a gesture that in one more able-bodied
would have been a bow, and, strange to say, she
recognised me at once. There was not a moment
to lose. I took courage from a certain wistful
look that gave softness to her eyes, and I spoke
out.

"'We shall never meet again,' I said; 'we
have crossed each other's paths, at such long
intervals, and on such strange occasions, but I
know this is the last of them! Why time stands
still for *you* is a secret I cannot fathom, but the
end must come some day, put it off however long
you will. Do you not think that when you
become as I am, a weary mortal, stumbling with
half-shut eyes on the edge of an open grave, it
would be well to have one good deed on which
you could look back, to have reprieved one out
of the many victims on whom you have inflicted
mortal punishment for the offence of loving you
so much better than you deserve? Far as it
stretches behind you, every footstep in your
track is marked with sorrow — more than one
with blood. Show mercy now, as you may have
to ask it hereafter. Life is all before this one,
and it seems cruel thus to blast the sapling from
its very roots. He is hopeful, trustful, and fresh-
hearted—spare him and let him go.'

"She was fitting the glove on her faultless

little hand. Her brow seemed so calm, so soft and pure, that for a moment I thought I had conquered, but looking up from her feminine employment, I recognised the hungry glitter in those dark, merciless eyes, and I knew there was no hope.

"'It is too late,' she answered, 'too late to persuade either him or me. It is no fault of mine. It is fate. For him—for the others—for all of us. Sometimes I wish it had not been so. Mine has been an unhappy life, and there seems to be no end, no resting-place. I can no more help myself than a drowning wretch, swept down by a torrent; but I am too proud to catch at the twigs and straws that would break off in my hand. I would change places with you willingly. Yes—you in that Bath chair. I am so tired sometimes, and yet I dare not wish it was all over. Think of me as forbearingly as you can, for we shall not cross each other's path again.'

"'And this boy?' I asked, striving to detect something of compunction in the pitiless face that was yet so beautiful.

"'He must take his chance with the rest,' she said. 'Here he comes—good-bye.'

"They walked away arm-in-arm through the golden autumn weather, and a chill came into my very heart, for I knew what that chance was worth.

"A few months, and the snow lay six inches

deep over the grave of him whose opening manhood had been so full of promise, so rich in all
that makes youth brightest, life most worth
having; while a woman in deep mourning was
praying there, under the wintry sky; but this
woman was his mother, and her heart was broken
for the love she bore her boy.

"His death had been very shocking, very
sudden. People talked of a ruptured blood-
vessel, a fall on his bedroom floor, a doctor not
to be found when sent for; a series of fatalities
that precluded the possibility of saving him; but
those who pretended to know best affirmed that
not all the doctors in Europe could have done
any good, for when his servant went to call him
in the morning he found his master lying stark
and stiff, having been dead some hours. There
was a pool of blood on his carpet; there were
ashes of burnt letters in his fireplace; more, they
whispered with meaning shrugs and solemn, awe-
struck faces—

> There was that across his throat
> Which you had hardly cared to see.

"You can understand now that I believe in
Vampires."

"What became of her?" I asked, rather
eagerly, for I was interested in this Madame
de St. Croix. I like a woman who goes into
extremes, either for good or evil. Great reck-

lessness, equally with great sensibility, has its charm for such a temperament as mine. I can understand, though I cannot explain, the influence possessed by very wicked women who never scruple to risk their own happiness as readily as their neighbours'. I wanted to know something more about Madame *de* St. Croix, but he was not listening; he paid no attention to my question. In a tone of abstraction that denoted his thoughts were many miles away, he only murmured—

"Insatiate — impenetrable — pitiless. The others were bad enough in all conscience, but I think she might have spared the boy!"

CHAPTER V

GOLD FOR SILVER

"The African Magician never minded all their scoffs and holloaings, or all they could say to him, but still cry'd *Who'll change old Lamps for new ones?* which he repeated so often about the Princess Badroulbondour's Palace, that that Princess, who was then in the hall with the four-and-twenty windows, hearing a man cry something, and not being able to distinguish his words, by reason of the holloaing of the mob about him, sent one of her women slaves down to know what he cry'd.

"The slave was not long before she return'd, and ran into the hall, laughing so heartily, that the Princess could not forbear herself. 'Well, Giggler,' said the Princess, 'will you tell me what you laugh at?' 'Alas! Madam,' answered the slave, laughing still, 'who can forbear laughing to see a fool with a basket on his arm, full of fine new lamps, ask to change them for old ones, which makes the children and mob make such a noise about him?'"

WHAT a fool they thought him, and no wonder. Yet surely a magician need not come all the way from Africa to teach the public this strange rate of exchange. In Europe, Asia, and America too, as far as it has yet been colonised, such one-sided bargains are made every day.

Old lamps for new, kicks for halfpence—heads

BONES AND I

I win, tails you lose—such are the laws of equity by which man deals with his neighbour ; and so the contest goes on, if, indeed, as Juvenal says, that can be called a contest—

> Ubi tu pulsas, ego vapulo tantum.[1]

The slave of the princess with the long name had passed more of her life in the palace than the streets, or she would not have found the magician's cry so strange : would have felt uncomfortably conscious that the day might come when she, too, would barter new lamps for old, perhaps humbly on her knees, entreating permission to make the unequal exchange. In all the relations of life, but chiefly in those with which the affections are concerned, we constantly see gold for silver offered with both hands.

That "it is better to give than to receive" we have Scriptural warrant for asserting, that—

> Sure the pleasure is as great
> In being cheated as to cheat,

we learn from Butler's quaint and philosophical couplets. I am not going to assert that the man who puts down sovereigns and takes up shillings has really the worst of it ; I only maintain that the more freely he parts with the former, the more sparing will he find the latter doled out to him in return.

[1] If that's a fight indeed,
Where you strike hard, and I stand still and bleed.

GOLD FOR SILVER

Perhaps the strongest case in point is that of parent and child.

In the animal world I know few arrangements of Nature more beautiful than the absolute devotion of maternity to its offspring, so long, though *only* so long, as its assistance is required. A bird feeding her young, a tigress licking her cubs, a mare wheeling round her foal — each of these affords an example of loving care and tenderness, essentially feminine in its utter forgetfulness of self. Each of these squanders such gold as it possesses, the treasure of its deep instinctive affection, on ingratitude and neglect. The nestlings gape with hungry little beaks, when they hear the flap of wings, not to greet the coming provider, but that they may eat and be filled. The cubs huddle themselves up to their mother's side, for warmth and comfort, not for her cruel beauty nor her fierce protecting love. The foal, when it gets on its long legs, will follow your horse or mine as readily as its dam. They take all, to give back nothing in exchange. And no sooner can the bird use its wings, the beast its limbs, than it abandons at once and for ever the parent whose sustaining care is no longer necessary to its existence.

With the human race, although I am far from affirming that, even in this age of bronze, filial piety has fled with other virtues from the earth, something of the same unequal barter holds good

in the relationship of parent and child. The
former gives gold, the latter does not always
return silver. Do not deceive yourself. You
love your children more than your children love
you. I can prove it in three words. They are
dearer to you than your own parents. And this
inequality of affection is but one more of the
beautiful arrangements made by that Providence
which bestows good so liberally in proportion to
evil. Under the common law of Nature, you are
likely to die first, and the aggregate amount of
suffering is, therefore, much less than it would
be did the course of domestic affection flow the
other way. So you toil, and slave, and scheme
for the child's benefit, forgiving its errors, repair-
ing its follies, re-establishing its fortunes, just as,
long ago, you used to rebuild with loving patience
those houses of cards the urchin blew down with
such delight. But, as of all human affections,
this, if not the strongest, is certainly the deepest
and most abiding, so, when wounded, does it
inflict on our moral being the sharpest and most
enduring pain. " Is there any cause in Nature
that makes these hard hearts ? " says poor King
Lear, forced, against his own instincts, to acknowledge the venomed bite of that serpent's tooth
with which elsewhere he compares a thankless
child. I have known men, and women too,
accept with courage every sample of misfortune
and disgrace—in the language of the prize-ring,

"come up smiling" after every kind of knock-down blow—but I cannot remember an instance in which the ingratitude of children has not produced wrinkles and grey hairs, in the proportion of ten to one, for every other sorrow of any description whatever.

There is no prospect of alleviation to amuse his fancy—no leavening of pique to arouse his pride. Hurt to the death, the sufferer has scarce manhood enough left to conceal his wounds.

In that conflict between man and woman which is perpetually going on, and without which the world, if more comfortable, would undoubtedly be less populous, gold is invariably given for silver with a lavish extravagance, akin to the absurdity of the whole thing.

Why is love like the handle of a teapot?—Because it is all on one side. The game has yet to be invented in which both players can win; and perhaps were it not for the discomfort, anxiety, worry, sorrow, and suffering entailed by the unequal pastime, it would cease to be so popular. As it exists at present, there is nothing to complain of on the score of flagging interest. At first, indeed, before the cards are cut, the adversaries sit down calmly and pleasantly enough. An hour hangs heavy on their hands, and they think thus to drive it agreeably away—beginning simply for "distraction," as the French call it, though ending in the English acceptation of that uncomfortable word. Ere the first tricks are turned, however, the game grows exciting. "I propose." "How many?" "Hearts are trumps." "I mark the king." The stakes increase rapidly in value, and presently gold comes pouring lavishly out of one player's pocket, against silver dribbling unwillingly from the other's. The winner, too, like all gamblers, seldom cares to keep the fruit of his good fortune, but loses it again at another table to some stronger adversary, who is beggared in turn elsewhere.

Yet still in all places, and under all circumstances, wherever this game is played there is the same inequality in the stakes. "Gold for silver." Such are the terms; and the old players, to do them justice, those who have lost and won many a heavy wager, are generally careful to begin at least by venturing the commoner metal. But even of these the discretion is not to be trusted as the game goes on. Touched by the magic rod, maddened by the spell against which Wisdom is often less proof than Folly, the sternest and the sagest will throw their gold about as recklessly as if every piece were not stamped with the impress of their honour and their happiness, precious as the very drops of life-blood at their heart.

Perhaps it is wiser to stick to any other pursuit in the world than the one in question; but if you must needs sit down to this beggar-my-neighbour kind of amusement, is it better to lose or to win? to give or accept the gold for silver passing so freely from hand to hand? Will you have the satisfaction hereafter of standing on the higher ground? of feeling you have nothing to reproach yourself with, nothing to be ashamed of? or will you take comfort in reflecting that while the storm raged above your head you had been careful to shelter cunningly from the blast? Will you exult in your forethought, your philosophy, the accurate knowledge of human nature, that has preserved you scatheless through the combat? or will you take pride in your generosity, your magnanimity, and the self-devoted courage that bids you accept the stab of ingratitude in addition to the pain of neglect? It depends entirely on character and temperament.

Men and women vary so much in this, as in every other phase of feeling. The latter, when they do take the more generous view of their position — when they can bring themselves to ⹁ choose the better part, accept it, I think, with a more complete abandonment of *pique* than the former. Perhaps their pride is of a nobler order: no doubt their vanity is less egotistical than our own. With us, except in the highest natures— and these, as has been well remarked, have ever a leavening of the feminine element in their organisation—there is always something of irrita-

tion left after a wound of the affections has healed
up—something that stings and rankles, and looks
to reprisals of one kind or another for relief. I
have read an old tale of chivalry so thoroughly
exemplifying this state of feeling, and affording
so natural an example of the changes and counter-
changes with which gold and silver are staked
against each other in the dangerous game, that I
cannot forbear quoting it here.

"A certain knight had long loved a damsel at
the court of the King of France; but she, albeit
accepting the service of none other, treated him
with such coldness and *duresse*, that he at length
obtained the title of the 'Patient Knight,' and
she of the 'Scornful Ladye.' In vain he sat at
her feet in hall; in vain wore her colours in the
lists; in vain added to his cognisance the motto
Sans espérance, above the representation of a
dungeon-grate, to signify the hopelessness of his
captivity. She looked upon him coldly as the
winter moon looks on a frozen lake; she turned
from him pitilessly as the bending poplar turns
from the south wind, whispering its longing and
its sorrows, wooing her even with its tears.

"So minstrels sang in their lays of his constancy, and knights marvelled at his subjection,
and ladies pitied—it may be despised him also a
little for his long-suffering: but still the Patient
Knight struck hard and shouted high for the
renown of her he loved; and still the Scornful

GOLD FOR SILVER

Ladye accepted his homage, and took credit for his deeds-of-arms with scant courtesy, and cruel neglect, and high imperious disdain.

"So the King bade his knights and nobles to a feast; and because there was to be a solemn passage-of-arms held on the morrow, he entertained them with a fight of wild beasts in the Carrousel, whereon lords and ladies looked down in safety from the galleries above. But many a soft cheek grew pale none the less, when a lion and a tiger were let loose to battle for their lives.

"Now even while they glared on each other ere they closed, the 'Scornful Ladye' dropped her glove between the beasts of prey. Quoth she, with a mocking smile, 'An I had a bachelor here who loved me well, he would fetch me back this glove that the wind hath blown from my hand.'

"Then the Patient Knight made no more ado, but drew his good sword and leapt lightly down into the Carrousel, where he picked the glove from the earth, and returning scatheless to his place, laid it in silence at her feet.

"Then the Scornful Ladye wept sweet and happy tears; for his great love had conquered at last, and she would follow him meekly now to the end of the world.

"But she shed bitter tears on the morrow, when he rode into the lists with another's sleeve in his helmet, another's colours on his housings,

and his shield blazoned with the fresh device of
a broken fetter and the motto, *Tout lasse—tout
casse—tout passe!*"[1]

So, you see, these adversaries changed places
at last; and you will probably be of opinion that
the Knight had the best of it in the end.

Perhaps it served her right. And yet to me
it seems that there may come a time when to
have given gold for silver in every relation of
life shall be the one consoling reflection that
enables us to quit it without misgivings for the
future, without regret for the past, — a time
perhaps of hushed voices, stealthy footsteps,
and a darkened room, growing yet strangely
darker with every breath we draw. Or a time
of eager comrades, trampling squadrons, short,
sharp words of command, a bugle sounding the
Advance, a cocked - hat glancing through the
smoke; a numb, sick helplessness that glues the
cheek into the dust where it has fallen, and a roll
of musketry, feebler, farther, fainter, and more
confused, till its warlike echoes die out in the
hush of another world. Or a time of earth-
stained garments, and bespattered friends proffer-
ing silver hunting-flasks in sheer dismay, and a
favourite horse brought back with flying stirrups,
dangling rein, and its mane full of mud, while the
dull grey sky wheels above, and the dank, tufted

---

[1] Another version of this story is given by Browning in his
ballad, *De Lorge.*—ED.

grass heaves below ; nor in the intervals of a pain, becoming every moment less keen, can we stifle the helpless consciousness that before our crushed frame shall be lifted from its wet, slippery resting-place, it will be time to die.

At such moments as these, I say, to have given gold for silver, while we could, can surely be no matter of regret.

I recollect a quaint old tombstone—I beg your pardon for the allusion—on which I once read the following inscription :—

"What I spent I *had*—what I saved I *lost*—what I gave I *have*."

Surely this sentiment will bear analysing. "What I spent I *had*." I enjoyed it, wasted it, got rid of it : derive from it now as much enjoyment as can ever be extracted from past pleasures of which self-indulgence was the motive—that is to say, none at all! "What I saved I *lost*." Undoubtedly. Mortgages, Consols, building leases, railway scrip—it was locked up in securities that I could by no means bring with me here. It has been an error of judgment, a bad speculation, a foolish venture, a dead loss. "But what I gave I *have*." Ah! There I did good business : took the turn of the market ; invested my capital in a bank that pays me cent. per cent., even now ; and this, not only for the dross we call money, but for the real treasures of the heart—affection, kindliness, charity, help to the needy, sympathy with the sorrowful, protection to the weak, and encouragement to the forlorn. The silver I had in return has been left long ago on earth: perhaps there was barely enough to make a plate for my coffin; but the gold I gave is in my own possession still, and has been beaten into a crown for me in heaven.

Yes. "It is better to give than to receive." With few exceptions the great benefactors of mankind have been in this world defrauded of their wages. Columbus died perhaps the poorest man in the whole kingdom he had spent his lifetime to enrich. Socrates sold the treasures of his intellect—the deductions of the greatest mind in antiquity—for a draught of hemlock on a prison floor. The fable of Prometheus has been enacted over and over again. Those who scale the heavens that they may bring down fire to enlighten and comfort their fellow-men, must not hope to escape the vulture and the rock. I have always thought that wondrous story the deepest and the most suggestive in the whole heathen mythology. Its hero was the first discoverer, the first freethinker, the first reformer. He was even proof against the seductions of woman, and detected in Pandora's box the multiplicity of evils that secured the presence of Hope within its compass, and prevented her flying back to the heaven whence she came. The only Olympian deity he would condescend to worship was the

Goddess of Wisdom; and she it was who taught her votary to outwit Jupiter, the great principle of what may be termed physical nature. By science man baffles the elements, or renders them subservient to his purpose. He was an herbalist, a doctor, a meteorologist, and universal referee for gods and men. He taught the latter all the arts necessary to extort a livelihood from the earth; showed them how to yoke their oxen and bridle their steeds. He was wise, laborious, provident, and paternal — the first philosopher, the great benefactor of his time, and—his reward was to lie in chains on Mount Ætna with a vulture sheathing her beak in his heart.

Can we not see in this heathen parable some glimmering of the Great Hope which was never entirely obscured to the ancient world?—some faint foresight of, some vague longing after, the Great Example which has since taught its holy lesson of self-abnegation and self-sacrifice? It is not for me to enlarge on a topic so sacred and so sublime. Enough for us and such as we are if, by lavishing gold for silver freely on our brother, we can cast but one humble mite into the treasury of our God.

There is much talk in the world about ingratitude. People who do good to others at cost or inconvenience to themselves are apt to expect a great flow of thanks, a great gush of sentiment in return. They are generally disappointed. Those natures which feel benefits the most deeply are often the least capable of expressing their feelings, and a speechless tongue is with them the result of a full heart.   Besides, you are sure to be repaid for a good action at some time or another. Like seed sown in the Nile, "the bread cast upon the waters," it may not come back to you for many days, but come back at last it most certainly *will.* Would you like your change in silver or in gold? Will you have it in a few graceful, well-chosen expressions, or in the sterling coin of silent love with its daily thoughts and nightly prayers ; or, better still even than these, will you waive your claim to it down here, and have it carried to your account above? I am supposing yours is not one of those natures which have arrived at the highest, the noblest type of benevolence, and give their gold neither for silver nor for copper, but freely without return at all. To these I can offer no encouragement, no advice. Their grapes are ripened, their harvest is yellow, the light is already shining on them from the golden hills of heaven.

CHAPTER VI

I HAVE been burning old letters to-night; their ashes are fluttering in the chimney even now; and, alas! while they consume, fleeting and perishable like the moments they record, each dying ember seems to have wrought its ghost upon my heart. Oh that we could either completely remember or completely forget! Oh that the image of Mnemosyne would remain close enough for us to detect the flaws in her imperishable marble, or that she would remove herself so far as to be altogether out of sight! It is the golden haze of middle distance that sheds on her this warm and tender light. She is all the more attractive that we see her through a double veil of retrospection and regret, none the less lovely

235

because her beauty is dimmed and softened in a mist of tears.

Letter after letter, they have flared, and blackened, and shrivelled up. There is an end of them—they are gone. Not a line of those different handwritings shall I ever see again. The bold, familiar scrawl of the tried friend and more than brother; why does he come back to me so vividly to-night? The stout heart, the strong arm, the brave, kind face, the frank and manly voice. We shall never tread the stubble nor the heather side by side again; never more pull her up against the stream, nor float idly down in the hot summer noons to catch the light air off the water on our heated faces; to discourse, like David and Jonathan, of all and everything nearest our hearts. Old friend! old friend! wherever you are, if you have consciousness you must surely sometimes think of me; I have not forgotten you. I cannot believe you have forgotten me even *there*.

And the painstaking, up - and - down - hill characters of the little child—the little child for whom the angels came so soon, yet found it ready to depart, whose fever-wasted lips formed none but words of confidence and affection, whose blue eyes turned their last dim, dying looks so fondly on the face it loved.

And there were letters harder to part with than these. Never mind, they are burnt and done with ; letters of which even the superscription once made a kind heart leap with pleasure so intense it was almost pain ; letters crossed and recrossed in delicate, orderly lines, bearing the well - known cipher, breathing the well - known perfume, telling the old, false tale in the old, false phrases, so trite and worn-out, yet seeming always so fresh and new.

The hand that formed them has other tasks to occupy it now ; the heart from which they came is mute and cold. Hope withers, love dies—times are altered. What would you have ? It is a world of change. Nevertheless this has been a disheartening job ; it has put me in low spirits ; I must call Bones out of his cupboard to come and sit with me.

"What is this charm ? " I ask him, "that seems to belong so exclusively to the past ?—this 'tender grace of a day, that is dead'? and must I look after it down the gulf into which it has dropped with such irrepressible longing only because it will never come back to me ? Is a man the greater or wiser that he lived a hundred years ago or a thousand ? Are reputations, like wine, the mellower and the more precious for mere age, even though they have been hid away in a cellar all the time ? Is a thing actually fairer and better because I have almost forgotten how it looked when present, and shall never set eyes on it again ? I entertain the greatest aversion to Horace's *laudator temporis acti*,[1] shall always set my face against the superstition that 'there were giants in those days'; and yet wherever I went in the world previous to my retirement here that I might live with you, I found the strange maxim predominate, that everything was very much better before it had been improved!

"If I entered a club and expressed my intention of going to the opera, for instance, whatever small spark of enthusiasm I could kindle was submitted to a wet blanket on the spot. 'Good Heavens!' would exclaim some venerable philosopher of the Cynic and Epicurean schools, 'there *is* no opera now, nor *ballet* neither. My good sir, the thing is done; it's over. We haven't an artist left. Ah! you should have seen Taglioni dance; you should have heard Grisi sing; you should have lived when Plancus was consul. In short, you should be as old as I am, and as disgusted, and as gouty, and as disagreeable!'

"Or I walked into the smoking-room of that same resort, full of some athletic gathering at Holland Park, some 'Varsity hurdle-race, some trial of strength or skill amongst those lively boys the subalterns of the Household Brigade; and ere I could articulate 'brandy and soda' I had

---

[1] Morose, complaining, and with tedious praise
Talking the manners of their youthful days.
Francis's Horace, A.P. 173.

A DAY THAT IS DEAD

Captain Barclay thrown body and bones in my face. 'Walk, sir! You talk of walking?' (I didn't, for there had been barely time to get a word in edgeways, or my parable would have exhausted itself concerning a running high leap.) 'But there is nothing like a real pedestrian left; they don't breed 'em, sir, in these days: can't grow 'em, and don't know how to train 'em if they could! Show me a fellow who would make a match with Barclay to-day. Barclay, sir, if he were alive, would walk all your best men down after he came in from shooting. Ask your young friends which of 'em would like to drive the mail from London to Edinburgh without a greatcoat! I don't know what's come to the present generation. It must be the smoking, or the light claret, perhaps. They're done, they're used up, they're washed out. Why, they go to covert by railway, and have their grouse driven to them on a hill! What would old Sir Tatton or Osbaldeston say to such doings as these? I was at Newmarket, I tell you, when the squire rode his famous match—two hundred miles in less than nine hours! I saw him get off old Tranby, and I give you my honour the man looked fresher than the horse! Don't tell me. He was rubbed down by a couple of prize-fighters (there were real bruisers in those days, and the best man used to win), dressed, and came to dinner just as *you* would after a five-mile walk.

Pocket Hercules, you call him — one in a thousand? There were hundreds of such men in my day. Why, I recollect in Tom Smith's time that I myself'—

"But at this point I used to make my escape, because there are two subjects on which nobody is so brilliant as not to be prolix, so dull as not to be enthusiastic—his doings in the saddle and his adventures with the fair. To honour either of these triumphs he blows a trumpet-note loud and long in proportion to the antiquity of the annals it records. Why must you never again become possessed of such a hunter as Tally-Ho? Did that abnormal animal really carry you as well as you think, neither failing when the ground was deep nor wavering when the fences were strong? Is it strictly true that no day was ever too long for him? that he was always in the same field with the hounds? And have not the rails he rose at, the ditches he covered so gallantly, increased annually in height and depth and general impossibility ever since that fatal morning when he broke his back under the Coplow in a two-foot drain?

"You can't find such horses now? Perhaps you do not give them so liberal a chance of proving their courage, speed, and endurance.

"On the other topic it is natural enough, I daresay, for you to yarn with all the more freedom that there is no one left to contradict.

A DAY THAT IS DEAD

People used enormous coloured silk handkerchiefs in that remote period, when you threw yours with such Oriental complacency, and the odalisques who picked it up are probably to-day so old and stiff they could not bend their backs to save their lives. But were they really as fond, and fair, and faithful as they seem to you now? Had they no caprices to chill, no whims to worry, no rivals on hand to drive you mad? Like the sea, those eyes that look so deep and blue at a distance, are green and turbid and full of specks when you come quite close. Was it all sunshine with Mary, all roses with Margaret, all summer with Jane? What figures the modern women make of themselves, you say. How they offend your eye, those bare cheek-bones, those clinging skirts, those hateful *chignons*! Ah! the cheeks no longer hang out a danger-signal when you approach; the skirts are no more lifted, ever such a little, to make room for you in the corner of the sofa next the fire; and though you might have had locks of hair enough once to have woven a parti-coloured *chignon* of your own, it would be hopeless now to beg as much as would make a finger-ring for Queen Mab. What is it, I say, that causes us to look with such deluded eyes on the past? Is it sorrow or malice, disappointment or regret? Are our teeth still on edge with the sour grapes we have eaten or forborne? Do we glower through the jaundiced eyes of malevolence, or is our sight failing with the shades of a coming night?"

Bones seldom delivers himself of his opinion in a hurry. "I think," he says very deliberately, "that this, like many other absurdities of human nature, originates in that desire for the unattainable which is, after all, the mainspring of effort, improvement, and approach towards perfection. Man longs for the impossible, and what is so impossible as the past? That which hath vanished becomes therefore valuable, that which is hidden attractive, that which is distant desirable. There is a strange lay still existing by an old Provençal troubadour, no small favourite with iron-handed, lion-hearted King Richard, of which the refrain, 'so far away,' expresses very touchingly the longing for the absent, perhaps only *because* absent, that is so painful, so human, and so unwise. The whole story is wild and absurd to a degree, yet not without a saddened interest, owing to the mournful refrain quoted above. It is thus told in the notes to Warton's *History of English Poetry*:—

"'Jeffrey Rudell, a famous troubadour of Provence, who is also celebrated by Petrarch, had heard from the adventurers in the Crusades the beauty of a Countess of Tripoli highly extolled. He became enamoured from imagination, embarked for Tripoli, fell sick on the voyage through the fever of expectation, and was brought on shore at Tripoli, half-expiring.

The countess having received the news of the arrival of this gallant stranger, hastened to the shore and took him by the hand.   He opened his eyes, and at once overpowered by his disease and her kindness, had just time to say inarticulately that *having seen her he died satisfied.*   The countess made him a most splendid funeral and erected to his memory a tomb of porphyry inscribed with an epitaph in Arabian verse.   She commanded his sonnets to be richly copied and illuminated with letters of gold, was seized with a profound melancholy, and turned nun.   I will endeavour to translate one of the sonnets he made on his voyage, " Yret et dolent m'en partray," etc.   It has some pathos and sentiment.   "I should depart pensive but for this love of mine *so far away*, for I know not what difficulties I may have to encounter, my native land being *so far away*.   Thou who hast made all things and who formed this love of mine *so far away*, give me strength of body, and then I may hope to see this love of mine *so far away*.   Surely my love must be founded on true merit, as I love one *so far away*.   If I am easy for a moment, yet I feel a thousand pains for her who is *so far away*.   No other love ever touched my heart than this for her *so far away*.   A fairer than she never touched any heart, either so near or *so far away*."'

"It is utter nonsense, I grant you, and the doings of this love-sick idiot seem to have been

in character with his stanzas, yet is there a
mournful pathos about that wailing *so far away*
which, well-worded, well-set, and well-performed,
would make the success of a drawing-room song.

"If the Countess of Tripoli, who seems also
to have owned a susceptible temperament, had
been his cousin and lived next door, he would
probably not have admired her the least, would
certainly never have wooed her in such wild
and pathetic verse; but he gave her credit for
all the charms that constituted his own ideal of
perfection, and sickened even to death for the
possession of his distant treasure, simply and
solely because it was *so far away*!

"What people all really love is a dream. The
stronger the imagination the more vivid the
phantom that fills it; but on the other hand,
the waking is more sudden and more complete.
If I were a woman instead of a—a—specimen, I
should beware how I set my heart upon a man
of imagination, a quality which the world is apt
to call genius, with as much good sense as there
would be in confounding the sparks from a blacksmith's anvil with the blacksmith himself. Such
a man takes the first doll that flatters him, dresses
her out in the fabrications of his own fancy, falls
down and worships, gets bored, and gets up, pulls
the tinsel off as quick as he put it on; being his
own he thinks he may do what he likes with it,
and finds any other doll looks just as well in the

same light and decked with the same trappings. Narcissus is not the only person who has fallen in love with the reflection, or what he believed to be the reflection, of himself. Some get off with a ducking, some are drowned in sad earnest for their pains.

"Nevertheless, as the French philosopher says, 'There is nothing so real as illusion.' The day that is dead has for men a more actual, a more tangible, a more vivid identity than the day that exists, nay, than the day as yet unborn. One of the most characteristic and inconvenient delusions of humanity is its incapacity for enjoyment of the present. Life is a journey in which people are either looking forward or looking back. Nobody has the wisdom to sit down for half an hour in the shade listening to the birds overhead, examining the flowers under foot. It is always 'How pleasant it was yesterday! What fun we shall have to-morrow!' Never 'How happy we are to-day!' And yet what *is* the past, when we think of it, but a dream vanished into darkness— the future but an uncertain glimmer that may never brighten into dawn.

"It is strange how much stronger in old age than in youth is the tendency to live in the here-after. Not the real hereafter of another world, but the delusive hereafter of this. Tell a lad of eighteen that he must wait a year or two for anything he desires very eagerly, and he becomes

utterly despondent of attaining his wish; but an
old man of seventy is perfectly ready to make
arrangements or submit to sacrifices for his personal benefit to be rewarded in ten years' time
or so, when he persuades himself he will still
be quite capable of enjoying life. The people
who purchase annuities, who plant trees, who
breed horses for their own riding, are all past
middle age. Perhaps they have seen so many
things brought about by waiting, more particularly when the deferred hope had caused the
sick heart's desire to pass away, that they have
resolved for them also must be 'a good time
coming,' if only they will have patience and
'wait a little longer.' Perhaps they look forward
because they cannot bear to look back. Perhaps
in such vague anticipations they try to delude
their own consciousness, and fancy that by
ignoring and refusing to see it they can escape
the inevitable change. After all, this is the
healthiest and most invigorating practice of the
two. Something of courage seems wanting in
man or beast when either is continually looking
back. To the philosopher 'a day that is dead'
has no value but for the lesson it affords; to the
rest of mankind it is inestimably precious for the
unaccountable reason that it can never come
again."

"Be it so," I answered; "let me vote in the
majority. I think with the fools, I honestly con-

fess, but I have also a theory of my own on this subject, which I am quite prepared to hear ridiculed and despised. My supposition is that ideas, feelings, delusions, name them how you will, recur in cycles, although events and tangible bodies, such as we term realities, must pass away. I cannot remember in my life any experience that could properly be called a new sensation. When in a position of which I had certainly no former knowledge I have always felt a vague, dreamy consciousness that something of the same kind must have happened to me before. Can it be that my soul has existed previously, long ere it came to tenant this body that it is so soon about to quit? Can it be that its immortality stretches both ways, as into the future so into the past? May I not hope that in the infinity so fitly represented by a circle, the past may become the future as the future most certainly must become the past, and the day that is dead, to which I now look back so mournfully, may rise again newer, fresher, brighter than ever in the land of the morning beyond that narrow paltry gutter which we call the grave?" I waited anxiously for his answer. There are some things we would give anything to know, things on which certainty would so completely alter all our ideas, our arrangements, our hopes, and our regrets. Ignorant of the coast to which we are bound, its distance, its climate, and its necessities, how can we tell what to pack up, and what to leave behind? To be sure, regarding things material, we are spared all trouble of selection ; but there is yet room for much anxiety concerning the out-fit of the soul. For the space of a minute he seemed to ponder, and when he did speak all he said was this—

"I know, but I must not tell," preserving thereafter an inflexible silence till it was time to go to bed.

CHAPTER VII

THE FOUR-LEAVED SHAMROCK

"WE are all looking for it ; shall we ever find it ? Can it be cultivated in hothouses by Scotch head-gardeners with high wages and Doric accent ? or shall we come upon it accidentally, peeping through green bulrushes, lurking in tangled woodlands, or perched high on the mountain's crest, far above the region of grouse and heather, where the ptarmigan folds her wings amongst the shilt and shingle in the clefts of the bare grey rock ? We climb for it, we dive for it, we creep for it on our belly, like the serpent, eating dust to any amount in the process ; but do we ever succeed in plucking such a specimen as, according to our natures, we can joyfully place in our hats for ostentation or hide under our waist-coats for true love ?

"Do you remember Sir Walter Scott's humorous poem called the *Search after Happiness* ? Do you remember how that Eastern monarch who strove to appropriate the shirt of a contented man visited every nation in turn till he came to Ireland, the native soil indeed of all the shamrock tribe ; how his myrmidons incontinently assaulted one of the 'bhoys' whose mirthful demeanour raised their highest hopes, and how

> Shelelagh, their plans was well-nigh after baulking,
> Much less provocation will set it a-walking ;
> But the odds that foiled Hercules foiled Paddywhack.
> They floored him, they seized him, they stripped him, alack !
> Up, bubboo ! *He hadn't a shirt to his back!*

"Mankind has been hunting the four - leaved shamrock from the very earliest times on record. I believe half the legends of mythology, half the exploits of history, half the discoveries of science, originate in the universal search. Jason was looking for it with his Argonauts when he stumbled on the Golden Fleece ; Columbus sailed after it in the track of the setting sun, scanning that bare horizon of an endless ocean, day after day, with sinking heart, yet never-failing courage, till the land - weeds drifting round his prow, the land-birds perching on his spars, brought him their joyous welcome from the undiscovered shore ; Alexander traversed Asia in his desire for it ; Cæsar dashed through the Rubicon in its pursuit ; Napoleon well - nigh grasped it after Austerlitz, but the frosts and fires of Moscow shrivelled it into nothing ere his hand could close upon the prize. To find it sages have ransacked their libraries, adepts exhausted their alembics, misers hoarded up their gold. It is not twined with the poet's bay-leaves, nor is it concealed in the madman's hellebore. People have been for it to the Great Desert, the Blue Mountains, the Chinese capital, the interior of Africa, and returned empty-handed as they went. It abhors courts, camps, and cities; it strikes no root in palace nor in castle; and if more likely to turn up in a cottage - garden, who has yet discovered the humble plot of ground on which it grows?

"Nevertheless, undeterred by warning, example, and the experience of repeated failures, human nature relaxes nothing of its persevering quest. I have seen a dog persist in chasing swallows as they skimmed along the lawn; but then the dog had once caught a wounded bird, and was there-fore acting on an assured and tried experience of its own. If you or I had ever found one four-leaved shamrock, we should be justified in cherish-ing a vague hope that we might some day light upon another.

" The Knights of the Round Table beheld with their own eyes that vision of the Holy Vessel, descending in their midst, which scattered those steel-clad heroes in all directions on the adventure of the Sangreal; but perhaps the very vows of chivalry they had registered, the very exploits they performed, originated with that restless longing they could not but acknowledge in common with all mankind for possession of the four-leaved shamrock.

> And better he loved, that monarch bold,
>   On venturous quest to ride
> In mail and plate, by wood and wold,
> Than with ermine trapped and cloth of gold
>   In princely bower to bide.
> The bursting crash of a foeman's spear
>   As it shivered against his mail,
> Was merrier music to his ear
>   Than courtier's whispered tale.
> And the clash of Caliburn more dear,
>   When on hostile casque it rung,
> Than all the lays to their monarch's praise
>   The harpers of Reged sung.
> He loved better to bide by wood and river
> Than in bower of his dame Queen Guenevere ;
> For he left that lady, so lovely of cheer,
> To follow adventures of danger and fear,
> And little the frank-hearted monarch did wot
> That she smiled in his absence on brave Lancelot.

"Oh! those lilting stanzas of Sir Walter's, how merrily they ring on one's ear, like the clash of steel, the jingling of bridles, or the measured cadence of a good steed's stride ! We can fancy ourselves spurring through the mêlée after the ' selfless, stainless ' king, or galloping with him down the grassy glades of Lyonesse on one of his adventurous quests for danger, honour, renown—and—the four-leaved shamrock.

"Obviously it did not grow in the tilt-yards at Caerleon or the palace-gardens of Camelot ; nay, he had failed to find it in the posy lovely Guenevere wore on her bosom. Alas ! that even

Lancelot, the flower of chivalry, the brave, the courteous, the gentle, the sorrowing and the sinful, must have sought for it there in vain.

"Everybody begins life with a four-leaved shamrock in view, an ideal of his own, that he follows up with considerable wrong-headedness to the end. Such fiction has a great deal to answer for in the way of disappointment, dissatisfaction, and disgust. Many natures find themselves completely soured and deteriorated before middle age, and why? Because, forsooth, they have been through the garden with no better luck than their neighbours. I started in business, we will say, with good connections, sufficient capital, and an ardent desire to make a fortune. Must I be a saddened, morose, world-wearied man because, missing that unaccountable rise in mule-twist, and taking the subsequent fall in grey shirtings too late, I have only realised a competency, while Bullion, who didn't want it, made at least twenty thou.? Or I wooed Fortune as a soldier, fond of the profession, careless of climate, prodigal of my person, ramming my head wherever there was a chance of having it knocked off, sticking to it like a leech, sir; never missing a day's duty, by Jove! while other fellows were getting on the staff, shooting up the country, or going home on sick leave. So I remain nothing but an overworked field-officer, grim and grey, with an enlarged liver, and more red in my nose than my cheeks, while Dawdle is a major-general commanding in a healthy district, followed about by two aides-de-camp, enjoying a lucrative appointment with a fair chance of military distinction. Shall I therefore devote to the lowest pit of Acheron the Horse Guards, the War Office, H.R.H. the Commander-in-Chief, and the Service of Her Majesty the Queen? How many briefless barristers must you multiply to obtain a Lord Chancellor, or even a Chief Baron? How many curates go to a bishop? How many village practitioners to a fashionable doctor in a London-built brougham? Success in every line, while it waits, to a certain extent, on perseverance and capacity, partakes thus much in the nature of a lottery, that for one prize there must be an incalculable number of blanks.

"I will not go so far as to say that you should abstain from the liberal professions of arts or arms, that you should refrain from taking your ticket in the lottery, or in any way rest idly in midstream, glad to

> Loose the sail, shift the oar, let her float down,
> Fleeting and gliding by tower and town;

but I ask you to remember that the marshal's baton can only be in one conscript's knapsack out of half a million; that wigs and mitres, and fees every five minutes, fall only to one in ten thousand; that although everybody has an equal chance in the lottery, that chance may be described as but half a degree better than the cipher which represents zero.

"There is an aphorism in everybody's mouth about the man who goes to look for a straight stick in the wood. Hollies, elms, oaks, ashes, and alders he inspects, sapling after sapling, in vain. This one has a twist at the handle, that bends a little towards the point; some are too thick for pliancy, some too thin for strength. Several would do very well but for the abundant variety that affords a chance of finding something better. Presently he emerges at the farther fence, having traversed the covert from end to end, but his hands are still empty, and he shakes his head, thinking he may have been over-fastidious in his choice. A straight stick is no easier to find than would be a four-leaved shamrock.

"The man who goes to buy a town house or rent a place in the country experiences the same difficulty. Upstairs and downstairs he travels, inspecting kitchen-ranges, sinks and sculleries, attics, bedrooms, boudoirs, and housemaids' closets, till his legs ache, his brain swims, and his temper entirely gives way. In London, if the situation is perfect, there is sure to be no servants' hall, or the accommodation belowstairs leaves nothing to be desired, but he cannot undertake to reside so far from his club. These difficulties overcome, he discovers the butler's pantry is so dark no servant of that fastidious order will consent to stay with him a week. In the country, if the place is pretty the neighbourhood may be objectionable: the rent is perhaps delightfully moderate, but he must keep up the grounds and pay the wages of four gardeners. Suitable in every other respect, he cannot get the shooting; or if no such drawbacks are to be alleged, there is surely a railway through the park, and no station within five miles. Plenty of shamrocks grow, you see, of the trefoil order, green, graceful, and perfectly symmetrical. It is that fourth leaf he looks for, which creates all his difficulties.

"The same with the gentleman in search of a horse, the same with Cœlebs in search of a wife. If the former cannot be persuaded to put up with some little drawback of action, beauty, or temper, he will never know that most delightful of all partnerships, the sympathy existing between a good horseman and his steed. If the latter expects to find a perfection really exist, which he thinks he has discovered while dazzled by the glamour surrounding a man in love, he deserves to be disappointed, and he generally is. Rare, rare indeed are the four-leaved shamrocks in either sex; thrice happy those whom Fate permits to win and wear them even for a day!

"What is it we expect to find? In this matter

of marriage, more than in any other, our anticipations are so exorbitant that we cannot be surprised if our come-down is disheartening in proportion.

> Where is the maiden of mortal strain
> That may match with the Baron of Triermain?
> She must be lovely, constant, and kind,
> Holy and pure, and humble of mind, *etc.*

(How Sir Walter runs in my head to-night.) Yes, she must be all this, and possess a thousand other good qualities, many more than are enumerated by Iago, so as never to descend for a moment from the pedestal on which her baron has set her up.   Is this indulgent? is it even reasonable? Can he expect any human creature to be always dancing on the tight-rope? Why is Lady Triermain not to have her whims, her temper, her fits of ill-humour, like her lord? She must not indeed follow his example and relieve her mind by swearing 'a good, round, mouth-filling oath,' therefore she has the more excuse for feeling at times a little captious, a little irritable, what she herself calls a little *cross*.   Did he expect she was an angel?   Well, he often called her one, nay, she looks like it even now in that pretty dress, says my lord, and she smiles through her tears, putting her white arms round his neck so fondly that he really believes he *has* found what he wanted till they fall out again next time.

"Men are very hard in the way of exaction on those they love.   All 'take' seems their motto, and as little 'give' as possible. If they would but remember the golden rule and expect no more than should be expected from themselves it might be a better world for everybody. I have sometimes wondered in my own mind whether women do not rather enjoy being coerced and kept down. I have seen them so false to a kind heart, and so fond of a cruel one. Are they slaves by nature, do you conceive, or only hypocrites by education? I suppose no wise man puzzles his head much on that subject. They are all incomprehensible and all alike!"

"How unjust!" exclaims Bones, interrupting me with more vivacity than usual. "How unsupported an assertion, how sweeping an accusation, how unfair, how unreasonable, and how like a *man*! Yes, that is the way with every one of you; disappointed in a single instance, you take refuge from your own want of judgment, your own mismanagement, your own headlong stupidity, in the condemnation of half the world! You open a dozen oysters, and turn away disgusted because you have not found a pearl. You fall an easy prey to the first woman who flatters you, and plume yourself on having gained a victory without fighting a battle. The fortress so easily won is probably but weakly garrisoned, and capitulates ere long to a fresh assailant. When this has happened two or three times, you veil your discomfiture under an affectation of philosophy

and vow that women are all alike, quoting perhaps
a consolatory scrap from Catullus—

> Quid levius plumâ? pulvis. Quid pulvere? ventus.
> Quid vento? mulier. Quid muliëre? nihil.[1]

But Roman proverbs and Roman philosophy are
unworthy and delusive. There *is* a straight
stick in the wood if you will be satisfied with it
when found; there *is* a four - leaved shamrock
amongst the herbage if you will only seek for it
honestly on your knees. Should there be but
one in a hundred women, nay, one in a thousand,
on whom an honest heart is not thrown away, it
is worth while to try and find her. At worst,
better be deceived over and over again than
sink into that deepest slough of depravity in
which those struggle who, because their own
trust has been outraged, declare there is no
faith to be kept with others; because their own
day has been darkened, deny the existence of
light."

"You speak feelingly," I observe, conscious
that such unusual earnestness denotes a conviction he will get the worst of the debate. "You
have perhaps been more fortunate than the rest.
Have *you* found her, then, this hundredth woman,
this prize, this pearl, this black swan, glorious

---

[1] What is lighter than a feather? Dust. What lighter than
dust? The wind. What lighter than the wind? Woman. What
lighter than woman? Nothing.

as the phœnix and rare as the dodo? Forgive my *argumentum ad hominem*, if I may use the expression, and forgive my urging that such good fortune only furnishes one of those exceptions which, illogical people assert, prove the rule." There is a vibration of his teeth wanting only lips to become a sneer, while he replies—

"In my own case I was *not* so lucky, but I kept my heart up and went on with my search to the end."

"Exactly," I retort in triumph; "you, too, spent a lifetime looking for the four-leaved shamrock, and never found it after all. But I think women are far more unreasonable than ourselves in this desire for the unattainable, this disappointment when illusion fades into reality. Not only in their husbands do they expect perfection, and that too in defiance of daily experience, of obvious incompetency, but in their servants, their tradespeople, their carriages, their horses, their rooms, their houses, the dinners they eat, and the dresses they wear. With them an avowal of incapacity to reconcile impossibilities stands for wilful obstinacy, or sheer stupidity at best. They believe themselves the victims of peculiar ill-fortune if their coachman gets drunk, or their horses go lame; if milliners are careless or ribbons unbecoming; if chimneys smoke, parties fall through, or it rains when they want to put on a new bonnet. They never seem to understand that every 'if' has its 'but,' every *pro* its *con*. My old friend, Mr. Bishop, of Bond Street, the Democritus of his day (and may he live as long!), observed to me many years ago, when young people went mad about the polka, that the new measure was a type of everything else in life, 'What you gain in dancing you lose in turning round.' Is it not so with all our efforts, all our undertakings, all our noblest endeavours after triumph and success? In dynamics we must be content to resign the *maximum* of one property that we may preserve the indispensable *minimum* of another, must allow for friction in velocity, must calculate the windage of a shot. In ethics we must accept fanaticism with sincerity, exaggeration with enthusiasm, over-caution with unusual foresight, and a giddy brain with a warm, impulsive heart. What we take here we must give yonder; what we gain in dancing we must lose in turning round!

"But no woman can be brought to see this obvious necessity. For the feminine mind nothing is impracticable. Not a young lady eating bread and butter in the schoolroom but cherishes her own vision of the prince already riding through enchanted forests in her pursuit. The prince may turn out to be a curate, a cornet, or a count, a duke or a dairy-farmer, a baronet or a blacking-maker, that has nothing to do with it. Relying on her limitless heritage of the possible, she feels she has a prescriptive right to the title, the ten thousand a year, the matrimonial prize, the four - leaved shamrock. Whatever else turns up, she considers herself an ill-used woman for life, unless all the qualities desirable in man are found united in the person and fortunes of her husband; nay, he must even possess virtues that can scarce possibly coexist. He must be handsome and impenetrable, generous and economical, gay and domestic, manly but never from her side, wise yet deferring to her opinion in all things, quick-sighted, though blind to any drawbacks or shortcomings in herself. Above all, must he be superlatively content with his lot, and unable to discover that by any means in his matrimonial venture, 'what he gained in dancing he has lost in turning round.'

"I declare to you I think if Ursidius[1] insists on marrying at all, that he had better select a widow; at least he runs at even weights against his predecessor, who, being a man, must needs have suffered from human weakness and human infirmities. The chances are that the dear departed went to sleep after dinner, hated an open carriage, made night hideous with his snores under the connubial counterpane, and all the rest of it. A successor can be no worse, may possibly appear better; but if he weds a maiden, he has

[1] Cogitat Ursidius, sibi dote jugare puellam,
Ut placeat domino, cogitat Ursidius.

to contend with the female ideal of what a man *should* be! and from such a contest what can accrue but unmitigated discomfiture and disgrace?

"Moreover, should he prove pre-eminent in those manly qualities women most appreciate, he will find that even in those they prefer to accept the shadow for the substance, consistently mistaking assertion for argument, volubility for eloquence, obstinacy for resolution, bluster for courage, fuss for energy, and haste for speed.

"On one of our greatest generals, remarkable for his gentle, winning manner in the drawing-room as for his cool daring in the field, before he had earned his well-merited honours, I myself heard this verdict pronounced by a jury of maids and matrons, 'Dear! he's such a quiet creature, I'm sure he wouldn't be *much use in a battle!*' No; give them Parolles going to recover his drum, and they have a champion and a hero exactly to their minds, but they would scarcely believe in Richard of the Lion-Heart if he held his peace and only set his teeth hard when he laid lance in rest.

"Therefore it is they tug so unmercifully at the slender thread that holds a captive, imagining it is by sheer strength the quiet creature must be coerced. Some day the pull is harder than usual, the thread breaks, and the wild bird soars away, free as the wind down which it sails, heedless of lure and whistle, never to return to bondage any more.   Then who so aghast as the pretty, thoughtless fowler, longing and remorseful, with the broken string in her hand?

"She fancied, no doubt, her prisoner was an abnormal creature, rejoicing in ill-usage; that because it was docile and generous it must therefore be poor in spirit, slavish in obedience, and possessing no will of its own.   She thought she had found a four-leaved shamrock, and this is the result!

"But I may talk for ever and end where I began.   Men you *may* convince by force of argument, if your logic is very clear and your examples or illustrations brought fairly under their noses; but with the other sex, born to be admired and not instructed, you might as well pour water into a sieve.   Can you remember a single instance in which with these, while a word of entreaty gained your point forthwith, you might not have exhausted a folio of argument in vain?"

He thinks for a minute, and then answers deliberately, as if he had made up his mind—

"I never knew but one woman who could understand reason, *and she wouldn't listen to it!*"

CHAPTER VIII

*R*OMÆ *Tibur amem, ventosus; Tibure Romam !*[1] quoth the Latin satirist, ridiculing his own foibles, like his neighbour's, with the laughing, half-indulgent banter that makes him the pleasantest, the chattiest, and the most companionable of classic writers. How he loved the cool retirement of his Sabine home, its grassy glades, its hanging woodlands, its fragrant breezes wandering and whispering through those summer slopes, rich in the countless allurements of a landscape that—

> Like Albunea's echoing fountain,
>   All my inmost heart hath ta'en ;
> Give me Anio's headlong torrent,
>   And Tiburnus' grove and hills,
> And its orchards sparkling dewy,
>   With a thousand wimpling rills,

---

[1] Inconstant as the wind I various rove ;
At Tibur Rome—at Rome I Tibur love.

as Theodore Martin translates his Horace, or thus, according to Lord Ravensworth—

> Like fair Albunea's sybil-haunted hall,
> By rocky Anio's echoing waterfall,
> And Tibur's orchards and high-hanging wood,
> Reflected graceful in the whirling flood.

His lordship, you observe, who can himself write Latin lyrics as though he had drunk with Augustus, and capped verses with Ovid, makes the second syllable of Albunea long, and a very diffuse argument might be held on this disputed quantity. Compare these with the original, and say which you like best—

> Quam domus Albuneæ resonantis,
> Et præceps Anio ac Tiburni lucus et uda
> Mobilibus pomaria rivis.

By the way, nobody who has not endeavoured to render Latin poetry into English can appreciate the vigour and terseness of the older language. Here are six lines in the one version and four in the other, required to translate three of the original, perhaps without producing after all so full a meaning or so complete a picture.

Nevertheless and notwithstanding his poetical predilections for the country, Horace, like many other people, seems of his two homes to have always preferred the one at which he was *not*. An unhappy prejudice little calculated to enhance the comfort and content of daily life. ·

Had he settled anywhere in the neighbourhood of our hermitage here, he need not have accused himself of this fickle longing, which he denounces by the somewhat ludicrous epithet of "ventose." He might have combined the advantages of town and country, alternating the solitude of the desert with the society of his fellow-men, blowing the smoke out of his lungs while inhaling the fresh breezes off the Serpentine, stretching his own limbs and his horses' by walks and rides round Battersea, Victoria, and Hyde Parks.

If you look for *rus in urbe*, where will you find it in such perfection as within a mile of the Wellington Statue in almost any direction you please to take? If you choose to saunter on a hot June day towards the Ranger's Lodge or the powder magazine, I could show you a spot from which I defy you to see houses, spires, gas-towers, or chimneys, anything, indeed, but green grass and blue sky, and towering elms motionless, in black massive shade, or quivering in golden gleams of light. A spot where you might lie and dream of nymph and faun, wood-god and satyr, Daphne pursued by Phœbus, Actæon flying before Diana, of Pan and Syrinx and Echo, and all the rustic joys of peaceful Arcady—or of elves and brownies, fair princesses and cruel monsters, Launcelot, Mordred, and Carodac, Sir Gawain the courteous with his "lothely ladye," the compromising cup, the misfitting mantle, all the bright pageantry, quaint device, and deep, tender romance that groups itself round good King Arthur and the Knights of his Round Table—or of Thomas the Rhymer as he lay at length under the linden tree, and espied, riding towards him on a milk-white palfrey, a dame so beautiful, that he could not but believe she was the mother of his lord, till undeceived by her own confession, he won from her the fatal gift of an unearthly love.   And here, perhaps, you branch off into some more recent vision, some dream of an elfin queen of your own, who also showed you the path to heaven, and gave you an insight into the ways of purgatory, ere she beckoned you down the road to Fairyland, that leads—ah! who knows where?   From this sequestered nook you need not walk a bowshot to arrive at the seaboard of the Serpentine ; and here, should there be a breath of air, if you have any taste for yachting, you may indulge it to your heart's content.   The glittering water is dotted with craft of every rig and, under a certain standard, of almost every size.   Yawls, cutters, schooners, barques, brigs, with here and there a three-masted ship.   On a wind and off a wind, close-hauled and free, rolling, pitching, going about, occasionally missing stays, and only to be extricated from the doldrums by a blundering, over-eager water-dog ; the mimic fleet, on its mimic ocean, carries out its illusion so completely that you can almost fancy the air off the water feels damp to your forehead, and tastes salt upon your lips.

An ancient mariner who frequents the beach below the boat-house feels, I am convinced, thoroughly persuaded that his occupation is strictly professional, that he is himself a necessity, not of amusement, but business. He will tell you that when the wind veers round like that, " suddenways, off Kensington Gardens, you may look out for squalls " ; that " last Toosday was an awful wild night, and some on 'em broke from their moorings afore he could turn out. The Bellerophon, bless ye, was as nigh lost as could be, and that there Water Lily, the sweetest thing as ever swam—she sprang her boom, damaged her bowsprit, and broke her nose. He was refitting all Wens'day, he was, up to two o'clock, and a precious job he had ! "

Everyone who constantly takes his walks abroad in the Great City, becomes a philosopher in spite of himself, of the Peripatetic School, no doubt, but still a philosopher ; so you sympathise mildly with the mariner's troubles ; for to you no human interests are either great or small, nor does one pursuit nor person bore you more than another. You hazard an opinion, therefore, that the Water Lily is somewhat too delicate and fragile a craft to encounter boisterous weather, even on such an inland sea as this, and find, to your dismay, that so innocent an observation stamps you in his opinion as not only ignorant, but presumptuous. He considers her both "wholesome," as he calls it, and "weatherly," urging on you many considerations of sea-worthiness, such as her false keel, her bulwarks, her breadth of beam, and general calibre. "Why, she's seven-and-twenty," says he, rolling a peppermint lozenge round his tongue, just as a real seaman turns a quid; "now look at the Sea-sarpent lying away to the eastward yonder, just beyond the point where the gravel's been washed adrift. She's fifty-two, she is, but I wouldn't trust her, not in lumpy water, you know, like the schooner. No. If I was a-building of one now, what I call for all work and all weathers, thirty would be my mark, or from that to thirty-five at the outside!"

"Thirty-five what? Tons?" you ask, a little abashed, and feeling you have committed yourself.

"Tons!" he repeats, in a tone of intense disgust—"tons be blowed! hinches! I should have thought any landsman might ha' knowed that—hinches!" and lurching sulkily into his cabin under the willow - tree, disappears, to be seen no more.

Later, when September has begun to tinge the topmost twigs with gold, and autumn, like a beautiful woman, then indeed at her loveliest, who is just upon the wane, dresses in her deepest colours, and her richest garments, go roaming

about in Kensington Gardens, and say whether
you might not fancy yourself a hundred miles
from any such evidences of civilisation as a pillar-
post or a cab-stand.

It was but the other day, I sauntered through
the grove that stands nearest the Uxbridge Road,
and while an afternoon mist limited my range of
vision and deadened the sounds of traffic on my
ears, I could hardly persuade myself that in less
than five minutes I might if I liked make the
thirteenth in an omnibus.

Alone? you ask—of course I was. Yet, stay,
not quite alone, for with me walked the shadow,
that, when we have learned to prefer solitude to
society, accompanies us in all our wanderings,
teaching us, I humbly hope, the inevitable lesson,
permanent and precious in proportion to the
pain with which the poor scholar gets his task
by heart.

Well—I give you my word, the endless stems,
the noiseless solitude, the circumscribed horizon,
reminded me of those forest ranges in North
America that stretch interminable from the waters
of the St. Ann's and the Batsicon, to the wild
waves breaking dark and sullen on the desert
seaboard of Labrador.

I am not joking. I declare to you I was once
more in mocassins, blanket-coat, and *bonnet-rouge*,
with an axe in my belt, a pack on my shoulders,
and a rifle in my hand, following the track of the

treboggans [1] on snow - shoes, in company with Thomas, the French Canadian, and François, the Half-breed, and the Huron Chief with a name I could never pronounce, that neither I nor any man alive can spell. Ah! it was a merry life we led on those moose-hunting expeditions, in spite of hard work, hard fare, and, on occasion, more than a sufficiency of the discomfort our retainers called expressively *misère*. There was a strange charm in the marches through those silent forests, across those frozen lakes, all clothed alike in their winter robe of white and diamonds. There was a bold, free, joyous comfort in the hole we dug through a yard and a half of snow, wherein to build our fire, boil our kettle, fry our pork (it is no use talking of such things to you, but I was going to say, never forget a frying-pan on these expeditions; it is worth all the kitchen-ranges in Belgravia), to smoke our tobacco, ay, and to take our rest.

There was something of sweet adventurous romance in waking at midnight to see the stars flash like brilliants through the snow-encrusted branches overhead, wondering vaguely where and why and what were all those countless worlds of flame. Perhaps to turn round again and dream of starry eyes in the settlements, then closed in sleep, or winking drowsily at a night-

[1] A narrow board, on which provisions, etc., are packed, to be dragged through the woods on these expeditions in the snow.

light, while the pretty watcher pondered, not unmindful of ourselves, pitying us, it may be, couching here in the bush, and thinking in her ignorance how cold we were!

Then when we reached our hunting-ground and came up with our game at last, though, truth to tell, the sport as sport was poor enough, there was yet a wild, delightful triumph in overtaking and slaying a gigantic animal that had never seen the face of man. The chase was exciting, invigorating, bracing; the idea grand, heroic, Scandinavian.

> An elk came out of the pine-forest;
> He snuffed up east, he snuffed up west,
> > Stealthily and still;
> His mane and his horns were shaggy with snow,
> I laid my arrow across my bow,
> > Stealthily and still;
> The bowstring rattled—the arrow flew,
> And it pierced his blade-bone through and through,
> > Hurrah!
> I sprang at his throat like a wolf of the wood,
> And I dipped my hands in the smoking blood,
> > Hurrah!

Kingsley had not written *Hypatia* then. Kingsley never went moose-hunting in his life. How could he so vividly describe the gait and bearing of a forest-elk stalking warily, doubtfully, yet with a kingly pride through his wintry haunts? Probably from the instinctive sense of fitness, the intuition peculiar to poets, that enabled him to feel alike with a fierce Goth sheltering in his snow-trench, and a soft, seductive Southern beauty, languishing, lovely and beloved, in spite of dangerous impulses and tarnished fame, in spite of wilful heart, reckless self-abandonment, woman weakness, and the fatal saffron shawl.

I tell you that I could not have been more completely alone in Robinson Crusoe's island than I found myself here within a rifle-shot of Kensington Palace, during a twenty minutes' walk, to and fro, up and down, threading the stems of those tall metropolitan trees; nor when my solitude was at last disturbed could I find it in me to grudge the intruders their share of my retreat. More especially as they were themselves thoroughly unconscious of everything but their own companionship, sauntering on, side by side, with murmured words, and loving looks, and steps that dwelt and lingered on the path, because that impossible roses seemed springing into bloom beneath their very feet, and that for them Kensington Gardens were indeed as the gardens of Paradise.

I knew right well for *me* the mist was gathering round, ghostly and damp and chill. It struck through my garments, it crept about my heart, but for these, thank God! the sky was bright as a midsummer noon. They were basking in the warmth and light of those gleams that come once or twice in a lifetime to remind us of what we might be, to reproach us, perhaps, gently for what we are. They did not speak much, they laughed not at all. Their conversation seemed a little dull, trite, and commonplace, yet I doubt if either of them has forgotten a word of it yet. It was pleasant to observe how happy they were, and I am sure they thought it was to last for ever. Indeed I wish it may!

But the reflections of a man on foot are to those of a man on horseback as the tortoise to the hare, the mouse to the lion, tobacco to opium, chalk to cheese, prose to poetry,

As moonshine is to sunshine, and as water is to wine.

Get into the saddle, leap on a thorough-bred horse, if you have got one. Never mind his spoiling you for every other animal of meaner race, and come for a " spin " up the Ride from Hyde Park Corner to Kensington Gate, careful only to steady him sufficiently for the safety of Her Majesty's subjects, and the inquisition, not very rigorous, of the policemen on duty. For seven months in the year at least this is perhaps the only mile and a half in England over which you may gallop without remorse for battering legs and feet to pieces on the hard ground. Away you go, the breeze lifting your whiskers from the very roots (I forgot, you have no whiskers, nor indeed would such superfluities be in character with the severe style of your immortal beauty). Never mind, the faster you gallop the keener and cooler comes the air. Sit well down, just feel him on the curb, let him shake his pretty head and play with his bridle, sailing away with his hind-legs under your stirrup-irons, free, yet collected, so that you could let him out at speed, or have him back in a canter within half a dozen strides ; pat him lovingly just where the hair turns on his glossy neck like a knot in polished woodwork, and while he bends to meet the caress, and bounds to acknowledge it, tell me that dancing is the poetry of motion if you dare !

Should it not be the London season—and I am of opinion that the *rus in urbe* is more enjoyable to both of us at the "dead time of year," than during the three fashionable months—do not, therefore, feel alarmed that you will have the ride to yourself, or that if you come to grief there will be nobody to pick you up! Here you will meet some Life-Guardsman "taking the nonsense " out of a charger he hates ; there some fair girl, trim of waist, blue of habit, and golden of *chignon*, giving her favourite a breather, ready and willing to acknowledge that she is happier, thus, speeding along in · her side-saddle, than floating round a ballroom to Coote and Tinney's softest strains with the best waltzer in London for a partner.

But your horse has got his blood up, and you yourself feel that rising within, which reminds

you of the merry youthful days, when everything
in life was done, so to speak, at a gallop. You
long to have a lark—you cannot settle down
without a jump or two at least. You look
wistfully at the single iron rail that guards the
footway, but refrain : and herein you are wise.
Nevertheless, you shall not be disappointed ; you
have but to jog quietly out of the Park, through
Queen's Gate, turning thereafter to your right,
and within a quarter of a mile you shall find
what you require. Yes, in good truth, our *rus
in urbe*, to be the more complete, is not without
a little hunting-ground of its own. Mr. Black-
man has laid out a snug enclosure, walled in
on all sides and remote from observation, where
man and horse may disport themselves with no
more fear of being crowded and jostled than in
Launde Wood or Rockingham Forest during the
autumnal months.   Here you will find every
description of fence in miniature, neat and new
and complete, like the furniture in a doll's baby-
house — a little hedge, a little ditch, a little
double, and a very little gate, cunningly constructed on mechanical principles so as to let you
off easily should you tamper with its top bar, the
whole admirably adapted to encourage a timid
horse or steady a bold one.

All this is child's-play, no doubt—the merest
child's-play, compared with the real thing. Yet
there is much in the association of ideas ; and a

round or two over this mimic country cannot but bring back to you the memory of the merriest, ay, and the *happiest*, if not the *sweetest* moments of your life. Mounted, with a good start, in a grass country, after a pack of foxhounds, there is no discord in the melody, no bitter in the cup—your keenest anxiety the soundness of the level water-meadow, your worst misgiving the strength of the farther.rail, the width of the second ditch. The goddess of your worship bids your pulses leap and your blood thrill, but never makes your heart ache, and the thorns that hedge the roses of Diana can only pierce skin-deep.

Wasn't it glorious, though you rode much heavier then than you do now,—wasn't it glorious, I say, to view a gallant fox going straight away from Lilburne, Loatland Wood, Shankton Holt, John-o'-Gaunt, or any covert you please to name that lies in the heart of a good-scenting, fair-fenced, galloping country? Yourself, sheltered and unseen, what keen excitement to mark his stealing, easy action, gliding across the middle of the fields, nose, back, and brush carried in what geometricians call a "right" line, to lead you over what many people would call a "serious" one! A chorus ringing from some twenty couple of tongues becomes suddenly mute, and the good horse beneath you trembles with delight while the hounds pour over the fence that bounds the covert, scattering like a conjurer's pack of cards, ere they converge in the form of an arrow, heads and sterns down, racing each other for a lead, and lengthening out from the sheer pace at which a burning scent enables them to drive along!

They have settled to it now. You may set to and ride without compunction or remorse. A dozen fields, as many fences, a friendly gate, and they have thrown their heads up in a lane. Half a score of sportsmen, one plastered with mud, and the huntsman now come up ; you feel conscious, though you know you are innocent, that *he* thinks you have been driving them ! You remark, also, that there is more red than common in the men's faces and the horses' nostrils ; both seem to be much excited and a little blown.

The check, however, is not of long duration. Fortunately, the hounds have taken the matter in hand for themselves, ere the only person qualified to do so has had time to interfere. *Rarpsody*, as he calls her, puts her nose down and goes off again at score. You scramble out of the lane, post-haste, narrowly escaping a fall. Your horse has caught his wind with that timely pull. He is going as bold as a lion, as easy as a bird, as steady as a rock. You seem to have grown together, and move like one creature to that long swinging stride, untiring and regular as clockwork. A line of grass is before you, a light east wind in your face, two years' condition and the best blood of Newmarket in his veins render you confident of your steed's enduring powers, while every field as he swoops over it, every fence as he throws it lightly behind him, convinces you more and more of his speed, mettle, and activity. What will you have? The pleasures of imagination, at least, are unlimited. Shall it be two-and-twenty minutes up wind and to ground as hard as they can go? Shall it be thirty-five without another check, crossing the best of the Vale, and indulging the good horse with never a pull till you land in the field where old Rhapsody, with flashing eyes and bristles all on end, runs into her quarry, rolling him over and herself with him, to be buried in the rush of her eager worrying followers? Would you prefer twelve miles from point to point, accomplished in an hour and a half, comprising every variety of country, every vicissitude of the chase, and ending only when the crows are hovering and swooping over a staunch, courageous, travel-wearied fox, holding on with failing strength but all-undaunted spirit for the forest that another mile would reach but that he is never to see again. You may take your choice. Holloa! he has disappeared!—he has taken refuge in his cupboard. Not even such a skeleton as mine can sustain the exorcism of so powerful a spell as fox-hunting! So be it! Who-whoop! Gone to ground? I think we will leave him there for the present. It is better not to dig him out!

CHAPTER IX

HUNDRED years ago there was scarce a decent country-house in England or Scotland that did not pride itself on two advantages—the inexhaustible resources of its cellar and the undoubted respectability of its ghost. Whether the generous contents of the one had not something to do with the regular attendance of the other, I will not take upon me to decide ; but in those times hall, castle, manor-house, and even wayside inn were haunted every one. The phantoms used to be as various, too, as the figures in a pantomime. Strains of unaccountable music sometimes floated in the air. Invisible carriages rolled into courtyards at midnight, and door-bells rang loudly, pulled by unearthly visitors, who were heard but never

seen. If you woke at twelve o'clock you were
sure to find a nobleman in court-dress, or a lady
in farthingale and high-heeled shoes, warming a
pair of ringed and wasted hands at the embers
of your wood fire; failing these, a favourite
sample of the supernatural consisted of some
pale woman in white garments, with her black
hair all over her shoulders and her throat cut
from ear to ear. In one instance I remember a
posting-house frequented by the spirit of an ostler
with a wooden leg; but perhaps the most blood-
chilling tale of all is that which treats of an
empty chamber having its floor sprinkled with
flour to detect the traces of its mysterious
visitant, and the dismay with which certain
horror-stricken watchers saw footsteps printing
themselves off, one by one, on the level, spotless
surface—footsteps plain and palpable, but of the
Fearful Presence nothing more!

"As with houses in those, so is it with men in
these days. Most of the people I have known
in life were haunted: so haunted, indeed, that
for some the infliction has led at last to madness, though, in most instances, productive only
of abstracted demeanour, wandering attention,
idiotic cross-purposes, general imbecility of
intellect, and, on occasion, reckless hilarity with
quaint, wild, incoherent talk. These haunted
head-pieces, too, get more and dilapidated every
day; but how to exorcise them, that is the

difficulty! What spells shall have power to banish the evil spirit from its tenement, and lay it in the Red Sea? if, indeed, that is the locality to which phantoms should properly be consigned. Haunted men are, of all their kind, the most unhappy; and you shall not walk along a London street without meeting them by the dozen.

"The dwelling exclusively on one idea, if not in itself an incipient symptom, tends to produce, ere long, confirmed insanity. Yet how many people have we seen going about with the germs of so fearful a calamity developing into maturity! This man is haunted by hope, that by fear,—others by remorse, regret, remembrance, desire, or discontent. Each cherishes his ghost with exceeding care and tenderness, giving it up, as it were, room after room in the house, till by degrees it pervades the whole tenement, and there is no place left for a more remunerative lodger, healthy, substantial, and real. I have seen people so completely under the dominion of expectation, that in their morbid anticipation of the Future, they could no more enjoy the pleasures afforded by the Present than the dead. I have known others for whom the brightest sunshine that ever shone was veiled by a cloud of apprehension, lest storms should be lurking below their horizon the while, who would not so much as confess themselves happy because of a conviction such happiness was not to last,—and for whom time being—as is reasonable—only temporal could bring neither comfort nor relief. It is rarer to find humanity suffering from the tortures of remorse, a sensation seldom unaccompanied, indeed, by misgivings of detection and future punishment; still, when it does fasten on a victim, this Nemesis is of all others the most cruel and vindictive. Regret, however, has taken possession of an attic, in most of our houses, and refuses obstinately to be dislodged. It is a quiet, well-behaved 'ghost enough, interfering but little with the ordinary occupations of the family, content to sit in a dark corner weeping feebly and wringing its hands, but with an inconvenient and reprehensible tendency to emerge on special occasions of rejoicing and festivity, to obtrude its unwelcome presence when the other inmates are gladdened by any unusual beauty of sight or sound.

"Discontent, perhaps, should hardly be dignified with the title of a ghost. He resembles rather those Brownies and Lubbers of northern superstition, who, unsightly and even ludicrous in appearance, were not yet without their use in performing the meaner offices of a household. If properly treated and never dragged into undue notice, the Brownie would sweep up the hearth, bring in the fuel, milk the cows, and take upon him the rough work generally, in an irregular, uncouth, but still tolerably efficient style. So perhaps a spirit of discontent, kept within proper bounds, may prove the unsuspected mainspring of much useful labour, much vigorous effort, much eventual success. The spur is doubtless a disagreeable instrument to the horse, and its misapplication has lost many a race ere now; but there is no disputing that it can rouse into action such dull, torpid temperaments as, thus unstimulated, would never discover their own powers nor exert themselves to do their best.

"But I should draw a wide distinction between the discontent which instigates us to improve our lot, and the desire, the *desiderium*, the poisonous mixture of longing and sorrow, defiance and despair, which bids us only rend our garments, scatter ashes on our heads, and sit down in the dust unmanly to repine. It is the difference between the Brownie and the Fiend. Of all evil spirits I think this last is the most fatal, the most accursed. We can none of us forget how our father Abraham, standing at his tent door on the plains of Mamre, entertained three angels unawares. And we, too, his descendants, are always on the lookout for the visitors from heaven. Do they ever tarry with any of us for more than a night's lodging? Alas! that the very proof of our guest's celestial nature is the swiftness with which he vanishes at daybreak like a dream.

But oftener the stranger we receive, though coming from another world, is not from above. His beauty, indeed, seems angelic, and he is clad in garments of light. For a while we are glad to be deceived, cherishing and prizing our guest, the more perhaps for those very qualities which should warn us of his origin. So we say to him, 'Thou art he for whom we have been looking. Abide with us here for ever.' And he takes us at our word.

"Henceforth the whole house belongs to the ghost. When we go to dinner, he sits at the head of the table. Try to shame him away with laughter, and you will soon know the difference between mirth and joy. Try to drown him with wine. No. Don't try that. It is too dangerous an experiment, as any doctor who keeps a private madhouse will tell you. Our duties we undertake hopelessly and languidly, because of his sneer, which seems to say, 'What is the use? Am I not here to see that you reap no harvest from your labour, earn no oblivion with your toil?' And for our pleasures — how can we have any pleasures in that imperious presence, under the lash of that cruel smile?

" Even if we leave our home and walk abroad, in hope to free ourselves from the tenacious incubus, it is in vain. There is beauty in the outside world, quiet in the calm, distant skies, peace in the still summer evening, but not for us—nevermore for us—

> Almost upon the western wave
> Rested the broad bright sun,
> When that strange shape drove suddenly
> Betwixt us and the sun.

Ay, therein lurks our curse. We bear the presence well enough when cold winds blow· and snow falls, or when all the landscape about is bleak and bare and scathed by bitter frosts. The cruel moment is that in which we feel a capability of enjoyment still left but for our affliction, a desire to bask in his rays, a longing to turn our faces towards his warmth—

> When that strange shape drives suddenly
> Betwixt us and the sun.

There is no exorciser from without who can help us. Alas! that we can so seldom help ourselves. The strength of Hercules could not preserve the hero from his ghastly fate. Our ghost is no more to be got rid of by main force than was Dejanira's fatal tunic, clinging, blistering, wrapping its wearer all the closer, that he tore away the smarting flesh by handfuls. Friends will advise us to make the best of it, and no doubt their counsel is excellent though gratuitous, wanting indeed nothing but the supplementary information, how we are to make the best of that which is confessedly at its worst.

Enemies opine that we are weak fools, and deserve to be vanquished for our want of courage —an argument that would hold equally good with every combatant overpowered by superior strength ; and all the time the ghost that haunted us sits aloft, laughing our helplessness to scorn, cold, pitiless, inexorable, and always

Betwixt us and the sun.

"If we cannot get rid of him, he will sap our intellects and shorten our lives; but there is a spell which even this evil spirit has not power to withstand, and it is to be found in an inscription less imitated perhaps than admired by the 'monks of old.'

"*Laborare est orare*, so runs the charm. Work and worship, and a stern resolve to ignore his presence, will eventually cause this devil to 'come out of the man.' Not, be sure, till he has torn and rent him cruelly—not till he has driven him abroad to wander night and day amongst the tombs, seeking rest, poor fevered wretch, and finding none, because of his tormentor—not till, in utter helplessness and sheer despair, stunned, humbled, and broken-hearted, the demoniac has crept feebly to the Master's feet, will he find himself delivered from his enemy, weary, sore, and wasted, but 'clothed, and in his right mind.'

"Amongst the many ghost stories I have read

there is one of which I only remember that it turned upon the inexplicable presence of a window too much in the front of a man's house. This individual had lately taken a farm, and with it a weird, long-uninhabited dwelling in which he came to reside. His first care, naturally enough, was to inspect the building he occupied, and he found, we will say, two rooms on the second floor, each with two windows. The rooms were close together, and the walls of not more than average thickness. It was some days ere he made rather a startling discovery. Returning from the land towards his own door, and lifting the eyes of proprietorship on his home, he counted on the second storey *five* windows in front instead of four! The man winked and stared and wondered. Knowing he was not drunk, he thought he must be dreaming, and counted them over again—still with the same result. Entering his house, he ran upstairs forthwith, and made a strict investigation of the second floor. There were the two rooms, and there were the four windows as usual. Day after day he went through the same process, till by degrees his wonder diminished, his apprehensions vanished ; his daily labour tired him so that he could have slept sound in a graveyard, and by the time his harvest was got in, the subject never so much as entered his head.

"Now this is the way to treat the haunted chamber in our own brain. Fasten its door; if necessary brick up its window. Deprive it of air and light. Ignore it altogether. When you walk along the passage never turn your head in its direction, no, not even though the dearest hope of your heart lies dead and cold within; but if duty bids you, do not shrink from entering—walk in boldly! Confront the ghost, and show it that you have ceased to tremble in its presence. Time after time the false proportions, once so ghastly and gigantic, will grow less and less—some day the spectre will vanish altogether. Mind, I do not promise you another inmate. While you live the tenement will probably remain bare and uninhabited; but at the worst an empty room is surely better than a bad lodger! It is difficult, you will say, thus to ignore that of which both head and heart are full. So it is. Very difficult, very wearisome, very painful, yet not impossible! Make free use of the spell. Work, work, till your brain is so overwrought it cannot think, your body so tired it must rest or die. Pray, humbly, confidingly, sadly, like the publican, while your eyes can hardly keep open, your hands droop helpless by your side, and your sleep shall be sound, holy, unhaunted, so that with to-morrow's light you may rise to the unremitting task once more.

"Do not hope you are to gain the victory in a day. It may take months. It may take years. Inch by inch, and step by step, the battle must be fought. Over and over again you will be worsted and give ground, but do not therefore yield. Resolve never to be driven back quite so far as you have advanced. Imperceptibly, the foe becomes weaker, while you are gaining strength. The time will come at last, when you can look back on the struggle with a half-pitying wonder that he could ever have made so good a fight. Do not then forget to be grateful for the aid you prayed so earnestly might be granted at your need ; and remember also, for your comfort, that the harder won the victory, the less likely it is you will ever have to wage such cruel battle again."

"Would it not be wiser," observed Bones quietly, "never to begin the conflict? Not to take possession of the haunted house at all?"

There is a pseudo-philosophy about some of his remarks that provokes me intensely.

"Would it not be wiser," I repeated, in high disdain, "to sit on the beach than put out to sea, to walk a-foot than ride on horseback, to loll on velvet cushions in the gallery, than go down under shield into the lists, and strike for life, honour, and renown? No. It would *not* be wiser. True wisdom comes by experience. He who shrinks from contact with his fellow-men— who fears to take his share of their burdens, their sorrows, their sufferings, is but a poor fool at best. He may be learned in the learning of the schools, but he is a dunce in all that relates to 'the proper study of mankind'; he is ignorant of human nature, its sorrows, its passions, its feelings, its hidden vein of gold, lying under a thick crust of selfishness and deceit; above all, he knows nothing of his inmost heart, nothing of the fierce, warlike joy in which a bold spirit crushes and tramples out its own rebellion—nothing of that worshipper's lofty courage who

> Gives the first watch of the night
> To the red planet Mars,

who feels a stern and dogged pride in the con-sciousness that he

> Knows how sublime a thing it is
> To suffer and be strong.

No; in the moral as in the physical battle, though you be pinned to the earth, yet writhe yourself up against the spear, like the grim Lord of Colonsay, who, in his very death-pang, swung his claymore, set his teeth, and drove his last blow home.

"Besides, if you are to avoid the struggle entirely, how are you ever to learn the skill of self-defence, by which a thrust may be parried or returned? the art of tying an artery or stanching a wound? How are you to help others who cannot help yourself? A man is put into this world to do a certain share of the world's work; to stop a gap in the world's fencing; to form a cog, however minute, in the world's machinery. By the defalcation even of the humblest individual, some of its movements must be thrown out of gear. The duty is to be got through, and none of us, haunted or unhaunted, ghost or no ghost, may shirk our share. Stick to your post like a Roman soldier during the watches of the night. Presently morning will come, when every phantom must vanish into air, every mortal confront that inevitable reality for which the dream we call a lifetime is but a novitiate and a school."

CHAPTER X

WEIGHT CARRIERS

FIFTY years ago, when the burning of a
bishop at Smithfield would scarce have
created more sensation in clerical circles than a
Ritualistic Commission or a Pan-Anglican Synod,
our divines took their share of secular pastime far
more freely than at present. It was the parson
who killed his thirty brace of partridges, and this,
too, with a flint-and-steel gun, over dogs of his
own breaking, on the broiling 1st of September.
It was the parson who alone got to the end of
that famous five - and - forty minutes from the
Church Spinneys, when a large field were beat
off to a man, and the squire broke his horse's
back. It was the parson who knew more about
rearing pheasants, circumventing wild ducks, otter-
hunting, fly-fishing, even rat-catching, than any-
one else in the parish ; and it was the parson, too,
who sometimes took the odds about a flyer at
Newmarket, and landed a good stake by backing
his own sound ecclesiastical opinion.

Concerning one of these racing divines I
remember the following anecdote :—

Returning from afternoon service on a Sunday,
he happened to witness a trial of speed between
two of his school-children. Unequally matched
in size, the big boy, as was natural, beat the
little one, but only by a couple of yards. The
parson stood still, watched them approvingly, and
meditated.

"Come here," said he to the winner. "Go into
my study, and fetch me my big Bible."

The urchin obeyed, and returned bearing a
ponderous quarto volume. "Now," continued
his reverence, "start fair, and run it over
again."

The competitors wished no better fun, and
finished this time with a dead heat.

"Good boys! Good boys!" said the parson
reflectively. "Ah! I thought the weight would
bring you together."

Yes ; how surely the weight brings us together!
How often have we not seen the universal handi-
cap run out over the course of daily life? Some
of us start so free, so light-hearted, so full of hope
and confidence, expecting no less than to gallop
in alone. Presently the weight begins to tell ;
the weight that we have voluntarily accepted,
or the weight imposed on us by the wisdom of
superior judgment. We labour, we struggle, we
fail ; we drop back to those whom we thought so

meanly of as our competitors; they reach us, they pass us, and though punishment be not spared, they gain the post at last, perhaps many, many lengths ahead! And even if we escape the disgrace of having thus to succumb, even if our powers be equal to the tax imposed on them, we are not to expect an easy victory; there is no "winning in a canter" here. Every effort tells on mettle, nerve, and spirits; on heart, body, and brain. We want them all, we summon them, we use them freely, and then, it may be within one stride of victory, comes the cruel and irretrievable breakdown.

Men, like horses, must be content to carry weight. Like horses, too, though some are far more adapted than others to the purpose, all learn in time to accommodate themselves, so to speak, in pace and action to their inevitable burden. How they fight under it at first! How eager, and irritable, and self-willed it renders them; how violent and impetuous, as if in haste to get the whole thing over and done with. But in a year or two the back accustoms itself to the burden; the head is no longer borne so high, the proud neck bends to the curb, and though the stride be shortened, the dashing, bird-like buoyancy gone for ever, a gentle, docile temper has taken its place, with sufficient courage and endurance for all reasonable requirements left. Neither animal, indeed, is ever so brilliant again; but thus it is that both become steady, plodding, useful creatures, fit to perform honestly and quietly their respective duties in creation.

We think we know a great deal in England of athletics, pedestrianism, and the art of training in general. It may astonish you to learn how a Chinese postman gets himself into condition for the work he has to do. The Celestials, it would appear, like meaner mortals, are extremely particular, not to say fidgety, about the due transmission of their correspondence. Over that vast empire extend postal arrangements, conducted, I believe, as in our own country, by some mandarin of high rank, remarkable for their regularity and efficiency. The letters travel at a uniform rate of more than seven English miles an hour; and as they are conveyed by runners on foot, often through thinly-populated districts in which it is impossible to establish frequent relays, the pedestrian capabilities of these postmen are of the greatest importance. This is how a Chinaman prepares himself to accomplish his thirty miles in less than four hours.

He has a quantity of bags constructed which he disposes over his whole person, like Queen Mab's pinches—

Arms, legs, back, shoulders, sides, and shins.

Into these he dribbles handfuls of flour before he starts for walking exercise, increasing the quantity little by little every day till the bags are quite full, and he carries clinging to every part of his body several pounds of dead weight, nor considers himself fit for his situation till he can move under it with the freedom and elasticity of a naked man. He will then tell you that, on throwing off his self-imposed burden, he finds all his muscles so invigorated by their own separate labours, his strength so stimulated, his wind so clear, his condition so perfect, that he shoots away over the plains, mountains, and tea-gardens of the Flowery Land less like John Chinaman with a letter-bag than an arrow from a bow. What would our old friend Captain Barclay, of peripatetic memory, say to such a system as this?

I doubt if the Chinaman's theory of training be founded on sound principles; but I am quite sure that in bearing our moral burden we cannot dispose it over too extended a surface, or in too many separate parcels. I see fathers of families carrying surprising weights, such as make the bachelor's hair stand on end from sheer dismay, with a buoyancy of step and carelessness of demeanour only to be accounted for by an equal distribution of pressure over the entire victim. A man who has his own business to attend to, his domestic affairs to regulate, half a dozen hungry children to feed, and a couple of poor relations or so to assist with sympathy, counsel, and occasional aid, finds no time to dwell upon any one difficulty, no especial inconvenience from any one burden, because each has its fellow and its counterpoise elsewhere. It is not only in pharmacy that the principle of counter-irritation produces beneficial results. A man with two grievances never pities himself so much as a man with one; and a man with half a dozen treats them all with a good-humoured indifference little removed from positive satisfaction.

Some people even appear to glory in the multitude of their afflictions, as though the power to sustain so much ill-luck shed a certain reflected lustre on themselves. I recollect, long ago, meeting an old comrade hanging about the recruiting taverns in Westminster. The man was a clean, smart, active, efficient non-commissioned officer enough, with the average courage and endurance of the British dragoon. A year before I had parted with him, languid, unhappy, and depressed, longing only to return to England but not yet under orders for home. Now he looked cheerful, contented, almost radiant. I stopped to inquire after his welfare.

"I landed a fortnight ago, sir," said he, with something of triumph in his voice, "and a happy home I found waiting for me! I haven't a friend or a relation left in the world. My father's absconded, my mother's dead, my brother-in-law's ruined, and my sister gone into a madhouse!"

It sounded melancholy enough, yet I felt convinced the man reaped some unaccountable consolation from his pre-eminence in misfortune, admired his own endurance, and was proud of his power to carry so heavy a weight.

Custom, no doubt, in these as in all other inflictions, will do much to lighten the load. There is a training of the mind, as of the body, to bear and to endure. With wear-and-tear the heart gets hardened like the muscles, and the feelings become blunted by ill-usage, just as the skin grows callous on an oarsman's hands. There is some shadow of truth in the fallacious story of him who carried a calf every day till it became a cow. None of us know what we can do till we try; and there are few but would follow the example of the patient camel, and refuse to rise from the sand, if they knew how heavy a weight is to be imposed on them ere they can reach the longed-for diamond of the desert, gushing and glittering amongst the palms! It is fortunate for us that the packages are not all piled up at once. Little by little we accustom ourselves to the labour as we plod sullenly on with the tinkling caravan, ignorant, till too late to turn back, of the coming hardships, the endless journey, or the many times that cruel *mirage* must disappoint our fainting, thirsting spirits ere we reach the welcome resting-place where the cool spring bubbles through its fringe of verdure—

where we shall drink our fill of those life-bestowing waters, and stretch ourselves out at last for long, unbroken slumbers under the "shadow of a great rock in a weary land."

But the worst method of all in which to carry our load is to build it up on the pack - saddle so as to attract notice and commiseration from those who travel alongside. The Turkish *hamals*, indeed, may be seen staggering about Constantinople under enormous bales of merchandise, twice the height and apparently three times the weight of the herculean bearer ; but a Turkish *hamal*, notwithstanding his profession, ignores the meaning of a sore back, moral or physical. Other jades may wince, but, under all circumstances, you may swear *his* withers are unwrung. To be sure, the first article of his creed is resignation. Fatalism lulls him like opium, though, kinder than that pernicious drug, it leaves no torment of reaction to succeed its soothing trance. Hard work, hard fare, hard bed, hard words, hard lines in general, a tropical sun and the atmosphere of a jungle, it is all in the day's work with *him*! *Backsheesh* he will accept with a smile if he can get it, or he will do without, consoling himself that it is *kismet*, for " There is one God, and Mahomet is His prophet." With this philosopher, indeed, "a contented mind is a perpetual feast," otherwise how could he sustain his stalwart proportions on a morsel of black bread and a slice of water-melon? His dissipations, too, are mild as his daily meals. A screw of weak tobacco, folded in a paper cigarette, wraps him in a foretaste of his anticipated paradise; a mouthful of thick, black, bitter coffee stands him in lieu of beer, porter, half-and-half, early purl, blue ruin, and dog's-nose. Once a week, or maybe once a month, he goes to the bath for two hours of uninterrupted enjoyment, emerging healthy, happy, refreshed, and clean as a new pin.

Perhaps it is his frugal, temperate life, perhaps it is his calm, acquiescent disposition, that enables him thus to carry weight so complacently. He never fights under it, not he! Through the narrow lanes of Stamboul, across the vibrating wooden bridge of the Golden Horn, up the filthy stairs, not streets, of Pera, he swings along with regulated step and snorting groans, delivered in discordant cadence at each laborious footfall; but he carries his weight, that is the great point—he carries a great deal of it, and he carries it remarkably well—an example of humility and patience, to the Christian who employs him, an object of comparison, not much in favour of the latter, between the votaries of the Crescent and the Cross.

When I protest, however, against making a display and a grievance of the load you have to bear, I am far from maintaining that you are to

keep it a profound secret, and hide it away in un-
suitable places under your clothes. A man can
carry a hundredweight on his shoulders with less
inconvenience than a few pounds about his heart.
If you doubt this, order cold plum-pudding for
luncheon, and you will be convinced! A secret,
too, is always a heavy substance to take abroad
with you, and your own seems to incommode
you more than another's, probably because you
are less indifferent about letting it fall. As for
attempting to dance lightly along with the jaunty
air of an unweighted novice, be assured the effort
is not only painful but ridiculous. No. Never
be ashamed of your burden, not even though your
own folly should have clapped an additional half-
hundred on the top of it. Get your shoulders
well under the heaviest part, walk as upright as
you may, but do not try to swagger ; and if you
have a friend who likes you well enough to give
his assistance, let him catch hold at one end, and so
between you move on with it the best way you can.

Some packages grow all the lighter, like a con-
traband trunk at the Douane, for being weighed
and examined, or, as our neighbours call it,
"pierced and plumbed." Some again gather increased proportions when we enlarge upon them ;
but it is only those of which we dare not speak,
those which no friend must seem to see, for which
no brother must offer a hand, that sink our failing
strength, that crush us down humbled and help-

less in the mire. There is but one place for such burdens as these, and we never lay them there till we have tried everything else in vain ; just as we offer the remnants of a life from which we expect no more pleasure, where we ought to have given all the promise and vigour of our youth, or take an aching, hopeless, worn-out heart back to our only friend, as the crying child runs to its parent with a broken toy.

> The ox toils through the furrow,
>   Obedient to the goad ;
> The patient ass up flinty paths
>   Plods with its weary load,

says Macaulay in his glorious *Lays of Ancient Rome*, and something in the nature of both these animals fits them especially for the endurance of labour and the imposition of weight. It is well for a man when he has a little of the bovine repose of character, a good deal of the asinine thickness of skin and insensibility to hard usage. Such a disposition toils on contentedly enough, obedient indeed to the goad so far as moderately to increase the staid solemnity of his gait, taking the flinty path and the weary load as necessary conditions of life, with a serene equanimity for which he has the philosophical example of the ass! The ways are rough, you know, and the journey long. Depend upon it these animals arrive at its termination with less wear-and-tear, more safety, and even more despatch, than the sensitive, high-spirited, and courageous horse, wincing from the lash, springing to the voice, striving, panting, sweating, straining every muscle to get home.

In the parable of the *Ancient Mariner*—for is it not indeed the wildest, dreamiest, and most poetical of parables?—you remember the hopelessness of the weight he carried when

> Instead of the cross the albatross
> About his neck was hung.

It was not his misfortune, you see, but his crime that bore him down. Its consciousness lay far heavier on his spirit than did his after-punishment, when, weary and desolate, he wailed that he was

> Alone, alone, all, all alone,
> Alone on a wide, wide sea,
> And never a saint took pity on
> My soul in agony.

The saints, indeed, might not have heard him; how do we know about that? but he *was* heard nevertheless, and thus he got rid of his burden to raise his head once more in the face of heaven.

He looked upon beauty, nature, animate life, the wonders of the deep, the creatures of his Maker, and "blessed them unaware!"

Enough. The hideous dream vanishes, the unholy spell is broken, and he cries exulting—

> That self-same moment I could pray
> And from my neck so free
> The albatross fell off, and sunk
> Like lead into the sea.

BONES AND I

I sometimes think that women bear their burdens with less apparent struggle, less toil or complaint, than men ; and this although they own more of the horse's anxious temperament than the sluggish nature of the ox and the ass. If they have less nerve than ourselves—less of the coolness which springs from constitutional insensibility to danger —they have more of that mettlesome spirit which is sometimes called pluck, that indomitable courage which acknowledges no failure for defeat, which never sleeps upon its post, which can bear up bravely even against the sickness and depression of unremitting pain. It is proverbial that in all phases of mere bodily suffering they show twice the patience and twice the fortitude of the stronger sex ; while who shall say how much of silent sorrow they can cherish and conceal in troubled hearts while they go about their daily business with smiles on their gentle faces, with a tranquil, staid demeanour seeming to chant in soft, harmonious cadence the watchword of All's Well ?

Do you not think they, too, keep their favourite skeletons (far less perfect than yourself) hoarded, hidden away, locked up, but not to be buried or forgotten for the worth of kingdoms ? Do you suppose they never bring them out to be hugged, and fondled, and worshipped, and wept over ?—

In the dead unhappy night, and when the rain is on the roof.

Bah! It is a world of shams. If a woman is not a hypocrite she must be a stone!

We should give them greater credit, though, could we learn more of the weights they have to carry. But their training is known only to themselves; their trials come off in secret; the saddles they wear are jealously locked up, and they take care to keep the key! I think the reason they run so kindly is that they apply themselves very frequently to the last resource of the Ancient Mariner when he saw no escape from his punishment, when he was over-weighted with his curse.

I know not: I only know that the quiet courage, the generous spirit, the untiring endurance with which they perform the journey of life is too generally ignored, unappreciated, and thrown away. How often have we not seen a thorough - bred horse ridden by a butcher — a being little lower than an angel submitting, gentle and patient, to a creature little higher than a brute?

CHAPTER XI

SHADOWS

"COMING events cast their shadows before," says a favourite adage of that proverbial philosophy which is often so quaint and truthful, sometimes so contradictory and far-fetched. In the present instance the maxim, I think, is contradicted by our individual convictions and general experience. For my own part I protest I am no believer in presentiments. That is a beautiful fiction of poetry, completely unsubstantiated by the prosaic events of life, which represents the predestined sufferer as one who

Still treads the shadow of his foe,

while the arm of the avenger, uplifted though unseen, intercepts the light of heaven ere yet its blow descends. Poets, no doubt, lay their foundations on a basis of truth, but, as befits their profession, do not scruple to raise a super-structure in magnificent disproportion to the limits of their ground-plan. I will appeal to nine people out of every ten whose lot it has been to sustain severe affliction—and I think it is nearly nine - tenths of the human race — whether they have not found themselves staggered or prostrated by blows as sudden as they were overwhelming; whether the dagger has not always been a more deadly weapon than the sword, the marksman behind the hedge a more fatal enemy than the battery on its eminence, the hidden reef a worse disaster than the adverse gale, and whether their hopes, their happiness, or their fortunes, have not failed them at the very moment when the false waves smiled serenely at the calm skies over-head—

> Like ships that on a summer sea
> Have gone down sailing tranquilly.

No; these forthcoming shadows need not disturb our repose. They owe their origin neither to heart nor brain, but proceed from the liver, and I should think must be quite unknown to him who "lives on sixpence a day and earns it!"

What a life we should lead if we could look an inch before our noses! Of all curses to humanity the bitterest would be the gift of foresight. I often think a man's progress towards his grave is like that of a sculler labouring up-stream, we will say from Richmond to Teddington Lock. By taking the established and conventional course he avoids collision with his kind, and proceeds in comparative safety. By certain side-glances and general knowledge of the river, which we may compare to the warnings of experience and the reasonings of analogy, he obtains an inkling, far removed from certainty, of much approaching trouble to which his back is turned. By observing the track of his own boat rippling the surface many a yard astern, he learns to guide his course, just as he would correct his conduct by the lessons of the past. Now the stream runs hard against him, and he must work his way foot by foot with honest, unremitting toil. Now he shoots along through slack water, much to his own content and self-approval, but under no circumstances, however formidable, must he completely relax his efforts, for the current would soon float him back to the place from whence he came. Many a scene of beauty, many a lovely nook, and sunny lawn, and fairy palace glides by him as he goes—fading, vanishing, shut out by the intervening point, to leave but a memory of their attractions, dispelled in turn by ever-recurring beauties of meadow, wood, and water.

So he plods steadily on, accepting the labour, enjoying the pleasures of his trip, and nearing with every stroke the haven he is to reach at last.

However healthy and invigorating the toil, however varied and delightful the passage, I think he will not be sorry to arrive at Teddington Lock, there to ship his oars, moor his boat under the willows, and so, lulled by the murmur of the ever-flowing waters, with folded arms, upturned face, and eyes wandering drowsily heavenwards, fall peacefully asleep.

But the shadows which cross our path to our greatest deception and detriment are those for which we so willingly abandon the substances whereof they are but the fading phantoms, as the dog in the fable dropped a piece of meat out of his jaws to snatch a like morsel from the other dog he saw reflected in the water. Every day men grasp at clouds as did Ixion, bartering eagerly for that which they know to be illusive the solid joys and advantages of life. How many people in the possession of sufficient incomes deprive themselves of common comfort in an attempt to appear richer and more liberal than they really are! How many forego the society of friends in which they find honest pleasure for that of mere acquaintances with whom they have scarce a thought in common, because the latter, perhaps themselves sacrificed to the same illusion, move in a higher and more ostentatious class of society! With one the shadow is a reputation for wealth, with another for taste. Here it is a house in Belgravia, there a villa on the Thames; sometimes a position in the county, a seat in parliament, or a peerage long dormant in a race of squires.

Whatever it may be, the pursuer follows it at the best speed he can command, finding, usually, that the faster he goes the faster it flies before him; and when he comes up with it at last to enfold the phantom in his longing embrace, behold it crumbles away to disappointment in his very arms.

I have seen Cerito dancing her famous shadow-dance; I have watched a child following its own retreating figure, lengthened to gigantic proportions in an afternoon sun, with shouts of wonder and delight; I once observed, perhaps the prettiest sight of the three, a thorough-bred foal gallop up to some park-pailings, to wince and scour away from the distorted representation of a racehorse it met there, in the wild, graceful freedom of a yet unbridled youth; and I have thought of the many shadows that lure us all, between the cradle and the grave, only to impose on us in their fullest signification . the different sentiments of disbelief, disillusion, and disgust. When Peter Schlemihl made his ill - advised bargain with the devil, that shrewd purchaser quietly rolled up his victim's shadow and put it in his own pocket. When Michael Scott, in the completion of his education at Padua, had mastered certain intricacies of the black art, his fellow-students observed to their consternation that while they walked in the college-gardens with the wise North-countryman,

> His form no darkening shadow cast
> Athwart the sunny wall.

SHADOWS

The first step in supernatural learning, the first condition for the attainment of superhuman power, seems to have been the dismissal of so inconvenient and unmeaning an appurtenance as a shadow.

How many people have I known, and these not the least endearing and capable of their kind, over whose whole life the shadow of a memory, though growing fainter day by day, has yet been dark enough to throw a gloom that the warmest rays of friendship and affection were powerless to dispel! Sometimes, indeed, that darkness seems dearer to them than the glories of the outer world; sometimes, and this is the hardest fate of all, they cling to it the closer that they feel the illusion has been to them a more reliable possession than the reality. There is a world of tender longing, bitter experience, and sad, suggestive pathos in Owen Meredith's lament—

> How many a night 'neath her window have I walked in the
> wind and the rain,
> Only to look on her shadow fleet over the lighted pane!
> Alas! 'twas the shadow that rested—'twas *herself* that fleeted,
> you see—
> And now I am dying—I know it! Dying—and where is she?

The shadow he had worshipped so fondly was not more fleeting than the dream on which he had anchored a man's honest hopes, and wasted a man's generous, unsuspecting heart.

Then we see our shadows at points of view so

peculiar to ourselves, in lights that so distort and disguise their proportions, it is no wonder if for us they become phantoms of formidable magnitude and overpowering aspect. The demon of the Hartz Mountains is said to be nothing more than the reflection or shadow of the traveller's own person, as seen under certain abnormal conditions of refraction against a morning or evening sky. Such demons most of us keep of our own, and we take care never to look at them but at the angle which magnifies them out of all reasonable proportions. When you see mine and I yours, each of us is surprised at the importance attached to his spectral illusion by the other. Yours seems to me a diminutive and contemptible little devil enough ; and doubtless, although you never may have entertained a high opinion of my mental powers or moral force of character, both are fallen fifty per cent. in your estimation since you have been brought face to face with the bugbear by which they are overridden and kept down. If we could but change shadows we should both of us get back into the sun. Alas! that all the magic art of Michael Scott himself would fail to effect such a trick of legerdemain. Alas! that we must bear as best we can, each for himself, the gloomy presence that makes us so dull of cheer, so sad of countenance, and so cold about the heart.

Men adopt a great many different methods to

get rid of their respective shadows, approximating more or less to the conclusive plan of Peter Schlemihl aforesaid, who sold his outright to the devil. Some try to lose it amongst a crowd of fellow-creatures, all with the same familiar attendants of their own; others struggle with it in solitude, and find themselves halting and maimed after the conflict, like him who wrestled of old with the angel at Peniel "until the breaking of the day." One thinks to stifle his tormentor in business, another to lull him with pleasure, a third to drown him in wine. None of these remedies seem to answer the purpose desired. Blue-books, bankers' books, betting-books are unable to break the spell; over the pages of each he throws the all-pervading gloom. Neither is he to be worsted by the gleam of many candles flashing only less brightly than the sparkle of Beauty's jewels and the lustre of her soft eyes in halls of dazzling light. On the contrary, it is here that, maybe from the force of contrast, he asserts his power with the greatest determination, coming out, as is but natural, under the vivid glare thrown on him in a stronger and more uncompromising relief. To steep him in wine is often but to increase his dimensions out of all reasonable proportions, and at best only gets rid of him for a night that he may return in the morning refreshed and invigorated to vindicate his sovereignty over the enfeebled rebel he controls. There are means of dispelling the darkness, no doubt, but I fear they are not to be found in the resources of study, certainly not in the distractions of dissipation nor the feverish delirium of vice. It must be a warm, genial, and unusually generous disposition which is not warped and dwarfed by a shadow cast upon it in youth, or indeed at any period of life; but for animate as for inanimate nature there are black frosts as well as white. The latter evaporate with the morning sun in light wreaths of vapour and perhaps a few tears sparkling like diamonds, to be succeeded by brilliant sunshine, unclouded till the close of its short winter's day; the former, grim, grey, and lowering, parch and wither up the life of every green thing, drawing her shroud, as it were, over the cold dead face of earth ere she is buried in the darkness of approaching night.

It is hard upon youth to see its rosy morning overcast by the shadow; but it has many hours yet to look forward to before noon, and can afford to wait for brighter weather. Far more cruelly does age feel the withdrawal of that light it had trusted in to cheer its declining day; a light it can never hope to welcome again, because long ere the shadow shall be withdrawn from the chilled and weary frame, its sun will have gone down for ever into the ocean of eternity.

People talk a great deal about that physical impossibility which they are pleased to term a broken heart; and the sufferer who claims their sympathy under such an abnormal affliction is invariably a young person of the gentler sex. I have no doubt in my own mind, nevertheless, that a severe blow to the fortunes, the self-esteem, the health or the affections, is far more severely felt after forty than before thirty; and yet who ever heard of an elderly gentleman breaking his heart? Anything else you please, his word, his head, his waistcoat-strings, or even his neck, but his heart! Why, the assumption is ludicrous. If you consult the statistics of suicide, however, you will be surprised to find in how many instances this most reckless of crimes is committed by persons of mature age, though it is strange that those whose span in the course of nature is likely to be so short should think it worth while to curtail it with their own hand. There is another shadow, too, which, apart from all finer feelings of the heart or intellect, has a pernicious effect on our interests and welfare. It is cast by our own opaque substances when we persist in an inconvenient attitude, commonly called "standing in our own light." Parents and guardians, those who have the care of young people, generally are well aware of its irritating persistency and disagreeable consequences. It is provoking to find all your efforts thwarted by the very person on whose behalf they are made. After much trouble, and the eating of more dirt than you can digest in comfort, you obtain for a lad a high stool in a counting - house, an appointment to the Indian army, or a berth in a Chinese merchantman, fondly hoping that in one way or another he is provided for, and off your hands at last. But after a while behold him back again, like a consignment of damaged goods! He has been too fast for the clerkship, too idle for the army, not sober enough for the sea. With a fine chance and everything in his favour, he "stood in his own light," and must abide by the gloom he has himself made. Or perhaps, though this is a rarer case, because women's perceptions of their own interest are usually very keen, it is your Blanche, or your Rose, or your Violet who thus disappoints the magnificent expectations you have founded on her beauty, her youth, her eyes, her figure, and her general fascinations. The peer with his unencumbered estate and his own personal advantages would have proposed to a certainty, was only waiting for an opportunity—he told his sister so—when that last ten minutes at croquet with Tom, those half-dozen extra rounds in the cotillon with Harry, scared this shy bird from the decoy, and he went off to Melton in disgust. Rose, Blanche, or Violet "stood in her own light," and must be content for the rest of her career to burn tallow instead of wax.

The shadows, however, which ladies preserve for their own private annoyance cast surprisingly little gloom over their pretty persons while they are before the world. A new dress, a coming ball, a race-meeting, or a picnic, are sufficient to dispel them at a moment's notice; and though doubtless when these palliatives are exhausted, when they put their candles out at night, the darkness gathers all the thicker for its lucid interval of distraction, it is always something to have got rid of it even for an hour.

That women feel very keenly, nobody who knows anything about them can doubt. That they feel very *deeply* is a different question altogether. In some rare instances they may indeed be found, when the light they love is quenched, to sit by preference in darkness for evermore; but as a general rule the feminine organisation is thoroughly appreciative of the present, somewhat forgetful of the past, and exceedingly reckless of the future.

For both sexes, however, there must in their course through life be shadows deep in proportion to the brilliancy of the sunshine in which they bask. "Shall we receive good at the hand of God," says Job, "and shall we not receive evil?" thereby condensing into one pithy sentence perhaps the profoundest system of philosophy ever yet submitted to mankind. The evil always seems to us greater than the good, the shadows more universal than the sunshine; but with how little reason we need only reflect for a moment to satisfy ourselves. There is a gleam in which we often fondly hope to dispel our shadows, delusive as the will-o'-the-wisp, a light "that never was on sea or land," which is cruelly apt to lure us on reefs and quicksands, to guide us only to eventual shipwreck ; but there is also a glimmer, faint and feeble here, yet capable of dispelling the darkest shadows that ever cross our path, which if we will only follow it truthfully and persistently for a very brief journey, shall cheer us heartily and guide us steadfastly till it widens and brightens into the glory of eternal day.

CHAPTER XII

MONGST all the works of our great poet, works in which criticism, searching diligently for flaws, discovers every day new beauties, surely this noble poem is the very crown and masterpiece.

"Compared even with the productions of his own genius, Guinevere always seems to me like a statue in the midst of oil-paintings. So lofty is it in conception, so grand in treatment, so fair, so noble, so elevating, and yet so real. As the Californian digger in his 'prospect' washes, and sifts, and searches, till from a mass of rubbish and impurities he separates the nugget of virgin ore, so from the lavish confusion of rich material to be found in that collection of early romance called *La Morte d'Arthur*, the Laureate has wrought out a poem precious in its own intrinsic merit as the purest metal that was ever beaten into a crown of gold. One other has been over the same ground before him, the great magician who with a wave of his wand has created for us gleaming blade and glittering hauberk, mail and plate, and managed steeds caparisoned, lances shivered to the grasp, sweet pale faces looking down on the mimic war beneath, and all the pomp, panoply, and *prestige* of an ideal chivalry when

> The champions, armed in martial sort,
>   Have thronged into the list,
> And but three knights of Arthur's court
>   Are from the tourney missed.
>
> And still those lovers' fame survives
>   For faith so constant shown ;
> There were two that loved their neighbours' wives,
>   And one that loved his own.

Alas! that the very first of these in arms, in courtesy, in personal advantages, and, but for the one foul blot, in honourable fame, should have been Lancelot de Lac, the ornament of chivalry. Alas! that the lady of his guilty love should have been that

> Flower of all the west and all the world,

whose rightful place was on the bosom of ' the stainless king.'

GUINEVERE

" Their fatal passion, that grew so insensibly in those fair May-days long ago, when the pair

> Rode under groves that looked a paradise
> Of blossom, over sheets of hyacinth,
> That seemed the heavens upbreaking thro' the earth,

has struck root now, deep, deep in the hearts of both, and spreading like the deadly upas-tree, has blighted every other sentiment and affection beneath its shade. There is no happiness for Lancelot without Guinevere, no sweetness in the breath of evening nor speculation in the stars of night, no gladness in the summer, no glamour in the greenwood, no glory in the day. Her whisper lurks in the hollow of his helmet when he shouts his war-cry, her image rouses his desire for fame, and points his trusty lance. But for the keen, unholy stimulant his arm would be nerveless and his courage dull, while all the time

> The great and guilty love he bare the queen,
> In battle with the love he bare his lord,
> Hath marred his face, and marked it ere his time.

Yes, there is retribution even here for the sweet, seductive sin. The worm that dieth not, the fire that is not quenched, begin their work long ere the cup has been emptied of its tempting poison ; and the one gnaws fiercer, the other burns deeper, in proportion to the capability of good from which the sinner has fallen—in proportion to the truth and tenderness of the tortured heart that seems meant for better things.

"And Guinevere. Who can fathom that woman's anguish, her shame, her self-reproach, her bitter, hopeless remorse, for whom the holy plighted love that should have made her shield, her honour, and her happiness through life, has been pierced, and shattered, and defiled by that other love which drags her to perdition, and to which she yet clings closer and closer with a warped instinct of womanly fidelity for the very sorrow and suffering it entails? The sense of personal degradation is perhaps the least of her punishment, for it is her nature when she loves to merge her own identity in another ; but what of her children, if she have any ? How can she bear the clear, guileless faces, the little hands clasped in prayer on her knee, the loving, trustful eyes of those simple believers to whom she, the sinner, is in the place of God? Many a woman, hesitating and hovering on the very brink of ruin, has been withheld by the tiny clasp of an infant's hand. If that last chance should have failed her, such failure has been ever after the heaviest and least endurable of the penalties she has brought on herself.

"But she may be childless, she may be spared the bitter pain of estrangement from those who are indeed part and parcel of her being. What, then, of her husband? The man whom once she believed she loved, who has cherished her, trusted her, given up for her sake many of the realities and all the illusions of life, whose care has surrounded her so constantly, every day and all day long, that, like the air she breathes, she can only be made sensible of its existence when withdrawn, whose indulgence was perhaps so unvaried as to escape notice, whose affection, expressed by deeds, not words, she has forgotten because it has not been repeated, like that other love, in burning whispers every hour. So she not only strikes him a deadly blow, such as his bitterest enemy would scarce deal in fair fight, but poisons her weapon besides, and leaves it sticking in the wound to burn and rankle and fester, that every passing hand in careless jest or wanton outrage may inflict on him mortal agony at will. Once perhaps she was proud of that brave, kind face, which she could not imagine blanched by fear nor clouded with shame. Can she bear to think of it now, quivering at the chance allusion of every idle tongue, warped into agony, like that of a man shot through the lungs, when her own name is spoken, purposely or otherwise, by some impertinent gossip or some rancorous, ungenerous foe? His sorrow has become a jest; that offence will soon pass away to make room for fresher scandal. His home is broken up; he can make himself another. The woman he loved has left him, yet there are plenty more as fond and fair ready to pity and console; but his trust is broken, and not even in an angel from heaven can he believe again. This is the worst injury of all. The strongest, the purest, the noblest of earthly motives to well-doing has failed him, and from henceforth the man is but a lamp without a light, a watch without a mainspring, a body without a soul. It is well for him now if he have some lofty aspiration, some great and generous object, to lift him out of his depth of sorrow, to rouse him from his apathy of despair. Thus only can he wrestle with the demon that has entered into his heart, thus only cast him out and, trampling on him, so rise to a higher sphere than that from which he has been dragged down. In self-sacrifice and self-devotion he shall find the talis-man to set him free, not at once, but, like other permanent results, gradually and in the lapse of time; so, mounting step by step and gaining strength as he ascends, he shall look down from the unassailable heights of forgiveness on the lesser souls that can never reach to wound him now—forgiveness, free, complete, and uncondi-tional as that which he himself pleads for from his God.

"And here it is that the character of Arthur, as drawn by Tennyson, exemplifies the noblest type of Christianity, chivalry, and manhood with which we are acquainted in the whole range of fiction. Poetry has yet to disclose to us a more godlike, more elevating sentiment than the king's pardon to his guilty and repentant wife. It breathes the very essence of all those qualities which humanity, at best 'a little lower than the angels,' is ever striving unsuccessfully to attain. There is courage, abiding by the award of its own conscience and appealing to a higher tribunal than the verdict of its kind; there is contempt for consequences; there is scrupulous, unswerving persistence in the path of duty, such as constitutes the soldier and the hero; there is large‑hearted, far‑seeing benevolence, that weighs its own crushed happiness and blighted life but as dust in the balance against the well‑being of its fellows. Above all, there is that grand trust in a better world and an immortal identity, without which man, despite his strength of will and pride of intellect, were little superior to the beasts of the field. Such is the diapason, so to speak, of this mighty march of feeling—the march of an un-conquered spirit and a kingly soul; while through it all, ever present, though ever modulated and kept down, runs the wild, mournful accompaniment, the wail of a kindly, tortured heart, of a love that can never die—

> And in thy bowers of Camelot or of Usk
> Thy shadow still would glide from room to room,
> And I should evermore be vext with thee,
> In hanging robe—or vacant ornament,
> Or ghostly footfall echoing on the stair.

For think not, though thou wouldst not love thy lord,
Thy lord has wholly lost his love for thee.
I am not made of such slight elements.
Yet must I leave thee, woman, to thy shame.

" How wonderful, how exhaustive, and how practical seems the familiarity of great poets with the niceties and workings of the human heart! It has been said of them, prettily enough, that

They learn in suffering what they teach in song.

" God forbid! If it were so, their lot would indeed be unenviable ; and what an eternity of torture would such a genius as Byron, or Shelley, or Tennyson himself have condensed into a single life! No, theirs must be rather the intuitive knowledge that springs from sympathy with all things, animate and inanimate, in summer and winter, in light and darkness, in sorrow and in joy—a sympathy receiving freely as it gives, and thus cozening them out of nine-tenths of their own private sorrows, which such finer temperaments as theirs would otherwise be too sensitive to endure.

" The wide scope of this sympathy, the facility with which genius can handle extreme contrasts of the same passion with equal skill, is, I think, finely exemplified in the two poems of *Maud* and *Guinevere*. I have already compared the latter to an exquisite piece of sculpture. The former seems to me like a wild, fanciful, highly-coloured painting, in which some true artist has striven to embody the unattainable conceptions of a dream. Was ever colouring mixed on palette more vivid and glowing than this description of a lover waiting for his mistress in her garden :—

> There falls a splendid tear
>   From the passion-flower at the gate ;
> She is coming—my love—my dear !
>   She is coming—my life, my fate !
> The red rose cries, She is near—she is near !
>   The white rose weeps,—She is late !
> The larkspur listens,—I hear—I hear !
>   And the lily whispers,—I wait !

"Is there not in these lines, besides grace, sentiment, pathos, tenderness, a wealth of pictorial fancy, such as Landseer himself has not outdone in his magical representation of clown and elves and stars and flowers grouped round Titania in Fairyland ?

"As in 'clear-faced Arthur' is rendered the ideal dignity of love, so in Maud's hapless suitor we find exemplified its mad enthusiasm and passion. With both, self is unhesitatingly sacrificed to the welfare of another. When the fatal shot has been fired, and the exile faces a foreign shore in utter hopelessness that he shall ever look on the face he loves again, the pity for himself that cannot but chill his sorrowing heart merges in anxiety and tenderness for Maud. Even now —perhaps now more than ever—in grief, danger, and privation, his first thought flies to the idol for whom he has built his life into a throne, that she may reign there unrivalled and supreme. May *his* be the shame, the sorrow, and the suffering! —such is his wild, pathetic prayer—and let the treasure of his heart go free. If there be danger, let it lower round *his* unprotected head. If there be punishment, let *him* bear it for both! Ay, though she may never reward him for it, never even know it; for in this world these two are surely parted not to meet again. What of that? She is still his queen—his goddess—his love— the aim of his existence, the darling of his care.

> Comfort her, comfort her, all things good,
> While I am over the sea;
> Let me and my passionate love go by,
> But speak to her all things holy and high,
> Whatever happen to me.
> Me and my harmful love go by,
> But come to her waking, or find her asleep,
> Powers of the height, powers of the deep,
> And comfort her though I die.

"Surely this is the pure, unadulterated metal. Alas! that it should sometimes lack the glitter of that counterfeit which women grasp at so eagerly in preference to the true gold. So, in extremity of danger, shattered in battle against the chosen friend and comrade whose treachery was only less galling to his noble heart than the disloyalty of his queen, beset by

> The godless hosts
> Of heathen swarming o'er the Northern sea,

stern old foes of himself and Christendom, erst by prowess of that 'glorious company,'

The Table Round,
In twelve great battles ruining overthrown,

now panting for reprisal and revenge, menaced with open rebellion by a sister's son, his army melting, his adherents failing, his sceptre sliding from his grasp, Arthur can yet provide tenderly and carefully for her safety who has brought down on him all this shame, ruin, and defeat.

And many more when Modred raised revolt,
Forgetful of their troth and fealty, clave
To Modred, and a remnant stays with me.
And of this remnant will I leave a part—
True men who love me still, for whom I live—
To guard thee in the wild hour coming on ;
Lest but a hair of this low head be harmed.
Fear not : thou shalt be guarded till my death.

"Well might the queen, when he had passed from her sight for ever, reflect bitterly on the comparative merits of lover and husband, having, like all such women, proved to extremity of torture the devotion of both.

I wanted warmth and colour, which I found
In Lancelot. Now I see thee what thou art—
Thou art the highest, and most human, too,
Not Lancelot, nor another.

"Could she but have seen him as he really was in the golden days long ago, when her court formed the centre of all that was bravest and fairest in the world of Christendom, when her

331

life seemed one long holiday of dance and revel in the lighted halls of Camelot, of tilt and tournament and pageantry of mimic war, held in honour of her own peerless beauty, in the lists of Caerleon, of horn and hound and rushing chase and willing palfrey speeding over the scented moors of Cornwall, or through the sunny glades of Lyonesse, of sweet May mornings when she went forth fresh and lovely, fairer than the very smile of spring, amongst her courtiers, all

> Green-suited, but with plumes that mocked the may,

to walk apart, nevertheless, with flushing cheek and eyes cast down, while she listened to *his* whispers, whose voice was softer and sweeter than fairy music in her ears! Could she but have known then where to seek her happiness and find it! Alas! that we see things so differently in different lights and surroundings— in serge and velvet, in the lustre of revelry and the pale cold grey of dawn, in black December frosts and the rich glow of June. Alas! for us, that so seldom till too late to take our bearings, and avoid impending shipwreck, can we make use of that fearful gift described by another great poet as

> The telescope of truth,
> Which strips the distance of its fantasies,
> And brings life near, in utter nakedness,
> Making the cold reality too real!

but still *reality*, and, as such, preferable to all the baseless visions of fancy, all the glitter and glamour and illusion of romance. We mortals must have our dreams; doubtless it is for a good purpose that they are so fair and sweet, that their duration is so short, the waking from them so bitter and forlorn. But at last most of us find ourselves disenchanted, weary, hopeless, memory-haunted, and seeking sanctuary after all, like Guinevere, when Lancelot had gone

> Back to his land, but she to Almesbury
> Fled all night long by glimmering waste and weald,
> And heard the spirits of the waste and weald
> Moan as she fled, or thought she heard them moan,—
> And in herself she moaned—'Too late! too late!'

".What a picture of desolation and despair! Mocking phantoms all about her, now gibing, now pitying, now goading her to the recklessness of despair. Before her, darkness uncheered by a single beacon; behind her, the sun of life and love gone down to rise no more, and, lifting helpless, hopeless eyes above,

> A blot in heaven, the raven flying high.

"Deep must be the guilt for which such hours as these are insufficient to atone!

"But the queen's penance hath only just begun, for the black drop is not yet wrung out of her heart, and even in her cloister at Almesbury it is remorse rather than repentance that drives the iron into her soul. As it invariably does in moments of extreme feeling, the master-passion takes possession of her once more, and 'my Lancelot' comes back in all his manly beauty and his devoted tenderness, so touching and so prized, that for him too it must make the sorrow of a lifetime. Again, she sees him in the lists, best, bravest, and knightliest lance of all the Round Table. Again, sitting fair and courtly and gentle among dames in hall, his noble face none the less winsome, be sure, to *her*, for that she could read on it the stamp of sorrow set there by herself as her own indelible seal.

"Again she tastes the bitter torture of their parting agony, and her very spirit longs only to be released that it may fly to him for ever, far away in his castle beyond the sea.

"This, with true dramatic skill, is the moment chosen by the poet for the arrival of her injured, generous, and forgiving lord—

> While she brooded thus,
> And grew half guilty in her thoughts again,
> There rode an armed warrior to the doors.

"And now comes that grand scene of sorrow and penitence and pardon, for which this poem seems to me unequalled and alone.

"Standing on the brink of an uncertainty more ghastly than death, for something tells him that he is now to lead his hosts in his last battle, and that the unearthly powers to whom he owes birth, fame, and kingdom, are about to reclaim him for their own, he stretches the hands of free forgiveness, as it were, from the other world.

"How short, in the face of doom so imminent, so inevitable, appears that span of life in which so much has been accomplished! Battles have been fought, victories gained, a kingdom established, a bulwark raised against the heathen, an example set to the whole of Christendom, and yet it seems but yesterday

> They found a naked child upon the sands
> Of wild Dundagil by the Cornish sea,
> And that was Arthur.

"Now in the height of glory, in the fulfilment of duty, in the prime of manhood, such sorrows have overtaken him as must needs whisper their prophetic warning that his task is done, and it is time to go. *Where*, he sees not, cares not. True to himself and his knighthood, he is ready now, as always, to follow the path of honour, wherever it may lead, and meet unflinching

> Death, or I know not what mysterious doom.

"Arthur, dethroned, ruined, heart - broken, mortally wounded, and unhorsed, will be no less Arthur than when on Badon Hill he stood

> High on a heap of slain, from spur to plume,
> Red as the rising sun with heathen blood,

and shouted victory with a great voice in the culminating triumph of his glory.

"For him too at this supreme moment the master-passion asserts its sway, and even that great soul thrills to its centre with the love that has been wasted for half a lifetime on her who is only now awaking to a consciousness of its worth. He cannot leave her for ever without bidding farewell to his guilty queen. So riding through the misty night to the convent where she has taken refuge, he looks his last in this world on her from whom in his great loyalty of affection neither her past disgrace nor his own approaching death shall part him for ever. With that instinct of pure love which clings to a belief in its eternity, he charges her to cleanse her soul with repentance and sustain her hopes with faith, that

> Hereafter in that world where all are pure
> We two may meet before high God, and thou
> Wilt spring to me, and claim me thine, and know
> I am thine husband.

"Thus, with all his soul flowing to his lips, this grand heroic nature blesses the guilty woman, grovelling in the dust, and moves off stately and unflinching to confront the doom of Fate.

"Then, true to the yearning nature of her sex, yearning ever with keenest longings for the lost and the impossible, Guinevere leaps to her feet, the tide of a new love welling up in her wayward heart, fierce, cruel, and irresistible because it must be henceforth utterly hopeless and forlorn. With her own hand she has put away her own happiness; and what happiness it might have been she feels too surely, now that no power on earth can ever make it hers again!

"Oh for one word more from the kind, forgiving voice! Oh for one look in the brave, clear, guileless face! But no. It is never to be. Never, never more! She rushes indeed to the casement, but Arthur is already mounted and bending from the saddle, to give directions for *her* safety and *her* comfort.

> So she did not see the face,
> Which then was as an angel, but she saw—
> Wet with the mists and smitten by the lights—
> The dragon of the great Pendragon-ship
> Blaze, making all the night a steam of fire.
> And even then he turned; and more and more
> The mooney vapours rolling round the king,
> Who seemed the phantom of a giant in it,
> Enwound him, fold by fold, and made him grey
> And greyer, till himself became as mist
> Before her, moving ghostlike to his doom."

"I think I like it better without your explanations and remarks," observed Bones. "There is a proverb, my friend, about 'refined gold,' and 'the lily,' that you would do well to remember. Hang it, man! do you think nobody understands or appreciates poetry but yourself?"

BONES AND I

Perhaps I have over-aired him lately; but it seems to me that Bones is a good deal above himself. If I can only get him back into the cupboard, I have more than half a mind to lock him up for good and all.

THE END

PRINTED BY MORRISON AND GIBB LIMITED, EDINBURGH